PRAISE FOR C

'There is a fresh and vital edge to this superior debut novel. Mason has much to say about relationships. Her women have resonant characters and recognizable jobs, which give depth to their messy lives. A bittersweet narrative and ambiguous outcomes make this much grittier and more substantial than standard chick-lit fare.'

Financial Times, UK

'It's got the raw realism of someone writing about a world she knows. A grand little book for the festive fireside.'

Irish Evening Herald

The
Shadow
Between
Us

ALSO BY CAROL MASON

After You Left
The Secrets of Married Women
The Last Time We Met
Send Me a Lover

The
Shadow
Between
Us

Carol
MASON

LAKE UNION
PUBLISHING

Published by Lake Union Publishing, Seattle

www.apub.com

Amazon, the Amazon logo, and Lake Union Publishing are trademarks of Amazon. com, Inc., or its affiliates.

ISBN-13: 9781542041867
ISBN-10: 1542041864

Cover design by Rose Cooper

Printed in the United States of America

For Sadie

ONE

When it happens, I am never doing anything out of the ordinary. Glancing in my car's wing mirror, bending over to lace up my running shoes, noticing a woman's billowy blonde hair. Suddenly, I will hear the distant rumble of a noise I can't pinpoint. Colours flash before me – green shot through with blue – a bit like when you glimpse the sky or the ocean through a thicket of trees as you're driving quickly past them. I will fill with debilitating dread. Disjointed scenes tumble into frame, scenes I want to make sense of but can't. The mind when it relives things has a way of amplifying details, of adding new and surprising ones. I might taste the blood from where I must have bitten the inside of my cheek, feel the half-moon indentations of fingernails in my palm. All that stuff they tell you to do – breathe, reorientate to your immediate surroundings, home in on something tangible to ground you – is as useless as if I were drowning and someone were telling me to swim at an angle away from the rip current, pointing towards shore. Then comes that same hard landing, the moment when I realise what it is I've done. Then everything stops.

Other times, like now, it's a shadow on the other side of the glass door, loose and amorphous, waiting for me to decipher it. This one is insidious and corporeal somehow. I will do anything to stop it fully forming – blast the house with CNN, fill my blender with handfuls of ice and hold down grind, pick up a cloth and begin a rampant cleaning jag. Keep on keeping on until I've managed to exorcise it, which leaves me with a frigid triumph. Or I'll phone someone, latch on to the anchor of a familiar voice. Just the act of searching for a number and punching it in is often enough to take the peal of panic down a peg or two.

By the time Jessica's phone has rung six times I know she's not going to pick up. I picture her on the other end of this umbilical cord of technology staring coldly at my name; it feels oddly demeaning. I wonder where she is now? Rome still, or is it Turkey? I told her there were certain countries I didn't want her visiting for safety reasons, but she just said, *Shit happens everywhere*, and she's not wrong. After her sing-songy 'leave a message!' I say, 'Hello, Jess. Look, it's Mum again.' Nerves have thickened my voice and I have to clear my throat. 'I hoped you might be there this time. I really just wanted to wish you a happy birthday . . . Anyway, I hope that whatever you're up to you're having a good time.' My cheeriness sounds put-on. I'm about to hang up then add, 'Look, at least text me. I just want to know you're OK . . . Love you.'

When she got it in her head to spend the summer waltzing around Europe we insisted she at least have a free international phone plan so she could keep in regular touch and we wouldn't be beset with worry.

Yup. That worked.

But then a thought rushes in. What if she's not answering because something's happened? All those crazy motorbikes in Rome! You have to have eyes in the back of your head. What if she didn't? If she's lying in a hospital bed hooked up to drips and beeping technology? If we haven't heard anything because she wasn't carrying ID? My diaphragm clutches; I can't let a breath out. The back of my neck prickles with cold sweat. Sometimes I get it from my groin to my knees and my clothes will be soaked in seconds.

Breathe. Sit down. Stop being so ridiculous. Of course she hasn't had an accident. She's just ignoring you because finally she can.

To distract myself I put the kettle on but I still feel discomfort prowling about inside my head. I stand there tap-tapping my fingernails on the fake granite. How many hours until bedtime? I used to do this with wine: wait until four o'clock, then I could sink the bottle. Now it's sleep, those magical nine or ten hours where I manage to give life the slip. At first I figured if I got up early I could call it a day early because evenings are always the hardest for me to be alone. It's after about 7 p.m. when I recognise I'm not quite the lover of my own company I always thought. But now I go to bed early and get up late because – who cares? There's no one around to see me anyway. From my half-open window I watch the rain as it bounces off the ground. Port Townsend is supposed to be in the Olympic Rain Shadow and get dryer, brighter weather than Seattle, but so far you wouldn't know it. All it's done is rain since I got here. I regret not packing more sweaters the day I walked out of my door, so certain of what I was doing, and yet at the same time not having a bloody clue. In the distance I can see the virtually uninterrupted expanse of cold, steel sea. The downpour has awakened the mature lavender and rosemary bushes, though. I can smell them in every room, which is nice: calming.

I look in the cupboard but there aren't any clean cups. I haven't washed dishes in days. I've never been much of a hausfrau. My modus operandi tends to be, watch the place become an utter disaster then wait one more week. I can't shake off the awful emptiness that's come over me since hearing Jessica's voice. When did this wedge come between us? Would it have happened to anyone in our circumstances? Did I allow it to occur in the slow, grey aftermath, because I was so into my own head that I almost forgot I even had a daughter? In my mind's eye I can see her lurking behind Mark as he poked his head around our bedroom door when I was pretending to read. 'We're going for a walk. Come with us. You've got to get some air.' Jessica standing there so still, her eyes monitoring every beat of my reaction, brimming with apprehension and the tiniest bit of hope. She doesn't know who I am any more. I am too many moving parts. Me saying, 'Leave me alone! Just *go!*' Then I heard the front door close and I was left with the low, steady hammer of my guilt. *Why am I being so unfair to them? Why can't I make an effort?*

The kettle whistles me back to life. I switch off the gas and continue to stand there, bewildered. I am in this familiar place again. The grabbing hands of depression. But as though the weather is trying to tell me something, there's a sudden break in the rain. I decide to put on my waterproof Barbour jacket, routing swiftly to the hall cupboard before I can talk myself out of it.

I have always liked the Pacific Northwest, in particular Port Townsend. For no sensible reason – because it's rainy, green, historic and on the water? – it reminds me of England, even though I grew up in the countryside, not on the coast. Mark and I came here once or twice when Jessica was a baby. I have retraced the gritty path of that happiness so many times lately. When I boarded the flight from Heathrow to Seattle, not much older than Jessica, off for a summer adventure after three years of uni, the last thing I imagined was that I'd meet an American the day I arrived and be pregnant six months later. Definitely not my big life plan, yet, oddly, everything felt like it was happening exactly as it was meant to. My baby rarely cried and was a remarkably good sleeper. Mark was a doting father, five years older than me, juggling his first promotion at Microsoft plus night school to get his patent engineer qualification. We were hopelessly unprepared and fudging it. Yet I was aware of being blessed, which must be the surest sign of having grown up. I can still see myself sitting on the top deck of that gently rocking ferry, eyes closed to the sun, my head tipped on to Mark's shoulder . . .

My rental house is way up the hill so it takes about twenty minutes to meander to Fort Worden State Park. I pass the same pretty houses as always, a mix of colourful A-frame, art deco, colonial and Cape Cod, making sure to look the other way if someone is out checking their mail and happens to glance up. With only just over nine thousand people living here, you have to make a rigorous effort not to get to know any of them.

Once I get down to the beach path I'm relieved to see there's not a soul out walking, not a single car in the parking area in front of the lighthouse that sits out on the nose of the beach. I stroll over the dunes towards the water's edge, welcoming the slap of waves and the salt-spiked air, then dig in my pocket for my phone. If I don't ring him I'm going to be plagued with images of him lying under a bus too, because, lately, if there's a worst-case scenario I'll find it.

'Liv!' he says.

It's funny, but with this single optimistic utterance of my name my eyes prick with tears.

'How are you?' He's slightly breathless. 'I've been thinking about you. I was going to call tonight when there was time to talk. It's been such a crazy busy day.' Mark has a certain mellow, artless, babe-in-the-woods way of speaking that might make you think he's not as bright as he actually is. Especially when he up-talks at the end of his sentences so his statements are like questions, making him sound like a teenager. He's also one of these rare people who can diffuse a crisis with his unex-citability, who can manage to good-humour his way out of any taut situation. Someone once told me they sensed Mark would cope with whatever you handed him. Little did they know.

'I'm not bad,' I say after a beat, buffered by the familiarity of his voice. 'Everything's fine.'

'Can you wait a minute. Let me . . . Give me two seconds, OK? I just got out of the shower.'

There's a clatter as he drops the phone then quietly curses. I imagine him hanging on to a white bath towel, dirty blonde hair limp on his brow. If he worked from home today, he'll have probably been out for a run – his latest fitness kick. Like many of his fads and fancies, he'll go at it with admirable zeal for about two weeks until he packs it in abruptly, never to be spoken of again. Mark has changed little over the years except for the bedazzling white smile. 'It's just a little bleaching,' he'd protested, coyly, when I'd gawked at him and said, 'What the heck?' He'd only gone in for a root canal. I couldn't help but wonder what was happening; we'd only been living in our new house for a short time and he'd already come home with the Mercedes SUV and a fitness member-ship at Orange Theory. I had a horrible sense he was morphing into one of our middle-aged neighbours – the very ones we liked to disparage when they'd pedal up their drives, beet red and panting in their Lycra that left nothing to the imagination. He later let it slip that his assistant had said, 'Too much coffee stains your teeth!' when he'd walked past her desk with his Starbucks grande Americano.

'I'm back,' he says. 'Sorry. Where were we?' More muffled sounds. He's probably struggling into a T-shirt. Mark isn't fond of being in the buff even if no one's looking. He once said that not having a great deal of manly body hair was something he'd been self-conscious about since he was sixteen.

'I rang Jessica,' I say. We always used to call her 'the wayward one', not because she really is – I don't even remember why we started it. But that was before all the humour had been wrung out of our lives, before making light of anything just felt wrong. 'All I wanted was to wish her happy birthday.'

Everything's gone quiet: whatever he's doing, he's stopped.

'Have you spoken to her?' I shouldn't be petty but I can't resist. Mark hates any implication he's the preferred parent, like it's some sort of contest. He hadn't approved of this travelling Europe lark. Not when she let it drop that instead of it just being for two months, she might delay her place at WSU if she was having a good time. 'It would only be for a year!' she'd argued, when he'd said, 'Of course you're going to have a good time! Who wouldn't? But you can do all that when you finish your education!' Mark is big on doing things in his idea of the proper order. He thinks we have all our lives to travel. Mark isn't always right.

Just when I wonder if he's gone, he says, 'Liv, look . . . can we not talk about Jess right this second? I'd like to talk about you. How *you* are. *Really* are.'

Something falters, like a small shifting of the earth underfoot. These days I can conquer the urge to break down when people are being tender to me, but it's still hard. After a moment or two I say, 'As I told you, I'm all right . . . I'm just out getting some air, you know . . . doing something with the day.' Two bald eagles pirouette overhead in perfect sync, emitting their high-pitched trill, and I watch them, envying them flight.

'The line's not very clear. It sounds like you're on a boat or something? Where are you?'

'Just down by the water. It's freezing. Blowing a gale, actually.' I'm aware of what it used to be like to talk to him. That constancy of sharing everything from the monumental to the trivial, the immunity you enjoy by having another person who is so wholly on your side, rare as a blue diamond.

'Can't you go back to the car? It'd be easier to have a conversation.'

'No, like I said, I walked.'

'Ah. Yes. So you did . . .'

It's just like we always were. I could be phoning him to ask what he thinks we should do for dinner, or to see if he remembered the 4.30 p.m. car service. Our life was a functioning hierarchy of work interspersed with weekends that mostly consisted of errands, take-out and the grand evening reward of Netflix, and I once had the luxury of thinking that it was mundane. Suddenly I fill with everything I have lost.

'I – I just needed to get out . . . It's been an endless day.'

'I know,' he says.

And for a second I could almost believe him. I want to hold it there – this idea of Mark knowing – like it's a fragile firefly and I'm getting to bask in its fleeting light. There is a long silence that I almost can't take. 'Say something,' I tell him. The eagles are keeping in step with me and now they're joined by a baby one. They're flying so low, I can hear the breathy waft of their wings.

'I don't know what to say . . .' he says, after a further hesitation. 'How will it change anything?'

The memory is there again, a shadow out at sea. Staring at it is dangerous because staring makes it take form, and all day I've said, *I will not think about this. If I can manage to not think about this, today of all days, then I'll have it under my control – instead of it having me.*

'Are you still there?' he asks. 'Liv?'

'Yeah, I'm here.' I am aware of a gentle sea spray on my face and I try to just focus on feeling it, letting it awaken nerve endings.

'Come home,' he says.

It slips out so quietly. With the weather wrapping around my ears I have to say, 'What?' But he doesn't repeat it. We hang there in suspenseful silence – me, bone still, windblown and confused – while the prospect of us being OK again flutters there like those birds. But then the birds disappear behind a cloud. Mark goes to say something else but I hang up.

'Why are you reading the *Eastbourne Herald*?'

I was sitting at the computer in the spare bedroom we'd turned into my office. I hadn't heard him come in and practically jumped out of my skin. 'For God's sake, stop sneaking up on me!' I said, and quickly clicked off the page.

But he knew why.

'Liv . . .' He clamped a big warm hand on my shoulder, squeezed.

There are times when I can still feel the imprint of Mark's fingers, the steadying reassurance, the low register of his despair. I can feel it right now as it happens. I actually believe I could reach up and touch the back of his hand.

The English newspaper is saved to my Favourites. In some ways I know more about a place I've never been to than the one where I've lived for most of my adult life. I do this by force of habit now, I think, which makes it feel harmless. But somewhere in the frontal lobe something tells me it should probably stop. Today would be a good day to make this the last time.

I usually need wine when I do this, so I make sure there's a decent glass at hand – not quite full, a shy seven ounces – then I click on the page. Up comes the red banner, the word *Herald* in big red letters. I go to *News,* scroll down, idly scanning the headings and subheads. *Winning sculpture pays tribute to pier fire.* There's an old photo of the famous Victorian pier with its blue and white dome engulfed in flames and black smoke. *Family thanks funeral cortège for 11-year-old Eastbourne boy.* A picture of a policeman on a motorbike leading a procession past terraced houses with multiple dustbins lined up like soldiers in postage-stamp-sized front gardens. I scroll through a few more pages, only half concentrating, not even sure what I'm doing, the heavy hand of tiredness creeping up on me.

I'm almost ready to log off when I see it.

For a split second my response mechanism shuts down. My eyes distrust what I'm seeing. It's too unlikely. Seriously – what are the chances? But the more I stare, the more my heart rages with adrenaline.

It's a photograph, probably snapped during an outing to the beach. To anyone else it's just a man in his thirties with a little girl with loose blonde ringlets, and a boy a couple of years older. The man has his arm around both children, the little girl tucking into his side. She looks cross, as she often can, but the boy is beaming the cheekiest of smiles and clutching an ice cream – he's got chocolate smeared all over his chin. His eyes are very much his mother's: strikingly dark brown against the fair hair, but the rest of him is every bit his dad.

I would know this man's face if we happened to find ourselves on the same Tube in central London, or if I stepped outside right now, on the other side of the Atlantic, and he were passing my gate. The strong smile lines, the slightly hollow cheeks. Something of a bygone era about him, like a young Frank Sinatra minus the twinkling blue eyes. You'd say he was handsome, in a spare, 'grew into his looks later in life' way. Staring at him is a chilling thing. He is holding my gaze the way photos do when you invite them to reach back at you. I am jailed by it. I can't break away, and nor, it seems, can he. I'm sure that if you put us in a room we would have a great deal to say to one another, or perhaps we would have nothing at all. It would be a test I would never want to face.

The headline says: *Doctor Admits 'I Made a Terrible Mistake'.*

I try to decide if those words can mean something else. The eyes are still looking at me as though it's important he monitors my reaction to this. My urge to read on is as strong as my dread. I pretty much take the first paragraph in one gulp then caution myself to resist skimming to get to the end in case I miss something crucial. By the time I finish, I have to remind myself to breathe. A lump the size of a small planet is lodged in my throat. I swallow but it won't budge. My muscles from my breastbone up have seized.

TWO

Nanette, my pint-sized landlady from the Philippines, is standing at my door peering at me through funky wire-rimmed glasses. 'Everything OK, Olibia?'

I try not to make it too obvious she just woke me up; I actually thought the knocking was in my dream. 'Everything's fine, thanks.' I plaster down bits of my hair with the flat of my hand. It's still raining. I'm guessing I've been zonked out for a couple of hours by the damp cotton-wool feeling in my head.

'You not well today, Olibia?' She searches my face, looking more concerned than she ought to be about a virtual stranger, which is unexpected and touching.

'No, no . . . I'm fine. But I put my foot through the deck last night. Look at my leg.' I hike up my Lululemons so she can see the network of scratches on my calf, the streaks of dried blood. 'There's so much raccoon dirt under there, too! It's a toilet. I almost needed stitches and a tetanus shot.'

'Oh no!' She slaps a hand over her mouth. 'Poor leg! I so sorry! So sorry 'bout this, Olibia!'

I suddenly feel bad for exaggerating. 'It's all right. Not to worry, I bathed it and it's totally fine.' I wave her inside and proceed through to the back of the house, hearing the short shuffle of her feet following.

When I answered her 'house to rent' ad two months ago she told me she's lived in the US for twenty years and has worked at the local library for most of them. 'Do you go to the library where you live?' she asked. 'Because I can pull string, get you temporary member card.' When I told her I did, she said, 'So where *do* you live, Olibia? Tell me, what bring you here to Port Townsend?' Clearly, I'd walked right into that one.

We step outside, stare at the hole. 'The wood's all rotted,' I say. She leans in for a closer look. Large drops of rain pockmark the white cotton of her shirt. I've noticed she's always in black trousers but wears them far too high up on her waist, giving her a 'long ass', as Jessica would say, and exposing a couple of inches of ankle at the other end; it makes me want to adjust them into their proper place. 'It's really disappointing. I'd been hoping I could sit out here in better weather.' I wave her back into the house, worried she's going to get soaked. I'm a big believer in perspective, so I'm trying to keep some, but I'm all for disclosure too; she should have told me the thing was falling apart.

'Ah, yes!' she says and shakes her head, meaning, *Well, that's not going to happen, is it!*

'You know, I really like it here . . .' I look up at the tall cedars rinsed with rain. The garden is a little private cocoon. I can hear the neighbours on both sides but can't see them. No need to make awkward small talk or have to look like a normal, together human being when I am feeling anything but.

'Your husband . . . Mr Chapman . . .' She utters his name like he's a state secret. 'Maybe he fix?' There's a flare of mischief in her eyes. I try to look away smoothly without appearing cowed by her curiosity.

I realise I'm a bit of an enigma. In small towns like this you can't be aloof without being a nut somebody needs to crack. I'm new, in my early forties, and while I wear a wedding ring, I don't have a man in tow. I'm definitely a city type because I dress well; it's a failing. Much as I always wish I could look *on trend* casual, I never feel I'm quite pulling off the look, so I end up resorting to smarter clothes – jeans paired with a three-quarter-sleeved black jacket, say – that might make me look more uptight than I really am. I'm certainly more British than I am American, meaning, while I'm polite and not unfriendly, I don't give much away. I neither welcome, nor over-answer, questions, nor do I bond easily; I need to trust someone a great deal before I'm ever going to put my heart on my sleeve or air my dirty laundry. All my life I've been one to push against the idea of having to give an account of myself – even back when I had nothing much to hide – and it's anathema to me now.

'A handyman could probably take care of this quite easily,' I tell her. 'It's just nailing together a few planks of wood. Even I could probably do it.'

She is shaking her head. 'Deck is rotted. Handyman fix now. Problem come back later.'

She has a point. No sense in throwing good money after bad, as my mother would say. I place a hand on my hip and stare out at the garden, aware of her scrutinising me like I'm visiting royalty. 'Rent very cheap!' she chirps.

'Yes, I know. But to be honest I'm not sure I can stay if I can't use the outdoor space.' I meet her fully in the eyes now. 'I'm not trying to be awkward. I'm really not. But I'm used to sitting out in a garden.' It sounds way more lady of leisure than I intended. I wonder what she'd think if she knew I'm used to a house three times this size, and that I'm already feeling claustrophobic and it's got nothing to do with the size of the property. That's why I need to be able to sit outside – I just need somewhere to go when I can't breathe. 'I suppose I just didn't expect the deck was going to be unusable, that's all,' I add, trying to sound less aggrieved by first-world disappointment.

'I can't build new deck,' she says, firmly. No hint of chummy agreeability now. 'Too much bills. Too much debt since my husband die.'

She told me it was sudden, that she'd had to move in with her daughter to rent this out for extra income. I felt sorry for her, and intrigued – she seemed more angry at her husband than anything else. Though I didn't want to show I was intrigued in case it gave her license to reciprocate.

'Well, we've reached a bit of a stalemate,' I say, affecting good-natured resignation to compensate for sounding so stuck-up. I really could leave as I'm travelling light and I've spotted plenty of other to-let properties as I've moseyed around town. But I really don't want to mess her around. Plus, I'm here now. It's furnished adequately – not modern, but cosy and cared-for. I adore the little view of the sea, and how the deer will actually come and graze in the garden while you're right there. A whole family visited just a few days back when I was sitting on the step; I felt like I had companions. And Nanette was very kind in trust-ing me when I told her that even though I had no references I could most certainly pay my rent – which she seemed to accept by scrutinising me up and down. So, really, the moral of the story is, if you want to earn a living as a confidence trickster, just invest in a pair of smart jeans and a nice handbag from Nordstrom Rack. A British accent might help too; everyone trusts people from countries where there's a reigning monar-chy. Plus the good thing is she's letting me pay month to month; I'm not bound by a one-year lease. Freedom for me right now is everything.

'The rent, I lower it,' she says, holding my eyes in bright despera-tion. A sweat has broken out on her brow, pooling in the folds of her wrinkles.

'No. I definitely couldn't let you do that. The rent's already very reasonable. That wouldn't be fair at all.'

'No?' She seems stunned.

'Of course not!' I'm hardly going to rip off somebody who's got nothing, if I'm going to rip off anyone at all. 'I'll go on paying what we agreed. If I decide to stay, I mean.'

She unleashes a smile. 'You good person, Olibia Chapman! Good person!' Her flattery makes me blush, despite the fact that the way she says *O-lib-ia* sounds like she's calling me a female private part.

'How about if I see if I can find someone to take a look at it?' The idea just comes to me. 'I've got some time on my hands.' I don't say that I could use the distraction, that the days are cruelly long and as each new one starts I have to talk myself down from the fear of wondering how I'm going to possibly fill it. 'If it's not ridiculously expensive I can maybe pay for the labour if you can cover the cost of the wood?' I have no idea where I'm getting this from. It's more than a little mad. But the area is pretty small: I can't imagine it's going to cost an arm and a leg. I'll get my use out of it, even if I only stay here for this summer. And, besides, Mark can afford it.

'Oooh!' She claps, and jumps up and down like a kid on a bouncy castle. The innocence of it makes me smile. 'You so kind! So kind! This is very nice offer! Very nice offer, O-lib-ia!'

'Not really.' I'm sure my cheeks are turning puce now. 'It's purely selfish. I just want to be able to enjoy the garden, that's all.'

'No!' She wags a finger. 'Selfish is bad person. You' – she reaches up and gives me a keen poke in the shoulder – 'are good person!'

After dinner – baked beans on toast from the can I opened a few nights ago – I contemplate another walk to deter me from pouring a second glass of wine that might easily become a third. But I don't really have it in me to traipse the roads again, on one more date with my own head-space. I don't feel like watching TV either, as I have a hard time concentrating, so I think, *Hang it! Just have another glass and get over yourself!* So I do. And then I open up my laptop. As I stare at my Favourites bar I think maybe if I click on it the article won't be there. It wouldn't be the first time I've imagined something. Part of me is looking forward to being proven right. But no. When I click on the article there it is – the photo, the faces, as real as day. I stare at him again. He's one of those people who could be thirty-five or forty-five, you can't quite tell. Something to do with the strong lines like parentheses either side of his mouth – they fool you into thinking his skin is older. The tips of his fingers peep just above his daughter's left shoulder. I've got an almost identical one of Mark doing that with Jessica when she was about the same age. But it's the sharp, soulful eyes I keep coming back to. Once again my own lock into his until they burn from lack of blinking. Before I re-read it I warn myself to affect an air of indifference. This could be anyone's misfortune, anyone's life. But it's impossible. When I'm done I'm devastated all over again, so many thoughts spooling in my head I don't know how to order them.

I'm not sure how long I sit here automatically refreshing the screen every time it goes dark, reviving his face. Finally I open up my email, click on 'Create New Message'. I punch in the first few letters of Mark's address then, when it auto-fills, copy and paste the link to the article. I try to think what to type in the subject line, and then it comes to me.

Consequences.

THREE

Port Townsend has changed so much since Mark and I used to come here almost two decades ago. I had no idea what I was expecting. I was driving north, in an unthinking void, subconsciously aware I'd have to find somewhere to base myself for a day or two until I could figure out my next steps, or I was going to end up in Alaska. I remembered how this place had always felt like a point of both destination and departure, which seemed somehow appropriate, though I'm not sure my decision was even that conscious – if I was clear-headed enough to think. I was on autopilot. In many ways I still am.

But when I was able to disconnect from my disconnect, and imagine myself as more of a tourist, I enjoyed discovering the town's new visage. It sadly never amounted to the name it was given in the 1800s – City of Dreams – when it was predicted to be the largest, most prosperous harbour on the West Coast, but its eclecticism somehow makes up for that. The main drag is a hodgepodge of unique and charming little shops catering mainly to middle class vacationers and day-trippers who are drawn to its remote, unexpected, historical charm. There's one that just sells premium olive oils and balsamic vinegars, and one next door that's into spices, sugars and salt from the far corners of the world. There are a couple of thrift stores whose windows are bursting with everything from old record players to vintage designer fashion, and even a store dedicated to all things British with a nature/hunting theme. So many times I've thought, *Oh I must text a picture of this to Jessica!* but something stops my hand. But then I was poking around in a shop and came across a gorgeous vintage belt – chunky, embossed leather in peacock blue. I thought, *Oh my! This has Jess written all over it!* I could see her pairing it with her jeans and oversized white peasant blouse. So I bought it and parcelled it up in brown kraft paper tied with jute twine. I'll hang on to it and give it to her as a little welcome home gift. Just the thought of her face when she sees it is already making me smile.

Then there is the café. What I like about Books and Beans is its trendy dilapidation, how it practically sits on top of the water through a curious feat of engineering, and that it's part coffee house, part used bookstore, which, being an English major who loves coffee, I think is quite ingenious. You can always grab a book and sit and read and no one hovers like a vulture for your table; people will happily sit on the old oak floor.

'You're not looking for work, are you?' Beth, the owner, looks up from writing on a piece of letter paper at the counter. I glance behind me to see who she's talking to, and she smirks. 'You see, once in a while people do get the courage to speak to you.'

She's always fresh with me and while it's bizarre she can be so familiar when she doesn't even know me it makes me feel human again. 'Hmm . . . Do they?' I pretend to frown. 'That's a shame.'

'Oh, you're English! I would never have guessed!'

Clearly she's taking her witty vitamins. She knows full well I'm English. I watch her painstakingly draw a decorative flourish on the paper right above the words, *The Correspondents' Club.* I wonder what that is.

From even the little time I've been here I could write a book on the people of this town and it wouldn't be a very flattering one. In fact, if it got published I'd probably turn up dead in a lavender field. I am slowly gathering that Beth is the frosty one whose armour never comes off. I'm sure we have nothing in common on any possible level, but it hasn't been helped by the fact that we got off on the wrong foot. Beth is a bit of a vegan tree-hugger, in her pocketless jeans, with her salt and pepper hair that's always braided and secured by scrunchies, which I believe should be put in a landfill along with baseball caps. Now, while I have a daughter who has put us through many a 'clean eating' phase, I am also the offspring of a farmer, and I believe that certain animals, so long as they are humanely raised and humanely killed, are part of the food chain. I told Beth this when she lectured me on all the ways Earth Balance is superior to butter. It only began because I asked what fat she used in her morning glory muffins because they were a little oily, though I didn't add that last part, but my face might have. It didn't end well.

'Fancy a treat with your coffee?' she asks me now, carefully placing the sheet of paper to the side and indicating the familiar tray of baked offerings that always look either sweaty or stale.

'It's ridiculously tempting but I'm good.' I feel her scrutinise me for some kind of sign that I've undergone a seismic personality shift, but the best I can manage is a twitch of my lips that I hope conveys sincerity rather than sarcasm.

On my first visit, I bought one of her sugar-free spelt vegan muffins but could barely get through half of it, despite the college try. So the next time I sneaked in a couple of McVitie's dark chocolate digestives. When she spotted me nibbling away in the corner like a nervous rabbit she gave me quite the public telling off about how she doesn't allow customers to bring in their own food. I tried to explain that it wasn't because I'm cheap; I'd just rather consume something simple that I enjoy. Besides, my body actually needs proper sugar, because of a strange disorder she really didn't need to know about (probably because I didn't know about it either; I was making it up as I went along). But it came out more insulting than I intended. I wasn't in a great place that day. I suppose since then we've each been doomed to think the other is on the spectrum.

I generally come here in the mornings before ten and lay claim to the sofa nearest the window. It's saggy and you can barely clamber out of it without showing your knickers, but it's more comfy than the almost classroom-sized tables and chairs that form a sterile row along the window. Just looking at them I am swept back to the little red-brick Victorian infant school of my childhood. I half expect to see lifting lids, inkwells and pencil grooves, and my mother at the door, smiling and waving when the bell rang, waiting to escort me home for lunch. The view out of the window is something else, though. Part of me could sit here all day watching the sea in shifting shades of light, and some days I almost have. On Sundays I will pick out a couple of books then on Wednesday exchange them for two others – they have an honour system that could only work in towns like this. I always make sure Beth sees me returning them, so she can't get me for stealing. And every time I do, you can somehow bet she has her eye on me.

'Thanks,' I say, when she puts my mug down, 'that looks wonderful.' She always pours my coffee how I like it: a double shot latte, with only half the amount of milk – 'You know, the kind that comes from a cow?' I once deadpanned as I wagged a container of soy at her. So I assume this is a sort of detente. I pull out my three dollars thirty. The day after the inane biscuit exchange I gave her a ten-dollar bill and told her to keep the change. Just to make the point that it wasn't about the money.

'I'm so understaffed,' she says, as I'm about to walk away. 'I was being serious about the job. Courtney has run out on me now she's got a boyfriend. And Thom's moved to Tofino for the surfing. Finding somebody trustworthy at short notice isn't as easy as you'd think.'

'Who says I'm trustworthy?'

There is a beat of hesitation where I think, *Here comes the sparkiness again*, then she says, 'Your face says.'

I'm about to thank her for the compliment when she adds, 'Then again I'm probably just desperate. But I figure you're fairly new round here, and you don't work for anyone I know of, because we've all talked about you. And I assume everybody has to work at some point, even though some of us don't necessarily look like we have to . . . ' She gives my dove-grey cashmere cardigan, paired with skinny jeans, the once over. I would never step out of the house without having made a token nod to fashion. Maybe it's the stiff-upper-lipped Brit in me, but no matter what kind of private hell I'm going through it's not going to be evident by my appearance.

I come late to something she's just said. 'Can I ask – why *are* you all talking about me?' I am genuinely curious.

At first she looks like she's wondering whether I'm being uppity, then she says, 'Well . . . it's just that Burt at the Night Watchman's Lookout said he thought you might have been a journalist type. He thought when you checked out so abruptly that a sudden assignment might have taken you elsewhere.'

If I were in the mood to find anything funny I'd probably laugh. 'Good heavens! Sounds very James Bond, doesn't it?'

Her spine straightens the way people rear up when they sense you're putting down their townspeople, and therefore them too. 'I believe he just thought you looked like you were here for a reason but you might have left for an even bigger one.' Her tone is clipped but she blushes.

I hadn't pegged Burt for being the town crier but clearly I should have. I am sure she knows he and I didn't exactly part bosom buddies. Though I'd booked five nights at the Night Watchman's Lookout, I only lasted two. I'd only checked in there because it was that or sleep in the car. I'd arrived on a long weekend without really having given much mind to it, and the few hotels in town were full. Burt had said he'd had a last-minute cancellation. He'd helped me bring my suitcase in to a tiny room that looked like it might have just been dusted off for my arrival, then he stood there, wedged in between the foot of the bed and the door, rattling on about the history of the house and how he was a direct descendent of the Prince of Wales. When I looked at him like he might possibly be off his head, he explained that white settlers in the 1800s had a hard time pronouncing the names of the native Indians who occupied the land, so they named them after British aristocrats and royalty. A couple of hours later, when I came out of the adjacent bathroom in my nightgown, he was hovering in the near dark and nearly gave me a heart attack. Apparently he needed to break the urgent news that if I required an extra blanket then I was out of luck; his wife had washed it and they were convinced one of the occupants of the neighbouring trailer park had nicked it from the line. When I did finally lay down my head once I was convinced Prince Burt wasn't drumming up any more bogus excuses to come pester me again, the gale force draught from the dreadfully old windows nearly blew me out of bed. And let's not talk about the ancient pillows that might as well have been filled with bricks. As soon as the only four-star hotel in town got a free room, I jumped ship. I was just so relieved to get away from overly gregarious fellow houseguests at the breakfast table asking what my plans were for my day, and Burt glancing down my shirt every time he topped up my coffee. But he wasn't exactly gracious about my leaving, insisting I pay for all five nights. I told him even the best hotels give you twenty-four hours' cancellation, so by all rights I should only be paying for two. But he was sticking to his guns, so I ended up just giving him his damned money to be done with it.

'We all just thought you'd be passing through, because we don't get too many people like you through these parts, certainly not on their own. But we're surprised to see you don't seem to be going anywhere in a hurry,' Beth says, as though this non-explanation accounts for why my existence begets all this curiosity.

'God,' is all I say, because there really are no words.

'Job's yours if you want it,' she adds as I'm walking over to the creamer stand.

I turn. 'Thanks. I'm really not looking for a job, but I appreciate you thinking of me.' Then I can't resist adding, 'But be sure to pass that on to Burt. So he can get on with his day.'

As I shake a packet of sugar into my drink I realise I'm trembling. It's as though by just talking about everyone's curiosity I'm somehow on the receiving end of it all over again.

'Just remember, if you ever change your mind it might be too late!' she hollers.

Beth is a last word sort of person. *Whatever floats your boat*, I think.

I take my coffee over to the bookshelves, relieved to disappear between them. I am sure my love for books and literature must stem from all those hours I spent with too much time on my hands, being an only child growing up with parents who were always too tied up with the farm to indulge me with much attention. It's still my favourite way of escaping the world. These days I'm not fussy what I read – my mind is only fifty per cent on it anyway – except I can't do sad stories. You'll find all kinds here – cookbooks, special interest books, how-tos, business books, and all manner of paperbacks recent and old. You'd think in the time I've been coming in I'd know them all off by heart, but the stock keeps miraculously changing. Today, though, something entirely out of the ordinary catches my eye. I home in on it hiding between Sidney Sheldon and Barbara Taylor Bradford. It's wedged in there quite tight; I have to do a lot of wiggling to get it out. I'm surprised to see it's a pocket-sized book of poems by Longfellow, bound in chocolate calfskin leather; exquisite but made to last, the way things were back then, the way things rarely are any more. One of those treasures you'd find in a bookstore in an old university town back in England, the kind that makes you stop what you're doing and sit cross-legged on the floor in homage to a bygone era, a lost art. When I hold it to my nose I detect cloves and leather gloves, maybe a hint of cigar. Fanning through the gilt-edged parchment pages, a loose one drops out. It's looks like it was torn from the front of the book then put back – why do people have to deface things of beauty? I can never understand. On it someone has written:

The tender word forgotten,

The letter you did not write.

The flowers you might have sent, dear,

Are your haunting ghosts tonight.

Margaret Elizabeth Sangster

It's as though someone is talking to me. I am the *you*.

A tingle travels the length of my spine, the top of my head prickling with dread. The beginnings of a fine sweat on the back of my neck make me stand bone still to see if it's going to travel to other parts.

The words have been written with a fountain pen, in a fine cursive hand – a woman's I'd guess. The skin of the page has absorbed the fat swells of ink, and, as I stare at the intricate lettering, I can almost hear the tiny scraping flourish of the nib in the expert hand of the writer. I read it again, unable to shake my conviction that this is some kind of sign, though I'm generally not a believer in these things – I can't speak for anyone else's mind but mine is messed up enough without that.

Haunting ghosts.

The coffee has suddenly turned me nauseous. There's a gumminess in the back of my throat, the kind that comes before you puke your insides up. I put the paper back where it dropped out from and close the book. But I can't unsee the words.

My instinct is to put it back on the shelf but instead, on a whim, I think, *No, I'd like to borrow it.* I place it in my bag, along with an Anita

Shreve – *The Pilot's Wife* – that I read many moons ago and is now ripe for a re-visit. I put my empty mug in the used dishes bin and walk to the door, deliberately avoiding Beth's eyes, which I sense are back on me like lasers. But as I go to leave I am powerfully aware of those astute little words throwing me slightly off balance.

On my way out there is a man coming in the door. It's that awkward moment where one of us has to give way and I'm curious to see if he's going to be a gentleman. Just as I'm thinking how life is a series of tests – some of them the ones that make you a better version of yourself, others immaterial like this – he holds the door open for me with an outstretched arm, and presses himself back to allow me to squeeze by him. He is tall, and of average build. I'm conscious of the pleasing smell of a well-worn leather jacket, mingled perhaps with faded aftershave or fabric softener, and of how he's blocking some of the light. As I try to slide past him our chests graze. I glance up to somehow apologise for the awkward bodily contact, but I can't see his eyes. He's wearing a pair of aviator sunglasses, the reflector kind; all I see is a slightly distorted image of my own head. I mutter 'thanks' and for some odd reason practically fizzle with relief when I get outside.

It's only when I've gone a few steps down the street that it hits me what it was about his face and I shudder.

FOUR

'I got your email,' he says.

I had almost forgotten I'd sent it.

'My God, Olivia . . . Are you ever going to move on?'

I open my mouth but a response just evaporates. I search for words but it's like I've had a crash course in a foreign language and forgotten what I learned.

'You're not, are you? You're never going to let this go.'

I'm not sure what's worse: his pity for me, or his complete inability to understand. I give up my task of trying to force a small plastic bag on to a large kitchen bin, pinch the bridge of my nose to stem that sense of going insane. 'He almost killed somebody,' I say. 'Somebody almost died because he wasn't fit to do his job.'

He sighs. 'It says he read the CT scan the wrong way round, performed the surgery on the wrong lung. When they opened the guy up he just assumed the clot had disappeared. They said it was an easy mistake.'

'They sent the guy home. He started spitting blood and his wife thought he was dying.'

'He ended up being fine! Why are you obsessing about this?'

'How can you be so casual about it?' I don't know whether he's trivialising it for my sake, or because he genuinely is this indifferent.

'He's fine, Olivia. End of.'

'End of?' My heart skips a beat then hammers out the next few. 'Glen Sullivan might never practice medicine again. The patient is claiming all kinds of—' The legal jargon escapes me. I'd had it all straight before.

'Yeah, that's what people do when they want to sue doctors for wads of money. They exaggerate.' The way he draws out his words makes him sound like he's trying to reason with an imbecile. 'Anyway, seriously, why are we talking about this?' He sounds genuinely bewildered. 'Why are you still trawling the Internet looking for stuff that's only going to torment you? You need to get help for this.' He sighs long and heavy through his nose.

My heartbeat is like a puff of breath in my ears. I ignore this annoying issue of my needing help. 'It's completely unfathomable to me that you seriously don't give a shit,' I say. You can't make a cold person care. I get up from the table and fling open the back door. We are here again, straddling the line between acquiescence and argument, reluctant to have a foothold in either, because we've been down both these paths many times before and it accomplishes nothing. I stand there looking out on to the rain, listening to the rhythmic rush and recede, filling my lungs with air and trying to steady my peripatetic thoughts.

'Of course I give a shit,' he says. 'But I give one about my wife. As for Dr Glen Sullivan, well, it's sad and I'm sorry, but it's not my problem and it's not yours.'

I disagree strenuously, but I don't have it in me to fight. My knee-jerk reaction is to wage war on everything Mark says because he is such an easy target and somewhere in me, where I still have the capacity, I know that's terribly wrong of me and extremely unfair. 'As usual, thanks for your understanding and your concern,' I say, a touch less strident. 'You're a real piece of work, you know that?'

'So you keep telling me.' There is a sad note of fondness and resignation in his tone that momentarily breaks my stride, and possibly my heart. After a protracted pause where neither of us seems to want to add anything, but neither are we rushing to hang up, he says, 'Anyway, can we stop talking about this for a minute and talk about something else? I want to know when you're coming home. It's crazy you not being here, where you belong . . . I miss you. The house isn't the same without you. Nothing is. *I'm* not. Not having you to come home to at the end of the day on top of everything, it's . . . well, it's a horrible existence, frankly.'

His candour makes my heart beat with a ravaged sadness, and yet I can't resist saying, 'You have someone else. Remember? How would that work, exactly?'

There's a small sigh, then silence, then, 'Seriously? This again?'

I think of myself saying to him that day – I was very calm, almost out-of-body – 'I'm leaving you. I can't forgive you.'

I was aware that once you've claimed this you can't really go back on your words without negating the damage somehow. Yet – it was so strange – I didn't feel fully committed to it. My words and my actions didn't line up. Leaving didn't equate to being unable to forgive; one didn't necessitate the other. It was a bit like being an actor speaking your lines: it's intense and you believe it wholeheartedly, but in the back of your mind you also know it isn't real. I remember him saying, in what seemed like genuine amazement, as he watched me pile my stuff into the car, 'Why are you doing this? I haven't done anything wrong!' As I slammed the door, a voice was saying, *Part of you believes him. Mark's not a liar. So why exactly* are *you doing this?*

'I thought you were going to call the realtor,' I say now. I have zero sentimental attachment to the place we bought almost four years ago. It's so barren of memories, except for one bad one – so lacking in everything that makes a house a home. It was Mark who pushed for it, as a measure of how far we'd come – or he had. If we'd never bought it none of this would have happened. Mark wouldn't have met her. I wouldn't have done what I did. I miss our old place, the one we scraped to afford, the one where I see memories of us as a family everywhere I turn. I miss it as though it were a human thing with a central nervous system and a steady strum of breath. Sometimes I can't get my head around the fact that we will never live in 4528 Cedars Avenue as a family again. The truest thing I have learnt is that you can't rewrite what's been written.

Someone has lit a barbecue and there is smoke in the air. It's stinging my eyes. Avenues for my thoughts to wander down stretch out ahead of me but I don't want to go down any of them at this particular moment. 'You said you were going to call the realtor,' I repeat, my voice quavering.

'That's not true. You said you wanted it sold. I said OK.'

'You said it would go up for sale before the end of the month! You promised.' I wipe my eyes.

'I was angry.'

'So you haven't done it, then?' I hear the wobble in my voice, the doubts, the belligerence, the building of anger I'm never properly able to release. It takes a certain gut-wrenching effort to push away the rush of *what used to be*. How do you accept that which you can't grasp and probably never will? It's still surreal to me. I cannot get my head around how this began, and how we got here so fast.

'No, I haven't done it, OK? I haven't done it because it's not going to solve anything, is it? You seem to think that if we make the house go away, everything goes away, and it doesn't. And you know that deep down. And I *know* you know it.'

I cling on to his words, the calm way he delivers them – on to this insight he has of me, born of knowing me almost better than I know myself, as though it's a lifeline back to the person I used to be. 'You promised,' I just repeat, less convincingly.

'Look . . .' His voice is quieter now. I can tell he is running out of space to give to this topic; his day won't accommodate it. 'If you want to end it, then go ahead. But I'm not doing it. There's no way I'm seeing my marriage break up because of—'

'Because of what?' My heart races with anticipation.

Carol Mason

'*Her*,' he says.

The way he outs her in a single sharp pronoun, practically spits it, stuns me. But of course now that he's done it he has put her there, right back in the middle of us, like this shadow. She is filling every space, starving me of air. I am completely ambushed by her. My heart is pounding.

When I don't speak, he says, 'Look, I'm going now, OK? I'm at work. I can't do this conversation here. I'm hanging up.'

Because Mark is always polite even when he's at the end of his rope with you.

FIVE

There's something about this ritual that's almost sacred now. I take a sip of my wine, my laptop balanced in the well of my crossed legs. I've put the gas fire on, not because it's cold, but because this is what Jessica and I always do on an evening when Mark is working late and we're settling in to watch one of our shows. It brings me a comfort that goes way beyond warmth.

Her Facebook page is public, the profile picture the same as always. The post at the top is also unchanged. The family trip to Spain. *Beautiful Seville!* she has written. Thirty-four photos in total, all candids – five of them you can see without clicking on the album. Pretty little Daisy in the pool in her pink water wings with her gaggle of cute, bare-chested cousins. Cheeky Henry sticking out his tongue; he's wearing his over-sized lime green sunglasses and his dad's Panama hat. Glen, lean and shirtless, batting a cricket ball. Someone is poised to catch – his brother, I think. Then there's the one that fascinates me the most. It's of the four of them watching a performance by flamenco dancers, their faces composed in that same transfixed expression. No one could deny they're a model family. Theirs are the kind of good looks you gaze upon with a certain reverence, that repeat themselves down the generations, that are almost unfair. Sarah is holding a glass of white wine. Her loose blonde hair is pinned back at the sides, showing tiny platinum bezel-set diamonds in her ears. What's so perfect about this one is, it's a family of four thinking the same thought, being moved in the same way, at the exact same time, and it's captured there, impossible to be recreated, long after the moment is gone, for all of forever. The last one is a picture of Sarah and Glen in a restaurant. I imagine Glen's brother and his wife were probably watching the kids. Sarah has her arm draped across Glen's back. I stare at the strong smile lines, the slightly sunken cheeks. He is saying something into her ear that has obviously tickled her by how she's laughing. They've been married since 2007. Anyone can see they're still very much into one another, which just makes this even harder to accept.

Twenty-nine other ones.

What gets me is, whether it's a close-up of Henry's absurdly long eyelashes or a frolicsome scramble for an airborne beach ball in the pool, there is so much humanity here, something almost more vital than life itself. Lots of people have liked and commented on them. Sarah has liked all the comments, and replied to most. Reading her words, her voice is so clear in my ear, so immediately recognisable: the gently lilting Welsh accent; her sparkly sense of fun. I cannot peel my eyes away from these vivid little narratives of somebody else's life. For the time it takes to go through them it's like I've been given a free pass to travel light, to feel the heat of a Spanish summer. I'm always a bit disappointed when I get to the end, though. When we are back to Daisy in her water wings in the pool.

I usually go to Sarah's older profile pics last. Eleven of them but one in particular always draws me: Sarah at a charity fundraiser. It's not just the floaty teal evening gown that shows how slim she is, and how gently toned her arms are. It's because she's so alive with personality in this one; someone has snapped her how she really is, so completely free of pose or pretence. She is reaching down to pluck the hem of her dress off the heel of her silver sandal where it's got caught, and she's pulling a face. There's a gigantic Christmas tree in the background. She looks flushed, like she's been tucking into the champagne.

By the time I go to click on her friends – she has 167 – I am smacked with, *Why am I doing this? What do I hope to find?* It's a strange thing to catch yourself recognising an element of lunacy in your own actions. I've long since given up scrolling through the whole lot of them, trying to connect the dots; all I can really conclude is that they are professionals – work or uni friends and acquaintances. Unfortunately, once you eliminate all the family members, there's not much evidence of Sarah's working-class roots on Facebook. Her bubbly bestie, Jo, has just updated her profile picture. I click on it. She looks a bit sad. Maybe because she recently got divorced and lost her job.

Once I've finished, there's the same frustrating hankering: why aren't there more? I'd give anything to have something fresh to pore over. It's the strangest thing to get an aperture on to someone's life and to recognise it's not nearly enough.

The message tab is there, though. It always troubles me how accessible we all are these days. How Facebook links the lives of old and new friends, even strangers, showing us surprising things we have in common, making us ships that pass in the night when we normally might not have been navigating the same waters. I get the same crazy thought. *What if I message her?* My heart races at the prospect. I have a sudden urge to top up my wine so I get up and go into the kitchen. I've managed to keep to my new rule of only drinking more than my allotted measure Fridays to Sundays, just so I can prove to myself I'm keeping a check on it.

When I get back to my laptop, good sense is taking over. I can't possibly write to her. It would be mad. Still, though, I stare at her current profile picture – a cropped version of the bigger one of her in the party dress, where she's pulling a face. I must sit like this for ages, finishing the wine without even tasting it. Then, somehow, without my brain even giving directions, I have scrolled to the message tab again.

Just click on it.

When I do, a reckless charge erupts in me; my limbs have a sudden energy and life of their own. Just catching myself doing this is like crossing a boundary already, like outing myself for a crime I've almost got away with. I stare at the little blue-bannered box, her name in white type, feeling the pounding of my blood.

Dear Sarah, I imagine writing. I am conscious suddenly of the wine having gone to my head, yet the idea of doing this is not diminished. My fingers levitate over the keypad. Dare I? I've got this far . . . Next, I am carefully tapping it out. My spine is locked in a shiver. I am oddly calm despite my heart beating hard. It feels good already, like a relief. But I've absolutely no idea what to say next.

SIX

The coffee shop is quiet this morning. I have a searing headache that I suspect isn't going to be improved by caffeine but I'm going to try anyway. I remove my sunglasses. Beth scans my face as though she's making something of its absence of make-up.

'Muffin?' She indicates the tray she's busy emptying.

'Thanks. I just ate breakfast.'

She continues to lift the remaining three or four with tongs and lays them in the display cabinet, in no great hurry, while I stand there like a potted plant. When she's done she fixes me with a steady stare. 'You know, I've been thinking . . . You look like you need something.'

I frown, unsure what she means. 'To eat?'

Her gaze doesn't flinch and her expression is set in a way that I don't like. Then she says, 'A purpose.'

I am blank for a second before the magnitude of her insult dawns on me. Then my heart gives several juddering beats and I hear myself saying, 'You know, that's actually seriously fucking rude.' The words fly out without my bidding. This is déjà vu.

She appears stunned. Her bottom jaw hangs there, slightly detached from the upper.

I am swept back to the parking lot near Bellevue Square mall. I'd been on my way to deal with our car insurance. It was the first day I'd actually left the house on my own in weeks. I had just got out of Mark's SUV and was pulling my bag from the back seat when I heard the shrill, raised voice of a woman. I noticed her then realised – oddly – she was addressing me.

'Aren't you listening?' She is small but there is something fierce and purposeful about her. 'I said that was a stop sign! You're supposed to come to a complete stop. You came to a *rolling* stop. There are kids walking through here at this time of day!' Her hand is planted on her hip. She is probably a few years younger than me, with an oversized Macy's sale bag hanging off one shoulder.

I frown. I did come to a full stop. I am ninety-nine per cent sure. I've always taken road safety with the utmost seriousness. I don't run amber lights, or go over the limit in a school zone. I am paranoid about reversing out of shopping centre parking stalls where people will just walk out behind your car, no mind to their own safety. Haven't we all, at some point, *almost* failed to see someone?

'I'm sorry,' I tell her, realising, at the same time, that she seems equally convinced of the opposite. 'I really thought I had but if I didn't—'

'You didn't!' she snaps.

Panic is tightening around me. 'OK,' I say. 'If you're sure . . . then I'm sorry. Like I said, if I didn't, then you're right – I absolutely should have.'

She stares at me wordlessly but hard. She was expecting more push-back. I've surprised her. I am busy thinking that's the end of it. I finish closing my door, hear the beep of my vehicle locking. I am walking over to the car insurance office. Then I hear, 'You know, it's because of irre-sponsible people like you that there are flowers and shrines at the side of the road. People not paying attention . . . on their phone, texting, chatting . . . People seeing stop signs but ignoring the law. Rules don't apply to them in their fancy cars . . .'

Each word is like a bullet in my back. I stand there, frozen, letting myself be peppered by them. But then suddenly I am turning. Rage rushes up my body with a force hitherto unknown. 'I said I was sorry!' I hear the defensive, indignant outrage in my tone. 'I'm certain I stopped! I always stop! But if I didn't stop then I said I was fucking sorry!' I am screeching, egged on by this rabid sense of having been wronged. How *dare* she? 'And anyway . . . I wasn't texting or talking! So I don't know what you're even going on about!'

I can tell immediately that this is going to escalate. Nothing about her body language says she's intending to let it end here. She goes to say something else, points an index finger at me, but I thrust out the palm of my hand. 'Back the fuck off!' I growl.

I don't recognise myself.

At first she is like a deer caught in my headlights, but the expression suddenly changes and I recognise what it is. Triumph. 'Are you threatening me?' she asks.

My heart rages. Somewhere, where there's a mote of sanity left, I am conscious of it being a pivotal question. What I say now will dictate what happens next. All my instincts tell me to walk away but I can't stop myself. 'If that's how you want to take it, then fine.' I say it quietly but it has the odd effect of sounding more menacing than if I had screamed.

She looks amazed for a moment. 'What?' Then, 'Right!' She digs in her pocket. 'I'm calling the police.'

With the mention of police, a dizzying, sickening sense of dread washes over me.

She is dialling numbers. A violent shaking begins. It grips me quickly and it stuns me how fast I am beholden to it. She is talking to someone now. My God. I can't even follow what's being said for my terror.

'What's your name?' she spits at me, presumably repeating what she's been told to ask.

'What's that got to do with anything?' I say, thinking, *Damn, Olivia! Why are you making this worse?* She holds her phone towards me to make sure the person on the other end of the line hears my belligerent response.

'How old are you?' she asks, eyes sending daggers. Then, 'She doesn't want to give her age.' She stares me up and down. 'I'd say she's about forty-six. Maybe forty-seven.'

She has just aged me by five or six years. I am vain enough for it to sting.

All I can now think is if the police are coming, then it's best I'm not standing here like this. So I start to walk towards the car insurance office as though this isn't happening. My legs are trembling violently, my heart leaping out of my ribcage. Once I get inside and sit down with the teller I'm so flummoxed I don't remember what I've come here to do.

It all takes ages because I can't concentrate on the paperwork for still feeling traumatised. When I step back outside, two cops are there waiting by my car. 'We've had a complaint that you've been acting aggressively towards a member of the public,' the younger, hugely overweight one says, when I reluctantly walk over to them. 'We're here to tell you that if it happens again we will have to take you in. Do you understand?' He doesn't quite look me in the eye, but slightly off to the side of my head.

All I can think is, *Thank God they're not asking my name. They're not going to know who I am.*

I nod, but then find myself saying, 'Don't you even want to hear my side of it?' I make a point of saying this quietly and calmly to show I'm not the psycho she's painted me as being, but it still comes out a little confrontational.

'Like I said' – the young cop barely meets my eyes – 'if it happens again we'll have to take you in. Do you understand?'

I stare at his face waiting for some sign of humanity but I'm not getting any.

Say it!

So I say, 'Yes. I understand.'

It's over. They turn and go back to their car. I go back to mine. I'm aware they don't immediately pull away. Perhaps they're waiting for me to, first. The woman is still standing there clocking all this. I can feel the smug satisfaction.

'She baited you in and she won,' Mark said, after. 'You gave her exactly what she was looking for.'

'Why, though? Why would anyone do that?'

'Because there are people like that in this world, Olivia. You don't know who you're dealing with, or what's going on in their lives that they've got nothing better to do than make yours a misery. You've got to be careful what you say to people because you never know how they'll take it.'

For days I could not get over how it had all escalated. Why *had* I implied I was threatening her? It was stupid, not to mention juvenile and beneath me. Why hadn't I handled it better with the cops? Turned the tables and told them *she* was the one behaving aggressively? Sometimes your best form of defence is a gentle, tactical offence. Or, better still, why hadn't I just ignored her in the first place, and walked away?

'Let it go,' Mark said, knowing it was mangling me. I had never had dealings with the police in my entire life until twice in a freakishly short span of time. It was just so humiliating. 'Believe me, if they'd wanted to arrest you they'd have done it. They were just doing their job. They clearly didn't think anything of it. And don't worry about her. She lived to tell the story . . .' Then he added, under his breath, in typical Mark fashion, 'To the entire neighbourhood.'

The memory dissolves and Beth is still staring at me. I don't want to make this worse but still feel the need to gently say, 'You don't know me. You have no idea what's going on in my life so you really shouldn't pass comments.' I try to say it levelly because one wobble and I'm going to break down.

She blanches, looks very uncomfortable then turns her back and starts to steam my milk. I just want to run.

Until it happens again with someone else? I can hear Mark saying. *You can't keep on running because this is going to outrun you, Olivia. Until you deal with what's at the core of this.*

So I stand there through the whizz and sputter of a coffee maker, weathering out my shame. As she reaches for a mug I try to say a friendly, 'To go, please,' my brain trotting out a heartfelt apology that I wish I could voice. Next thing, she is handing me my drink in a paper cup with a sleeve on it. 'No charge,' she says, meeting my eyes flatly with either displeasure or remorse. I hurry out a 'Thanks, that's kind,' and try to exert mind control over the wobble of my hand.

As I'm about to walk away, she says, 'That was actually just my really unfortunate way of telling you that I'm still looking for help. If you've changed your mind?'

'Oh . . .' I freeze, wanting the ground to swallow me again. Is she making this up to save face? I half glance in her direction, try to attempt a smile but my cheeks are set in concrete. 'Well, I'm sorry . . .' I say. 'I really am.'

Over at the creamer station I spend an inordinate amount of time shaking a packet of sugar on to the foam and watching the golden grains blur into the white. Don't cry. God, don't cry! I try to breathe, the sense of hands tight around my neck loosening fractionally.

As I'm putting a lid on my cup, I notice something on the board right in front of me. Among the desktop-published flyers advertising book clubs, Port Townsend's residents looking to take in boarders, photos of missing cats, details about the Lavender Festival and the Wooden Boat Festival, is a sheet of writing paper, the quality of good old English Basildon Bond. I recognise it right away.

The Correspondents' Club

If there is something you would like to say, to someone who might like to hear from you. Or if you remember, with fond nostalgia, the lost art of writing a letter and putting it in the mail, the simple pleasure of receiving one — then we are a small group who will be meeting here, in Port Townsend's Books and Beans café on the first and third Tuesday of every month. Our mission is to make time to put good old-fashioned pen to paper, for whatever reason that calls us, and perhaps to make new friends in the process. Come along at 7 p.m. Supplies will be provided.

I can't stop staring at the small decorative flourish drawn next to the title, and picturing Beth intently drawing it that day.

Hmm . . . a letter-writing circle, I think, once I get outside and begin walking down the street. Somehow the angst of five minutes ago has waned, allowing a pleasant thought to enter in.

It's a lovely idea.

For civilised people. Not that I am one of them, of course.

SEVEN

The salesman in the canary yellow shirt is clearly not used to dealing with a woman.

'Depends on what you're looking for. Are you thinking cedar? Pressure-treated? Composite?'

I pull the sample of wood from the bin bag and tell him my grand plan.

He takes it off me and is already shaking his head, rubbing it with his pointy thumbnail as bits slough off on to the floor. 'Cedar rots fast in our rainy climate. This hasn't been resealed. Deck's probably no more than ten years old. I'm not even sure you'll be able to nail new wood to rotting. There'll be nothing to hold.'

A woman's squawky voice comes over the terrible sound system announcing a sale on kitchen appliances. 'OK.' I try to talk over the top of the garbled message. 'Want to tell me my other options and the costs?' I hand him some hasty measurements scrawled on the back of an envelope.

Listening to his lengthy monologue, I am besieged with the strangest of realisations. It's possible I've never been in a home hardware store without Mark. Out of the two of us, I am the handier, though that's not saying much. I've refinished antique tables, upholstered the odd chair. My most adventurous undertaking was subway-tiling the backsplash in our old kitchen and we got endless compliments about it. I can still hear him telling friends, 'Oh yes, *we* did it over the weekend.' *We?* Ha! And he'd smile that slightly self-satisfied smile that said the credit really was all his. If I needed to go and buy paint Mark would be there telling me he was pleased I'd gone with the arctic grey because that was the one he'd originally suggested. If it was vaguely man's work, even by outdated definitions, Mark would be there, hanging about, waiting to put his rubber stamp on things – acting the part of the handy husband, trying to be what every other husband we seemed to know already was. It was equal parts endearing and maddening.

And yet . . . he was *there*. I've never really considered what that meant, or what the absence of that would feel like. I hadn't ever imagined it being any different.

'Are you OK?' I vaguely register that the salesman is looking worried.

When I touch the back of my neck I am drenched around my hairline. Mark would have been here. Mark would have an opinion on the wood.

For an instant I imagine he's just over in aisle eight looking at barbecues. He'll poke his head around the corner any minute, ready to give the yay or nay. But knowing he isn't – that Nanette's house isn't some little cottage retreat we bought and are renovating, where we will see out our old age, with visits from Jess and our grandkids – delivers the most stupefying smack of reality. We're not going to drive home together and stop off for a spontaneous nice dinner. He won't stick a plant in front of it when my project is an epic fail. He will never again try to fix our gurgling toilet with dental floss, or stop the leak under our old kitchen sink with one of his Happy Socks. I won't ever have to watch him fiddling under a cabinet with pipes, saying 'shit, fuck, bastard' every time he bangs his head. Or listen to, 'Why don't you do something to *help me*?'

Then something surreal happens. I turn around and he's there. He is looking at me and when I smile at him, he smiles back. I am held there by the spell of hopeful surprise. Only then I realise he isn't smiling at me. 'What do you think about this?' I hear a woman's voice ask, from just behind me. 'Perfect,' he replies, like they are in the early days of playing house and he's on his best behaviour, being all agreeable. Then he walks past me as though I'm not there and places his big arm around her waist.

The salesman is still staring at me. My hand is slapped over my mouth. I back up, turn, almost bump into someone then practically break into a run. After a few frustrating attempts to exit through an entrance door, aware my little meltdown is attracting the attention of people checking out at the tills, I manage to flee through the correct one.

In the car, I slam the door shut. It's uncharacteristically warm today, like summer arrived overnight. In no time I'm engulfed in heat. The sensible thing would be to get the air conditioning going. But for a short time I just sit here and imagine what it would be like to suffocate.

EIGHT

Beth has her 'Wet Floor' sign up. I shake off my old wax Barbour jacket at the door. When I venture inside, there are one or two customers at the counter, and a young couple on *my* sofa, but they're too into one another to be here for a letter-writing club. I don't know what I was expecting. The whole town to turn out?

I am not a coffee drinker beyond noon so I decide to order a hot chocolate just to give me something to hold. I walk over to the counter, wondering where Beth is – mopping sweat off the muffins? Suddenly someone taps my shoulder and says, 'Hi! I'm Amy! Are you here for the Correspondents' Club?' I turn and find myself staring at a woman with a face like a smiling moon. She has tiny, button-like green eyes, and bluish-white teeth that are made more dazzling by very matte, brick red lipstick. As she hangs there waiting for my response, the expectation that I might be her new best friend slowly dies on her face.

'Olivia,' I say, a little stunned. 'And . . . yes, I suppose I am here for the club.' Saying it is what suddenly makes it real.

Next I find myself pinned to the counter, this Amy's nose so close to mine I must be turning cross-eyed. 'Isn't this fun! Who are you going to write to? I love writing letters and these clubs are so popular now if you look online. Everything comes full circle . . .' She babbles on. Her breath isn't the most pleasant and I find myself leaning backwards over the counter. But the more I do, the more she leans in, until I'm trapped and beginning to panic.

'This is Bernie.' She thrusts her iPhone at me and there's a small white poodle on the screen. I can feel Mark nudging me and smiling: *Why do all the crazies love you?* 'Now, I'm a reasonable person. I believe in live and let live. Dogs bark. Dogs have rights just like people. But I can promise you no dog barks like Bernie. Bernie barks at squirrels, at the mail man, at a train rumbling by. Bernie barks at my *curtain* if it twitches. All day and all night . . . This dog never stops. Every time I try to bring it up with his owner, the man just slams the door in my face! Oh! I am at my wits' end.' She finally removes her hand from near my face, and I think, *Good Lord, woman! It's you who needs a muzzle, not the dog!* 'So I decided I'm going to write to Bernie's owner. No one can interrupt a letter.'

'Good luck,' I tell her. She backs up a fraction and I slide out from under her and make a beeline for the door.

It happens again. As I am on my way out, a man is on his way in. I am almost butted against the same leather jacket, conscious of the same pleasing smell, and the same diminishing of light and air. Time stretches, then he says, 'I'm starting to take this personally.'

I look up but once again see only my head disproportionately reflected in the aviator shades.

'I was joking,' he says, awkwardly, perhaps because I have hesitated. My surprise has robbed me of my wit.

'Sorry – I . . .' Heat rushes to my cheeks. 'I know you were.'

Neither of us moves.

'I'm here for the club.' He removes his glasses and two warm brown eyes meet mine; one of them – his left – is painfully bloodshot. 'You?' And now I see more clearly what shocked me before. It looks like he may have suffered burns to one side of his face. He has particularly prominent scars on the lower portion of his left cheek, running down his neck and disappearing under his collar, and a few paler patches of mottled pink skin on his forehead. I don't know whether it's the thought of flesh on fire, or the fact that his eyes are scoping out my face as though he's just landed from another planet and I am the first human he's seen, but suddenly his proximity is overwhelming.

'Well, I was,' I say, 'but I'm leaving.'

'Oh . . .' He continues to stand there then says, 'Sorry to hear that.'

I am guessing he's in his early thirties, at most. He has one of those accents that sounds like he's from nowhere in particular. Our bodies are still way too close for comfort. We must both recognise this at the same time because I step left and he steps right, then we repeat this the other way and end back in the same place. I wave a hand, meaning, *Seriously, can I get past you?*

He steps aside while I consciously stand still to ensure we won't repeat this farcical dance again. Once I'm past him and outside, I let out a small sigh of relief.

I walk briskly along the path, but I can't rid myself of the spatial memory of his body, nor can I unsee that face. I slow down only when I turn on to Water Street. Now what? I don't feel like going back to the house; I am suddenly highly charged and restless. I walk to the end of the block but reach it too soon. Now where? Annoyance strums in me. Why am I always running? No one knows the first thing about me; I don't know why I have to act so bizarrely.

When I go back inside, Beth and this Amy are laughing. For a second I think it's at me and I'm just about to do a U-turn, when Amy says, 'Ah! You're back! We thought we'd scared you off!' She cackles. She's built like a barrel and is wearing the gayest of pink and green shoes to match an overly colourful 50s-style dress. If I took a sneak picture and sent it to Jessica she would shriek laughing. Just the thought makes a smile almost break out.

'Not really,' I tell her. 'I thought I'd dropped something.'

'Your money or your uppity attitude?' Beth looks like she's weighing me to see how I'm going to take it.

'My keys.' I smile, and tug at the linen scarf looped around my throat.

I am saved by the opening of the door. A dapper-looking older man and a young boy come in. The man appraises the room as though he's pleased with what he finds. The little boy looks cautiously curious but then suddenly hides behind the older man's back.

'What's the matter, Daniel?' He reaches around to pat the boy's head.

The child peeps out and I see where he's looking. The guy with the burns is sitting in the corner by the window where the young couple were. He looks like he's trying desperately hard to blend in. 'What happened to your face?' the boy says.

'I'm sorry.' The old man looks over at him. 'My grandson asks too many questions.'

'It's OK,' the guy replies. Then, to the little boy, who has returned to hiding behind his granddad's leg, 'Hey, you don't have to be scared of me.'

The kid emerges again, stands there as though he has reluctantly found himself on stage and has forgotten his lines. 'But why do you look like that?' he asks, shyly.

Suddenly Beth stops steaming milk. After a beat or two of hesitation, during which you could hear a pin drop, he says, 'I had an accident.' He says it quite matter-of-factly, but the way he's clutching his sunglasses indicates otherwise. 'I was in a war. In Afghanistan. I was blown up.'

'Oh my gawd!' Amy says.

The soldier glances at me, but before I can even react Daniel is saying, 'I know about the Afghanistan war! The people in those countries, well, they are *always* fighting and sometimes America has to go and help them sort it out.'

His granddad pats his head and catches my eye.

'But how did you get blown up?'

I'm starting to find this kid annoying.

The soldier looks at me again. Does he want rescuing? 'I was in a Humvee that went over a land mine,' he says, and my blood runs cold.

Daniel's eyes become saucers. 'Wow! How did that feel?'

The soldier releases his grip on his glasses and puts them on the table with an air of purpose, but I sense he might be buying time. I notice his hands are badly scarred, more so than his face. He has taken off his jacket and is wearing a long-sleeved T-shirt made of soft grey jersey material. It hugs him enough to see that he's fit but not the beefcake build you'd normally associate with someone in the military. He has chestnut-coloured hair – a crew cut without any parting, and a nicely shaped head with ears that stick out slightly, reminding me of tiny, cupped hands. 'Well, fortunately for me, I don't really remember,' he says.

I realise I've fallen into a state of mild catatonia and need to snap out of it. 'Maybe Daniel would like a muffin?' I pick up a tray of sweaty offerings and hold it out to the kid.

Daniel couldn't care less about a muffin. 'Are your scars going to heal?' he asks.

Good heavens! To think I was upset that Nanette asked if I was a member of a library!

'They are healed.' I watch this man inspect his own hands – perhaps for want of somewhere to put his eyes. 'I sustained burns to over forty per cent of my body. I've had countless surgeries to improve how I look, but I won't get any better than this, unfortunately.'

It intrigues me how objectively he is talking about something so utterly unimaginably awful. Daniel looks like he's going to cry. His granddad and I exchange a knowing glance that says, *He's annoying, but he's just a child!*

'Here.' I offer him the tray again, feeling bad for being irritated by him. 'These are really delicious. Try one.'

He reaches out and, after a brief calculation, selects the big chocolate one.

His granddad says, 'We're here for the Correspondents' Club. I hope you don't mind that one of the participants is a child. Sometimes a trying one.' When he sees what Daniel has in his hand, he says, 'Daniel, you know, perhaps you should ask first before you take the biggest and the last of something. It would be good manners.'

'But I'll probably eat it all. And that's good manners too, isn't it?'

'He's got a point there!' I laugh. 'But it's not my club, if that's what you're thinking. Perhaps because I'm giving out the food?'

'Sorry.' The old man blanches. 'We don't live in town. We just dropped in one day and saw the notice. I just assumed it was. You have the look of a proprietor about you.'

When I turn, the soldier is right behind me. I think I feel the proximity of him immediately before our eyes connect. 'I'm Ned Parker by the way.' He holds out a badly burned hand. 'As we keep running into one another in doorways.'

I've never been so powerfully aware of a hand before I shake it.

'Olivia.' Now that I'm over the shock of his scars I can look at him more objectively. If you extrapolate an entire face from the one side that seems to have fared better than the other, it's pretty obvious he'd have been quite the head-turner.

Then I think, *Have been?* How awful that I just referred to him in the past tense.

'Bet you wish you'd never come back.' His tone is trying to be light, and I find myself warming to his stiff attempt at humour despite the shiver that's still running up my spine.

'The thought did cross my mind.'

'I'm glad you did,' he says, not in a flirty way, just more matter-of-fact.

Conversation sharply falls off. Perhaps because I don't know where else to take it. How do you make casual chit-chat with someone who has suffered burns to forty per cent of his body? Then again, maybe he doesn't even want me to. 'Muffin?' I pick up the tray I set down earlier and hope he doesn't note my trembling hand. I wonder what it is about the sight of burned skin that can do this to you.

'Thanks. They look great. Did you bake them?' He takes one.

'Please!' I pull a face. 'I'd do a much better job than this.'

He makes a better attempt at smiling now, though it doesn't quite reach his eyes. If I were a guessing person, I'd say it's not something he does too often. I find myself returning it.

After another awkward moment he goes and sits at one of the school desks. I watch him fidgeting for a bit to get comfortable and I get an overwhelming urge to snap a sneak photo and send it to Jess.

Beth has set up a supplies table by the creamer stand and the old man and the little boy are perusing it. There is assorted writing paper, notepads, flip pads, clipboards, postcards, envelopes, local and international stamps. There are Post-it notes, pencils with erasers, ballpoint pens in different colours, even old-fashioned liquid paper and a couple of pocket dictionaries. On all of the little desks are economical borderless picture frames with quotes in them. To give me something to do, I work my way up the line, reading a few of them: *Emily Post said never send an angry letter.*

More than kisses, letters mingle souls. John Donne. I love that!

This is not a letter but my arms around you for a brief moment. Katherine Mansfield.

When I get to the soldier's table, I pick up his little quote and read it, aware of him observing me doing so. *Your handwriting is like your face. It is personal. It is you.* Good grief. I carefully put that one down, trying to be casual about it.

'Oh, look at this!' I suddenly notice an old post box like the ones we used to have in England.

'I bought it off Amazon.' Beth pats its top. In the background I can hear that annoying Amy recounting the dog story to the old man.

'Apparently antique mailboxes are quite a collector's item. I thought that after we write our letters we can pop them in there and I'll send them off tomorrow.'

'That's a wonderful idea,' I tell her. 'There's literally nothing you haven't thought of!'

'Be careful,' she says. 'That sounds dangerously like a compliment.'

We smile.

'Daniel is going to be writing to his pen pal.' The old man introduces himself as York. I'm sure he's relieved to have escaped Amy's clutches.

'Granddad found me one on the Internet.' Daniel grins.

'It's not as irresponsible as it sounds.' York looks amused. 'It's through a charitable organisation. Daniel is going to be writing to a little boy in a Bosnian orphanage. Apparently he wants to improve his English, and Daniel could use that too – well, his written English. Clearly there's nothing wrong with his spoken word.'

'Who are you going to write to?' Daniel asks Beth, while he beats the top of his head with two pens like he's playing the drums.

Beth says, 'Oh! Well, I have a sister. She lives in Austria. We haven't spoken in thirty-five years.'

'Thirty-five years is a long time!' Daniel stops the drumming business. 'What did she do wrong?'

Beth stares at him for a second as though he's telepathic. 'It's a very long and complicated story.'

'Who are you going to write to?' he asks Ned.

I didn't know we'd be having some sort of discovery session. He'd better not ask me.

Ned rapidly waggles the foot that's resting across his opposite knee. 'Well, there's a guy I was in Kuwait with. And maybe some others. I'll see how it goes.'

'Who are the others?'

'Daniel!' his granddad says. 'It's none of your business!'

Daniel beams a cheeky smile then sits down at the first desk. 'This is cool! I've never had a pen pal before!'

I sit at the desk immediately behind the soldier. I watch Amy walk over to him, pull out her phone and say, 'Let me tell you a story about man's best friend . . .' and I can't resist mumbling, 'Oh God.'

But then I pick up my little framed quote. Rather remarkably it says, *Reading your old letters reminds you of the person you used to be.* I gaze out of the window, far across the water. I wrote so many letters to Mark when I had to go back to England for my dad's heart surgery, just a few months after we'd met. I'd just found out I was pregnant. My mother was horrified and thought it the end of life as I knew it. There was an entire letter devoted to breaking the news to Mark. International phone calls were expensive back then; I'd never have dreamed of saddling my parents with a bill. I wrote something like, *I know it's a shock. Please don't tell me we're too young . . . With or without a baby I am going to make my life a success . . .* Blah. Blah. But I remember the last line quite clearly. *Please think your response through carefully, because what you say will shape the way I'll remember you for the rest of my days.* Because I'd just found wisdom I was convinced I must have invented it. Not all that long ago I stumbled upon it in a shoebox filled with old photographs, CD sleeves, and some other paraphernalia from my younger days and I showed it to Mark. I watched his face as he read it. It's so true that your old letters transport you to a chapter in your life in a way that nothing else can. Something so fugitive is captured – a chime of your old conscious self, the embodiment of who you were in the palpable moment. Nothing else is quite like it; not even a photograph. Mark is wary of over-sentimentality. I could tell he was trying to mask the fact that he was overwhelmingly moved by it. 'Yup.' He smirked at me, giving me his best loving look. 'Melodramatic as ever! What's changed?'

'Eat the muffins.' Beth's hand on my shoulder startles me from my daydream. 'Be warned, if there's any left over you're just going to have to take them home.'

'Forewarned is forearmed,' I say and we smile.

I turn my attention out of the window again, oddly grateful I can be here rather than on my own in that little house with a bottle of wine and a laptop.

Beth switches on some music. 'Let the ink flow and cell phones be idle. May the force of Goddess Iris be with us.'

It occurs to me that you know when a cultural art form is dying when people make a point of celebrating it. And I think there is something sad and beautiful in that.

I was going to make another stab at writing to Sarah. That was my reason behind coming here – the hope that the nature of the gathering, the shared purpose, would make it easier to focus and find the right words. But now the moment is upon me I don't feel I can; I am blunt, blank, and I can't bear to think about her right now. So I decide I'll write to my mother, instead. I'll tell her all about Jessica being in Europe – the baby she always thought I was too young to have. Describe it all in magnanimous detail. What I don't know, I'll invent.

'Who is Goddess Iris?' a little voice pipes up.

NINE

I spot him sitting near the lighthouse, staring out to sea. He has his back to me. There is something about the perfectly aligned neck and head, the close cut of his hair, that makes him immediately recognisable. A couple of old fishing boats bob on the water, but other than that everything is postcard still and serene – and so is he.

I'm about to sneak off but my arrival disturbs some seagulls who were sleeping on the stones. As they disperse in a flurry of wings he glances around and notices me. 'Hi,' he says, his tone carrying only a trace of surprise.

I am taken aback by the sight of his burns once again and hope my face doesn't show it. I walk over and try to perch casually on the end of the log beside him, and he joins me in staring out to sea as though this were some sort of mutual meditation we're participating in. 'You know, this is my favourite place to sit on this entire beach,' I tell him.

'By the lighthouse?'

'This very log, actually.' I pull off my sunglasses and we meet eyes, briefly. 'You're sitting in my seat, says Papa Bear.'

'Ha,' he says, without any mirth. He studies my profile as though feeling he's obliged to say more, but not knowing what. Then he says, 'Well, I can move. I mean, if you're one of these people who likes to spread out.'

I tilt my face to the sun, enjoying how nice it feels now that it seems to be sticking around. 'It's OK. You can stay.'

'Anyway, I was here first.' There is a note of playfulness in his voice.

I find myself smiling. The act of it makes my shoulders relax, because I realise they've been up by my ears – a bad, headache-triggering posture I ended up having to get acupuncture for around the same time that I accepted I couldn't live off a diet of wine and Tylenol. We sit like this for a while without speaking, our faces to the sun. 'Did you get any writing done last week?' he asks.

I think about this, and our tentative common ground of the Correspondents' Club.

'Hmm . . . Not really. Attempted one to my parents.'

> Jessica is in Italy and we hear she's having a fantastic
> time! Sorry I haven't written in so long. The good news
> is Mark and I are doing fine now. It was very hard for
> a long time but you'll be pleased to know I am much
> the old me again.

When I came to putting it in an envelope it ended up in the bin instead.

'I'm not the best at staying in touch,' I add. 'My parents never use email, and I'm not always in the mood for phone calls . . . It's a funny thing, though, when you're not used to writing; the pen was like a foreign object in my fingers. And my handwriting is awful now. Can't believe I used to get gold stars for it in school.'

'I never ever saw myself as being a member of any writing club,' he says, 'but I've written letters my whole life. I grew up in the tech age but I hate everything computers represent and I can't stand all that shallow texting shit. I think I just like the process of putting words on paper with a pen. In many ways I communicate better that way. You have to kind of reach into yourself and think, which is a cool exercise.'

'You'd be quite at home with my parents then.' I look over at the seagulls, who are back, facing the same direction, gathering like they're at church. 'I know what you mean, though. It might seem very old-fashioned but there's an intimacy about writing a letter, isn't there? A sort of self-consciousness that's been lost with modern communication. A letter is such a physical, lasting thing that you feel it deserves the very best words you can bring to it . . .' I smile. The way he is studying me makes me think I've gone a bit esoteric on him, so I say, 'Amy's a character, huh? Oh my God, the dog story!'

'Ha,' he says, after perhaps absorbing the shift from serious to playful. 'I'm just glad I'm not the guy who lives next door.'

I snort. We look at one another and smile. In the bright sunlight his bloodshot eye appears angry against the pallor of the burned areas of skin. I wonder if it's painful. Then he turns serious again. 'I drafted a letter to my old friend who I was in Kuwait with. To kinda flex my writing muscle a bit. But then I didn't know what to say after all these years. I'm not great at small talk at the best of times, and how do you write the bigger stuff in a letter when it's coming pretty well out of the blue?'

I am suddenly reminded of that poem about unwritten letters and haunting ghosts. Distantly off on the horizon I see faces. Words flickering like tiny meteors somewhere between their world and mine.

'You make a start, I think. Everything has a beginning, right? Even things we think have ended are never as over as we believe.'

This seems to give him pause. 'In Afghanistan I wrote a lot of letters home. I even wrote them for all the other guys . . . They said I had a way of phrasing things. They'd tell me approximately what they wanted to say, then leave it up to me to package it.'

There is a wistfulness about him – for his buddies? I don't know. What I can't grasp is that he will have witnessed things most of us wouldn't even begin to stomach imagining and yet there is a certain untainted, almost naive quality in his eyes that's way more befitting of his age than his experience.

'I hope you charged them. That sounds like quite the undertaking,' I say.

'Yes. I should have thought of that . . . Probably could have got rich . . . It wasn't always easy, I'll tell you. You've got to make each one sound like it's still coming from them. I could hardly have all their letters to their wives sound like they were written by Ned Parker.'

'Or they would probably never have dared go home.'

He looks at me for a moment as though he doesn't quite get it. Then he says, 'Ha. True . . .' He gazes out to sea again and seems to turn nostalgic. 'It was how we passed time, or so we kidded ourselves. I'm sure what we were really doing was making sure we were leaving something behind . . . you know . . . in case we didn't come home. Like you say, letters are physical things.'

'Oh my.' I recognise it's an inadequate response. It strikes me that this consciousness of your own mortality in someone so young leaves me feeling a little helpless. He is watching me with an openness about him which makes me say, 'I sometimes think I've spent way too much time around an awful lot of sheltered people. I'm not meaning this cruelly; you can't really blame people because they haven't led a tortured existence . . . I just sometimes wonder, what's the darkest thing that friends, people around me, have ever experienced? I mean, *is* there stuff? Do they just not talk about it? I know a lot about their diets, their proud parent moments, their vacations, naturopaths, politics, Pilates, but I don't know what eats away at their conscience late at night. I don't know if there's anything to know about them that you couldn't put on a bumper sticker or a car decal.'

I stare at the seagulls and suddenly think, *Yes, flock behaviour,* I have shied away from it at the best of times, and it was truly something to run from at the worst. I guess I could never have hacked being a bird. 'Sometimes I've just longed to say to people, *What's the one thing you would undo if you could?* But I'm frightened of finding out there's nothing.'

'Wow,' he says, and I realise that was way too much of a ramble to a virtual stranger.

'Sorry,' I tell him. 'How did I get on to all that?'

'I don't know,' he says, 'but it's some deep shit.'

I meet his eyes again, and we smile.

'Daniel's something else, eh?' As soon as I've said it I think, *Why is he making me so nervous that I'm gabbling? Can't I just shut up? He's going to think I'm awful.*

'He's a kid with a lot to say, I guess. And that's either going to work for him in the future or be his downfall.'

'Watch out, world!' When I glance at him his face registers something between fascination and surprise. 'You think I'm cruel. I suppose we are bad-mouthing everybody.'

'We? Not me. You.'

I briefly hide my face in my hands. 'Sorry. I'll be kind now . . . Well, once I've said my piece about Beth.'

He says, 'Ha,' again. No actual laugh, just a voiced expression of vague amusement. I've noticed he does this; it's his thing. My sudden realisation that I know a quirk about him bobs there between us for a moment. I don't know him. He's led a life I can't even begin to fathom. And yet there's something very pared down about him that makes him easy to talk to. It's been a very long time since I had a proper conversation with someone without feeling like they're looking at me but only seeing what I did. Without knowing they're avoiding every possible topic that might hit a nerve.

'Daniel really looks up to you,' I say. 'There's part of him wants to be you, and yet he's seen what that can mean now and he's terrified.'

'Well, everywhere I go people want to know how I got to look like this and kids are no exception. I guess it's natural. I'd be doing the same. I suppose I thought if I came to a small town, once everybody had got their fill they'd eventually just leave me alone.'

'Has it worked?'

'I've only been here ten days. I've not had much interaction with any-one.' For a moment he seems solemn. 'He reminds me a bit of my son.'

'You have a son?' I glance at his left hand. I thought I hadn't noticed a wedding ring. Perhaps he's divorced.

'Jamie. He's eight.' He tilts his head back, closing his eyes to the sun again, so I can look at him without feeling conspicuous. I wonder how his scar tissue responds to changes in the weather. If it does better in rain or sunshine. If it tans or burns. If it has no feeling at all.

'He's with his mother. We're not exactly together.'

I want to ask more, but I'm going to sound as bad as Daniel. So I settle for 'That must be hard.' There is a tramline of hairless new skin in his crew cut. I'm guessing it's not a fashion statement; perhaps he's had surgery on his head, too. A shiver travels up my spine.

'I was deployed a lot. If you're not doing that you're doing work-ups, training, pre-deployment exercises. You're away sometimes ten months in the year. But I suppose the difference in all of those cases is that I was always coming back to them – so long as I was alive, anyway.'

'I can't really imagine what it must be like to go to war,' I say. 'I can't pretend that I know what to say to you. I have a hunch everything would sound uneducated or highly simplistic.'

'Don't worry. You can't imagine until you've been there.' He leans forwards, resting his elbows on his knees. I look at the ground where he's staring. Our feet. My small, white Converse and his big, brown Merrells. 'War is a testament of failure in diplomacy, in the ability to compromise. It defies human decency. The military spends three to six months training kids how to kill and sends them off as these tremen-dous patriots without properly preparing them to mentally deal with the emotional impact of killing or coming to terms with their own mortality. Or they're older, they've messed up their lives, made a few mistakes and they see the military as an opportunity to get sorted out, and they've got no idea what that's going to mean.'

'Did you ever regret signing up? I mean, you must have. I'm guessing. At some point.' *When you lost your face.*

'Not sure that's the word. Regrets are really just lessons we're slow in learning, aren't they? The military is so much a part of who I am. Being a SEAL was everything I wanted and admired. In many ways I am who I am because of the path I chose, and a lot of good things came of that. But a lot of bad did too . . . But I'm alive and I know many guys who aren't sitting here saying that. They weren't as lucky as me, though don't get me wrong, I don't always feel so lucky.'

'I didn't realise you were a SEAL.' I'm aware it's somewhat of an unfinished remark, and a bit of a conversation-stopper for me. What do I think a naval officer of Sea, Air and Land looks like? Bigger? Meaner?

He doesn't elaborate so I say, 'I'm glad I had a girl. If I'd had a son and he'd wanted to sign up I'd have put him under house arrest. I know wars have to be fought but I wouldn't want my child doing it. Maybe it's not politically correct, but in my opinion nothing is worth dying for and war should never be thought of as the only way. I could start quoting some of the war poets I studied in university that had such a profound impact on me, but best not to get me started!' He is watching me again as though I'm either massively fascinating to him or he's pitying my idiocy. When he doesn't say anything, I find myself flooding with embarrassment. I hope I haven't offended him. Mark has often told me I shouldn't always voice what I think.

'How old is she?' he asks.

It takes me a second or two to realise he's talking about Jessica. 'She just turned nineteen,' I say, after a moment. I gaze far out across the water, to the horizon, wishing I could grasp on to what lies beyond it, if anything does. 'She's in Europe. It was supposedly just for the summer, then she was going to be off to Washington State University . . .' I am aware of how light my voice suddenly sounds just by speaking of her, of a burgeoning of pride at the idea of her determining her own path, regardless of what her dad wants. Jessica having this marvellous free rein to follow her whims and desires, and her doing exactly that.

'Nice . . . So she's not going to college now?'

'Ah . . . Who knows? I will probably be the last to find out, if I'm being honest. We had a bit of a falling out over it.' How shiny the truth looks when we varnish it. 'Her dad didn't support her wanting to defer her place and spend a year travelling. I was fine with it . . . but in the end it was *me* she thought was being unsupportive.' I realise we are venturing down a path I hadn't intended to take. 'It's a long story,' I say, hoping that will end it. I lean forwards and stare at the tops of my shoes, trying to focus on the criss-cross of the off-white laces, the silver grommets, one of them that's bent, the smudge of dirt on the left one, by the toe. When I look up I'm a little light-headed; everything looks rearranged, the sun brighter, the sea too much like glass. He is watching me closely. Too closely. 'Sorry,' I say. 'Not sure how we got on to all that . . .' I fake looking at the time. 'I should probably make some sort of move . . .' I stand up, perhaps a little too quickly, and feel the blood draining from my face.

'Are you OK?' he asks. 'Hope I didn't say something wrong?'

I shake my head. 'No, I'm fine.' I try to say it chirpily but there's a distinct edge of un-fine-ness about me. 'Like I say, though, time to go and put my day to good use.' What did Elizabeth Taylor say? *Pour yourself a drink. Put on some lipstick. Pull yourself together.* I hate to think how many times I've drawn upon the wisdom of a seven-times married movie star recently. 'I'm supposed to be building a deck. It's a great day for it.'

'Deck?'

'Well, more like repairing.'

'Yourself?'

'Don't look so shocked.'

'Sorry. You're just so tiny. I wouldn't have thought . . .'

I must seem a little edgy or something because he adds, 'Sorry, I didn't mean to sound sexist or to insult you.'

'You didn't. Not at all,' I say, once I can drag a response out of myself. Or did he? I don't even know. What I do know is we have wrong-footed somehow. He feels it too, and is suddenly out of his depth. Good heavens, I am probably a decade older but right now it feels like a million years.

'I suppose it is a bit shocking, even to me,' I say, trying to salvage it. 'I've never actually built anything that other people have to stand on before. It was one of those "seemed like a good idea at the time" things. Anyway . . .' I shrug, affecting casualness, but it's an untold effort. 'See you later,' I say, and start to walk away.

'If you need an extra pair of hands . . .' I glance over my shoulder and he's flexing his left one. 'Mine used to be pretty capable. They haven't been tested in a while.'

I smile again, weakly, by way of saying thanks in the spirit that the offer was meant: not seriously. 'Don't tempt me. You might regret you offered.'

'You might regret I did too,' he says.

TEN

I really didn't see myself doing this so soon.

The butterflies start up the instant I indicate to turn left off the main arterial road into our tree-lined suburb. I have to put a hand on my stomach to try to quell the sickening sense of dread. Abigail Avenue meanders for about a quarter mile, off-shooting into several no through roads and cul-de-sacs, the third one being ours. When we first drove here to meet the listing agent there was no denying the entire neighbourhood had a certain upmarket charm. In a green belt, just minutes from the lake, with trails in every direction, you could still walk to the shops and be in downtown Seattle in about twenty minutes. There were some beautiful character homes on slopes or hidden among trees, some with direct access to the lake. The one we had come to see – the taupe house – was on the mountainside and already pushing our budget. In the photographs, with its strong architectural lines and three-car garage with sectional glass doors framed in black aluminium, it was too contemporary and not homey enough for me. I'd hoped I'd see it differently in person, but turning into the drive that day with the realtor left me with a *Hmm, still not crazy about this place!* feeling that somehow never fully went away. The inside was shiny and fresh, to be expected of a new-build. The endless taupe colour scheme and dark wood cabinetry might have been modern and neutral to some but to me it was drab and cold. But Mark loved its clean lines, high ceilings, its wide, light, open spaces – all 4,000 square feet of them – the gazillion pot-lights and monster-sized stainless fridge. Admittedly the bathrooms were nice and spacious, the finishings high quality, and it did have a perfectly manicured, private back garden – in many ways it would have felt ungrateful to dislike it. Plus, as Mark reminded me, it was near Whole Foods for me, and work for him, and Jessica didn't have to change schools. By the time we left that day I was feeling a bit better about it, or perhaps it's just in my nature to make the best of things. Had Mark walked away, I'd probably not have given it a backwards glance. But I only had to look at him to see how taken he was with the place. With his latest promotion at work bringing him into the big leagues of high-tech patent engineering, the house reflected how Mark saw himself now, and somewhere in the core of him, he even liked it for all the right reasons. I would have had to find it fundamentally objectionable on a level I could not live with to tell him I hated it and ruin his dream. Then Jessica got to know she would be getting a bedroom twice the size of her old one. With a walk-in closet. That's when I was officially outvoted.

Now that I'm turning into our drive I still can't fully equate it with home, but it's tempered somewhat by the relief that, despite there being an accident on the I5 so that I am later getting here than I intended, school is still not out for the day, the kids haven't started trickling home, there are no cars in driveways, no mums ambling back from their afternoon dog walks. The neighbourhood hasn't come out of hibernation. I am getting away with no one seeing me.

Going inside is a strange experience. The place feels cavernous, unlived in, oddly silent. I drop my bag by the front door and hear the short echo of my feet as I walk into the great room, noting immediately how show-home-like the kitchen looks. Of course, Wednesday. Josie, our cleaner, will have been yesterday. But it's more than that. It hits me immediately what it is. The place is missing Jessica. The chairs lack piles of school files and discarded clothing detritus. There are no shoes kicked off by the coffee table, no half-eaten apples, balled-up pairs of fluffy socks, errant hair elastics. Just for the hell of it, I call out, 'Jess?' imagining her responding, fantasising about us going back, way back, in time – or even to just a little over a year would do – when we were a normal, happy family. But there is nothing. Just a barren, bewildering silence.

I dump my car keys and phone on the granite island. The only thing about this house that drove Mark mad was that it's got one of those hanging pot racks above the island, the kind you see in the kitchens of TV chefs. Mark was always dinging his head on a pan. I can't look at it without thinking of Jess and me laughing at him when he got in a tizzy about it. There is a build-up of mail sitting by the fruit bowl, like no one has paid any attention to it for a while. I contemplate flicking through it, hoping to see a postcard from Jess, but decide not to bother. I notice that Josie has placed my container of cooking oils right beside the stove again; I've told her countless times you don't keep oil near 22,000 BTUs of heat unless you want it to turn rancid. I like it right behind me on the island within arm's reach of where I'm cooking. She finally did as I asked, but has clearly reverted to her wilful ways. I never wanted a cleaner. It felt a little lazy or elitist, not to mention an invasion of privacy. Besides, who needs aerobics with free weights when you can scrub a bathtub? But once we moved in Mark wanted our place to be as denuded of life as the neighbours'. We were supposed to be turning over a new leaf in a new house. Though I was never convinced there was anything wrong with our leaf the way it was.

I wander over to the windows and stare out at the lawn, thinking of how just days before it happened Jessica and I had been laughing because a raccoon kept using our gutters as its personal toilet – Mark had gone up the ladder and got out his iPhone. 'Daaad! Why are you taking pictures?' He gave her that look that said, *Haven't you anything better to do than watch me?*

'He's going to use it as evidence when he takes the raccoon to court,' I teased, and elbowed Jess in the ribs. 'Or maybe he just wants the photo in his back pocket, you know, for when he and the raccoon have the serious talk.' We had cracked up. Makes me smile just remembering it. We were often united in mocking the one person we smugly saw as being less evolved than the pair of us. It was a girl thing. Mark had given me that face. We never found out why he'd photographed it.

I look over at the Waxmans' next door. Urgh! All I can see is the hideous Fourth of July weekend. I hadn't wanted to go to any party just six weeks after what happened. I made the effort for Mark, to prove I was doing better than he thought I was, to show I was at least trying. Bill said it was going to be a low-key affair – just the five couples from the cul-de-sac and some of the younger kids. But when we walked in it seemed like he'd invited half the neighbourhood. No sooner had I put my fig, blue cheese and prosciutto canapés on the table than Phyllis Chappell, who has never said more than 'hello' to me in the past, was hugging me and saying how brave it was of me to be here, how she couldn't imagine what it must be like to be me. I remember standing rigid like a tree trunk, wanting it to be over. Then I was trussed by another pair of well-meaning arms, shrinking into myself until I had nowhere else to go. The music was loud – a tune from my growing up, Feargal Sharkey's 'A Good Heart'. You don't hear it much in North America. Ordinarily I'd have sung along in my mind, been swept back with dewy-eyed nostalgia to the days of my youth. But the music couldn't penetrate, couldn't reach the part of the brain where the feel-good chemicals live. Music then and music now makes me feel nothing; I am utterly dead to it. Mark rescued me and I wanted to say, *I need to go home!* But then I spotted Barb Norman, who, just days after it happened, somehow ended up in my kitchen saying, 'I know you suffer terrible remorse. Remember that God is our refuge and our strength, an ever-present help in times of trouble. Let Him give you strength. Psalm

46:1.' She had squeezed my clenched hands, held hers fast over mine, almost as though we were praying for me together. Then she'd got up and left, with the same busybody entitlement she'd arrived with. Seeing her here released a flurry of dread in the pit of my stomach. I already felt defensive and she hadn't as much as looked in my direction yet; tension was gathering around my ears like a storm. If she came over . . . If she repeated one more Godly platitude . . . She'd get it in the neck just like the woman in the parking lot.

'Wine?' Mark was at my side again, gently ushering me outside to the drinks table. My husband, who I'd shown such little appreciation for over the previous weeks. I'd been finding myself looking for a chance to attack him for reasons I didn't even understand. The guilt about this was just around the corner waiting to make me feel worse about myself than I already did. I spent a painful eternity meandering from one table of food to the next, wishing my friend Deanna would arrive, gazing with feigned interest at platters of raw vegetables, picking at pitta and dip – anything to give myself something to do other than have to stare into somebody's face and wait for them to say something that was going to hit a nerve. I still hadn't regained my appetite; just the look of food made me want to throw up. I was skinny – had dropped twenty-five pounds in six weeks. I'd never had a huge bottom but now when I turned sideways in the mirror I was a straight line; my neck felt bird-like and loose-skinned. Even my shoes were like boats; my feet had shrunk! I remember overhearing Stephanie, who lives directly opposite us, gushing to Tanya about how her beautician had started ordering Marc Jacobs' Jealous Glaze nail polish after Stephanie had raved about it to her. How could I remember so little about the terrible thing I'd done, and yet days later I could still recall the name of a nail polish like it was my own name? I stood there grasping for something to add, inwardly decrying them for being this shallow and self-absorbed. Then Bill cracked a joke about something and everybody was suddenly high-fiving and falling around laughing. Everyone but me. I remember the laughter suddenly dissipating when they must have noticed that I was a block of stone. Then, out of the blue, Bill stunned me by giving one sharp smack to my back, like a man might do to his buddy. 'Come on, Liv! Put a smile on that face!' The hard thump and his words reverberated through the weightless shell of me.

There was complete silence, then a low rumble of disapproval. Distantly I was aware of Mark saying something to Bill, though I didn't know what, and then they had sailed on to some other topic – their kids, their golf, their hair, their trip to the Canadian Rockies. Bill's boorish behaviour was forgotten about and I was the only one somehow still stuck in the moment, pulsing with shame.

I walked to the corner of the yard, to where he stored the barbecue when it wasn't in use, still feeling the impression of his hand on my back. What I did next wasn't really me. I was outside my body, watching myself, almost fascinated; I saw myself turning on the garden hose. Wren, Bill's springer spaniel, was the only one who seemed to be aware of this: dogs and water. He started barking and trying to bite the end of the hose. Before anyone knew what had hit them I'd aimed the water right at Bill. The long jet of it was super-powered: I could hear the force of the water blasting the cotton of his colourful checked shirt; the fabric ballooned, like a sail caught by wind. He leapt and shouted, covered his face with his hands, but I wasn't aiming for his face. I was aiming for his middle as though his big fat gut was the bullseye in my private target practice. But then I was turning it on everybody. I was going after anything that moved. I remember blankly watching the women run for cover, the sound of their squeals melding with Earth, Wind and Fire singing 'September'. I remember vaguely thinking how amiss this very sight before my eyes was. But all in all I was just blank, just vaguely conscious that my head and my hands weren't connected – my intentions and my actions hadn't got it together. It wasn't me who was commanding this evil water torture. I was too busy being transfixed by a beautiful rainbow that was suspended in the particles of water, in a shaft of sunlight.

I suddenly heard '*What the fuck?*' as though life's volume had just been turned up. Bill was soaked to his skin and was glaring at me like I was the evil outlier. This was a person who had dined in my house, who had sat on my sofa until the wee small hours and playfully flirted in that inoffensive way that we tend not to mind because it reminds us we are living, sexual beings rather than just husbands and wives. And now he was staring at me like I was a Martian. The kids were laughing like this was the best thing they'd ever seen. Wren kept on trying to bite at the water just a few inches from my hand. Then I heard Mark saying something to him again. But it wasn't what I thought. I realised Mark wasn't defending me, he was *apologising* for me, bumbling out an excuse for my behaviour – not a word of criticism of Bill's. Then his blonde, handsome head was coming towards me . . . barging through my aim, wrenching the thing out of my hand. It fell to the ground, quickly saturating my pale green ballet flats. Next I was being frogmarched back across the soggy lawn past my enemies, through the gate, back to our side of the fence. As he hauled me into the silence of our house, tears suddenly began to stream down my face – or maybe it was only then that I was feeling them, along with the clench of each individual one of his fingers on my bare arm.

'Liv.' I heard his voice. 'Liv.'

I was numb yet stinging. I was so sore. Inside and out. I was as mortified as if he had stripped me bare in front of them.

I remember feeling the dying of love. All those years – good heavens, nearly a lifetime – of esteeming him so highly, all of it leaving me. What overlaid everything was the stigma of having been so publicly let down.

'Liv.' I hear it again.

Echoes of the garden party fade. No one is there; I am staring at an empty yard.

The noise in my head has abruptly stopped, replaced by dull confusion. I turn from the window. Mark is standing right by the island. 'You're back?' His suit jacket is hanging off his right shoulder from a fingertip. 'You're home.' The questioning tone when it isn't a question. He is buoyed up, optimistic.

'I thought you'd be at work . . .' I say. I'm puzzled. How long could I have been standing here, so powerfully pinned by a memory? He's wearing a lilac dress shirt. With his fair, lightly tanned skin he suits the colour very much. I am struck by how tired he looks, and older – something I've never noticed before. In all these years his collar-length hair has never been either longer or shorter than it is now. As though his hair might point to time having stood still, if only his face didn't contradict it. And for a moment I imagine what it would be like to be back. If this – him standing here, his cautious optimism – were the bridge. 'I came to get some more of my stuff. And a few things from my desk.'

The promise, the hope, or whatever it was I believe I saw in his eyes, dwindles. He drops his jacket into a chair; it lands with the clunky weight of too much paraphernalia in pockets. 'I took the afternoon off.'

The air has lost its charge. I glance quickly out of the window again, to where it all was, and see only a pretty garden. And yet moments ago it had all been so vibrantly real.

'Wasn't feeling like it today . . .' He looks black, sad, shrugs.

Dust motes are trapped in a shaft of light that stretches between us. There is a wedge of silence that neither of us knows how to fill. 'D'you want a glass of wine?' he says, after a moment or two of us holding eyes, trying to work out where we now stand in each other's estimation, probably with neither one of us coming off too high.

'Wine? No. I'm driving . . .'

'But you just got here.'

'I'm not staying. I just need to get a few more of my things. Work stuff.' Stuff I've managed not to deal with for over a year. I don't know why it has suddenly become so important now.

71

I continue to stand there, rooted, as does he. 'She said she was going to Florence,' I say. 'Didn't she? If I'm not mistaken it was going to be Rome first, then Venice, then Florence for a longer spell to allow her to tour around Tuscany. Am I right?' In the absence of being told anything first-hand, I am just struggling to get a picture.

After a while he nods, says, 'Yes.'

I am a little brighter suddenly. Jessica is in my favourite city right now! Mark watches me, appearing stilled by my comment, clearly struck with nostalgia, too, at the mention of the city where we honeymooned. It's funny how you can go through the worst possible hell with someone, they can disappoint you in ways you never bargained for, and yet with one small reminder of the good times, the bad times crumble before your eyes; for a moment you wonder if they were ever there. Still he looks at me. But I break the spell by remembering what I'm doing here and heading towards the stairs. He stands without moving until I am almost past him. Then his eyes follow me with the slightest turn of his head until I am no longer in his range of vision. I climb the first few, pause and glance at his back. He is staring into the space where I just was.

The bad times are more easily remembered than the good, but in some ways they're also easier to forget, and it strikes me that this is both a blessing and a curse.

As I climb the stairs, it occurs to me, like it did when I was driving here, that I might find things in our bedroom that aren't mine and I've about twenty seconds to prepare myself for this. I remember him saying, *If you're so convinced I cheated then maybe I should have! And me thinking, Nice head game you're trying to play with me.* A wave of nausea and dread rock me as I push open the bedroom door. I can't take any more discoveries, any more bad things happening.

'She's just a friend,' he said at first, that day when I told him I knew he was having an affair and I even knew who with: I had seen them. 'I work with her. That's all.' He said it so convincingly. I remember staring at him, thinking, *How can an honest person lie so easily?*

The room looks much the same: very little on either of our night tables; the bed's unmade on his side, tightly tucked on mine. Josie will have washed the sheets yesterday. I love a newly laundered bed. I have a sudden longing to climb into it and sleep for all eternity. I had to tell her about using too much laundry detergent, though – I kept getting a rash and finally twigged why. Telling her felt like a big ordeal at the time. That was back when those sorts of things were all I really had to get het up about. Has Mark brought anyone else into this house? This bed? Would he do that? I can't really see it, and yet I can't stop staring at the mattress, picturing his body entwined with someone who isn't me. His hands appreciating someone else's ass – *her* ass. I have always loved witnessing which parts of my body turned him on. Someone else being cherished, prioritised, put first, in all the ways I have known and held dear – and expected to continue for many years. His feelings for me being irrevocably changed simply because he loves someone else now, because she makes his life feel manageable again. He loves her with that fresh, exciting certainty he once felt for me. And he does it because I have driven him into her arms.

I happen to glance in our full-length mirror and see he's right behind me. We hold eyes through the glass as though he's trying to read my mind. His face looks slightly distorted and yet there is still a glimmer of optimism in it; he has hope for me that I don't have for myself. I break the spell by going into the bathroom. A quick scan of the double sinks, the side of the bathtub. Nothing out of the ordinary. A pink razor blade by the soap dish. Mine. I throw a few things from the vanity into my bag – a beloved brand of dry shampoo that I used sparingly because it had been discontinued, before I gave up caring about whether or not I had clean hair. My electric toothbrush – one more thing I've surprised myself by living without.

I pluck my bathrobe from a hook behind the door. 'Don't,' he says, standing in the doorway, blocking me as I go to pass him. 'Please, Liv . . .' I wiggle by, then he pads after me to my chest of drawers. 'Can we just talk?'

'Talk?' I glance in his direction. 'I wanted to talk for a very long time. You weren't there.'

He frowns, caught in the act of processing this, then looks intensely wounded. 'That's not true. You know it's not. Why would you even say that?'

I can't look at him right now. It hurts too much.

'I was there. I've always been there. And I still am. I'm still here, Olivia.' His tone is strident, almost defensive. 'You're the one who left.'

Our conversations are like a game of solo squash. I fast serve. The wall stays. I try to manoeuvre differently. 'I've rented a little house,' I say. 'Signed the lease for a year.'

For a moment he just looks at me blankly, then he says, 'Shit.' He sucks in a sharp breath. In all these years of marriage I have never seen Mark have a fit of anger. Mark never lays into people, never wants to kick a wall. He has an amazing ability to take the steam out of a situation just by being present in it. But recently I have wondered, is it just because he doesn't ever feel anything deeply enough? Is that why I can't reach a certain part of him – because those places don't exist? We are complicated human beings. There are so many layers to us. But I've recently thought that perhaps there aren't that many layers to Mark.

He puts a hand to his mouth, rubs his palm across it. 'Jeez, Olivia . . . Tell me that's not true.'

'Well, obviously, I couldn't keep staying in a hotel. It was costing a small fortune.'

Something in his face has changed. He is looking at me as though I'm some sort of potential threat, an alien, as though he can't even begin to fathom me because he's just come to the conclusion I am not even human.

'It's a nice little place. I think I'll be happy there.' I absorb the frequency of his reaction.

'You've won, Olivia.' He shakes his head as though he is smarting from my words. 'If this was what you wanted . . . you've got me. You win.'

This concept of winning – as though any of this is a game – reverberates and hurts. His eyes hurt. Once again I can't look at them. I don't know what to say. I don't understand our dynamic any more. I no longer know who either of us is. I go back to pulling T-shirts from a drawer. I don't get very far. There is part of me that so badly doesn't want to do this that my arms are like lead weights, preventing me. I hold my tangerine tank top between both hands, stare at it for way too long. I stroke it with my thumbs, trying to smooth out the ribs in the cotton, combing over them and over them and over them until they blur and I can't distinguish the lines any more. I can't make them out for my tears. When I come round again, I am on my own. Mark has gone back downstairs.

I must sit on the floor for a very long time, or it feels that way, gazing into the carpet, the tiny whorls of cream wool, my brain loosely making shapes and patterns out of them and spinning thoughts. When I can't stand the bottomless ache any longer I get up, go into my office and rake through drawers, forgetting at first what I'm even looking for. On my way back down I'm passing Jessica's room and my feet instinctively stop at the door. I try to picture something: on the other side is Florence. Jess outside the Duomo, lingering at that little stall where you can try tiny samples of local olive oils and knobby Parmigiano, wearing her favourite fuchsia cardigan. She turns to me and smiles . . .

When I open the door, the room feels a little foreign to me, and stuffy, yet I can still detect a hint of the nice new Jo Malone perfume she'd started wearing. It makes my missing her so desperately raw. I'd hop on a flight right this minute if I could. For a second I hold it there as an idea. My eyes go to some pictures on her nightstand – the Keith Urban concert where she's laughing with a few friends; the first time she put pink streaks in her hair. Surprisingly, it looked really good with the platinum blonde. On her dresser is her dog-eared mohair teddy we bought for her second birthday, sitting splay-legged. That teddy went everywhere with her. *Why didn't you take your teddy with you, Jessica?* I think. *Were you trying to make the point: I'm all grown up now. I'm not a child! Because if you were, you've succeeded.*

When I go back downstairs he is sitting on a stool at the island. He's got his head down like I've seen him do when he is both despairing and thinking hard. He's opened a bottle of white wine, poured himself a large glass. Mark is a Scotch drinker and only ever drinks wine if we are having a special dinner out and I am desperate to order something a notch up from the measly 'by glass' selection. 'Scotch is a solitary drink,' he once said. 'Wine is meant to be shared.' He doesn't seem to hear me come down, or be aware of me standing there. Then he looks up as though I've been there all along, the heatedness of what just happened between us upstairs dissolved. He too has pressed some sort of reset button on things, it seems. He gets up and goes to the cupboard, pulls out another glass. I am aware of the chime of crystal meeting granite, the chinkle of a bottle top being unscrewed. I take a small sip of what he pours. It's cold and buttery: the only kind of white I can drink. Then I push the glass away. Tentacles of yearning for our old life try to wrap around me and part of me thinks, *What would coming back really look like now that everything is different?*

'I've joined a letter-writing club,' I say, out of the blue. I don't really know why I'm telling him this. For want of something to follow it, I shrug.

He studies me as though I am a new object for his discovery, not the woman he's been married to for nearly twenty years. But it's not a pursuit he wants. He was happy with the me I used to be.

'It's called the Correspondents' Club, which makes it sound quite old-worldly and grand.' I smile. 'Like I'm in a turn-of-the-century novel . . . I thought it might be therapeutic for me. Force me to put some order in my mind.'

'I remember your letters,' he says, with an air of nostalgia again. One side of his mouth tries to cock a smile. 'When you were pissed with me, you used to write me those diatribes. Remember?'

I peer down the dim path of memory. 'No. I don't think so. I wrote to you that time I had to go back to England. When I found out I was pregnant.' Reaching so far back to the early days of us makes my brows knit with emotion.

'There was that one, yes . . . But there were others. It was how you communicated your annoyance. When I'd done something to piss you off there was always a long written analysis of it, saying what this meant for you, me and mankind at large.' There is a note of amusement and sentimentality in his voice but his eyes quickly mist over.

I open my mouth to protest but think, *God! Maybe he's right!* I do remember doing that once or twice, now he's mentioned it. He's always had a better memory than me. How many times have I said to him, 'If I end up with dementia, who'll be there to give a damn about me? To make sure I don't get mistreated in a care home?'

'I will,' he'd say. 'Always. So long as I don't get it too. Or then we're fucked.'

'Maybe you're right,' I say now. I vaguely recall him once jokingly saying I was like Churchill's wife, Clementine. She used to write to him when she was annoyed because it was the only way she could express her side without him butting in. 'I may have done it once or twice.'

I'm not really sure what he's referring to when he says I was annoyed with him, though. Our disagreements were never about anything major. We could spat over a lot of silly stuff – who left the car window open when it was forecast to rain? Is anything other than three-ply toilet paper just false economy? Why did I have to agree to dinner with Laurel and Mike when he thought we were taking a social breather for a weekend or two? But on the bigger, important things, we were almost freakishly eye to eye. We were compatible with each other, supporters of each other, right for each other in the least cloying, least clichéd way possible; neither of us is overly sentimental or romantic. And that's why, without him, every time I stand I stumble. Why I feel so easily defeated unless he's quietly encouraging me to be stronger than I want to be.

'It'll probably be good for you.' I realise he's talking about the club again. 'You'll meet some people. You know, new ones.'

Who don't know.

'Believe me, that's the last thing I'm looking for right now. Friends.'

'Don't let people's shitty behaviour make you a cynic,' he once said. 'That would be a waste of all that you are.'

'Well,' he says. 'You like your own company better, anyway, don't you?'

I want to say, *You're right and you're wrong.*

'Are you seeing her?' I ask. I have to ask it.

I remember him saying that day, 'Of course we're not sleeping together! She's married. *I'm* married.' As though to remind me that those two positives could never make the particular negative I was accusing him of.

He stares at me now for a second or two while I wait for his answer, then he unscrews the bottle again, slowly refills his glass to the top. 'My wife walked out on me, accused me of something she had no actual proof of, and now she's telling me she's rented a house for a year . . .' He screws the lid back on again, sets the bottle down, looks at me. 'If I were, I'd have a right to, don't you think, Liv?'

A lump forms in my throat. I try to swallow. My mouth has gone dry. 'It's not really an answer, though, is it?' It just feels like a lot of smoke and mirrors.

He goes on staring at me, levelly. 'You left me and I tried to see around why you would feel you needed to do that – to go that far. You called me some shitty things I'm trying not to dwell on . . .'

'But it's still not as shitty as what you did to me, is it?' I say it quietly and calmly. I have no stomach for an argument about this right now.

'What did I do?' he says defiantly. And then, with a stronger note of challenge, 'What did I do, Olivia?'

I want to say to him, *How do you even have to ask?* But I cannot find my voice, cannot dig for the words. All of this leads to the place I can't go. Despite the fact that I should, or that I need to, I just can't do it.

I had never, ever, checked Mark's phone, searched his pockets, questioned his nights out with clients, or imagined anything he told me might be an alibi. We didn't have that sort of relationship. I am not suspicious by nature. I had never taken Mark for a liar. Not because he's incapable of dishonesty. Aren't we all able to distort the truth when we need to? But because I'd made certain assumptions about my marriage. I'd been unwavering in my conviction that we were happy. I was certain his definition of loving someone was the same as mine. It meant that the thought of being with someone else, whenever that thought occurred, was only that – a pleasing image in the quiet of the mind's eye that made you feel good about how you viewed yourself for a moment. Never a significant temptation. Never a threat.

'You've never got your head around the fact that I'm going through hell too,' he'd said when I found the texts, after he'd told me nothing had happened, like he's essentially still telling me. He'd said that I'd seen what I wanted to see that day, because I was messed up and I was angry and I needed someone to lash out at. That I was making it my excuse. 'You've been so wrapped up in how *you* feel about everything that you've forgotten about everybody else, Liv. Have you stopped to think that's maybe the real reason people don't want to be around you?'

Yes, I'd thought. *Deflect it. Clever. Prey on my guilt. Put the blame back on me.*

From the texts alone there was no evidence it was anything more than what he said. The most incriminating thing I could find was:

HER: *Loved our lunch! LOVE how we talk so easily. Look forward to many next times . . .* (with a winky face emoticon)

HIM: *I know . . . And . . . thanks. Cheers.*

And yet I know what I saw that day. It was not the interaction of *friends.*

'Maybe we should talk about us making our separation official,' I say now, my conviction that I'm being messed with renewed, that he's trying to gaslight me. That same feeling I had then: profound confusion, like my head is scrambled fudge. That same thought: *Mark is one step ahead of me; maybe he always has been. Maybe every truth between us has been a lie in disguise.* 'Deep down, I'm sure you think it's for the best, and I could use a fresh start. I'm in a new place. I've even got a job now. I need to move on, for my own sanity. Maybe we both do.'

He takes a drink of his wine almost purposefully slowly, sets the glass down, doesn't look at me. After a moment or two he says, 'If that's what you want, then go initiate it. You're a big girl. Nothing's stopping you.' He meets me hard in the eyes. 'And if you do it, Olivia, if you take those steps because you genuinely feel there's no coming back from this for us, or it's what you need to do for your sanity, then I promise you I'll try to accept it. I won't stand in your way. But don't make it about something it's not.'

'Fine then,' I say, to a rampant tick-tick of my heart, a reckless daring. 'If you're not sleeping with her, then why is her necklace on our bedroom floor?'

ELEVEN

The café is quiet on Sunday afternoon.

'You don't need to tamp so hard.' Beth takes the portafilter from my hand. 'Try again.'

'I'm deliberately trying to be useless so you won't ask me back tomorrow.'

She titters as she watches me dump the coffee and fill the basket again.

'That's right. Light touch . . . There. You got it.'

'Have I? I can undo this perception in two seconds flat.'

We smile.

One or two regulars are seated by the window reading the newspaper. I am grateful there hasn't been a stampede. On the floor by the creamer station are three boxes of book donations. Beth explains she places ads in the *Leader*, picks through estate sales, garage sales, church bazaars and the like. Most donations come directly from the local community; in exchange, she offers them a coffee card. 'It seems to work.' She shrugs. 'Of course there's no end to how serious you can get about the books side of the business but my intention's not to bite off more than I can chew . . .' Later, once I've got comfortable pulling espresso,

I'm supposed to sort and shelve them. 'You'll be having me cleaning the toilets next,' I quipped.

'That's for Thursday!'

I agreed to do this for one week. One week, I told her. Sometimes she has a knack of acting like she doesn't hear.

She pulls on a cardigan, arranges her long braids very properly over her shoulders like a scarf. 'I'm off out to pay some bills. If it gets too busy just don't walk off the job.'

'Thanks,' I say. I've only been here two hours and I'm already minding shop. 'Good to have a tip in crisis management.'

He is dressed in light jeans and a navy-blue hoodie. Just as I notice him I catch him walking towards me looking like I might be amusing him. 'Hi,' he says. 'Wow . . . From deck builder to barista. Who knew? Cool . . . How's it all going?'

'Deck builder? Ah . . . ' I groan. I had almost forgotten about that. 'Well, the deck is doing many things, but *going* isn't really one of them.' I nudge my hair off my face with the back of my wrist. 'The intention was to have it done for summer. But now I'm thinking *next* summer.'

He glances down at the shiny-plated silver apron I bought from the cooking shop across the way and that somehow makes me look like a Dalek. 'Why aim high when you can aim low and not be disappointed?'

'My sentiments exactly.' I dig a fist into my hip, grappling for an explanation as to what I'm doing here serving coffee, but the urge to supply it passes. He's not asking for one. 'Whoosh . . .' I hear myself say, suddenly feeling warm. 'What can I get for you? Please don't ask for anything too complicated.'

'How about a black coffee? If that's not too challenging. If it is I can settle for bottled water.'

I cock my head. 'If you're going to insult me, maybe you get nothing.'

He does that *ha* thing again, his verbalised laugh. 'How about a muffin, too?' He casts his eyes over the tray of baked goods.

'Personally I think they should come with a government health warning, but the decision's yours.'

'The blueberry orange one looks pretty innocuous.'

'I should have you sign a waiver.' I reach into the cabinet with my tongs, pulling out the one at the back, which is the freshest, then I pour his coffee.

He slides a hand into the pocket of his jeans and pulls out his wallet.

'No.' I shoo his hand away. 'On me.'

He cocks me a curiously impressed look. 'Won't that get you fired?'

'I'm seriously hoping.'

He smiles. It would be a broad smile, only the left side of his mouth doesn't have quite the same range of mobility as his right. *I was blown up . . . a Humvee that went over a landmine.* Suddenly, out of nowhere, a tingle travels down my spine and grips and builds. Then, the room starts moving – a wall of green and blue sliding faster and faster past my eyes. I find myself trying to latch on to detail, attempting to make sense of what it is, but the voices start whispering again, and now I'm too lost in struggling to hear what they're saying.

'Are you all right?' I hear one above the rest. Or did I hear it?

Focus on something tangible. I cast around but can't see anything to get a hold of with my eyes. There is a metallic taste in my mouth. I'm aware of smacking my lips, trying to get rid of it, of being unable to stop myself.

'Olivia?'

The voices fade somewhat against the strength of this one. It grounds me a little. I'm aware of the smell of coffee, which leads me to reconnect in the smallest way with where I am. Muffins under glass.

Once I see them I stare at them, forcing myself not to look away. My hands are locked, fingers numb with my grip. After a moment I look down at them, at the white knuckles, deliberately try to unclench them. Everything else is fading.

'Olivia?'

I see shoulders and a navy-blue zip-up. The moving room is subsiding further, everything slowing, even my heart rate. I am conscious of waiting to make sure the feeling is going to leave. 'I'm fine,' I say, like it's a reflex. Part of me is telling me to listen to my own words.

'You sure?'

I nod. I have come out in goosebumps. Every hair feels like it's standing up. His voice draws me back to the now. The nape of my neck is soaked when I lay a hand there, and so is my lower body from my crotch to my knees.

'You're sure you're sure?' I hear the genuine concern in his voice. His warm, kind eyes stay fixed on me, and I let them provide an anchor.

'Positive.' I let my lips part a fraction and breathe out slowly and steadily without making it obvious. I have a vague sense of having stepped off a boat from a choppy sea, on to steady land. This one was faster than they normally are, over more manageably. 'Thanks,' I tell him.

I'm expecting him to go, but still he stands there. I refocus away from his eyes, run a hand down my wet leg; it's like I went swimming in my jeans. 'Well, enjoy your coffee,' I say, but my words seem to come out one step ahead of me. My voice sounds torqued. I need him to not be standing here. I could badly use air.

'Well . . . OK . . .' he says, perhaps getting the message. 'And, um, thanks for not charging.' He still looks reluctant to move.

'I won't make a habit of it,' I hear myself saying.

'No.' He half smiles. 'And don't worry, your wild act of rebellion is safe with me.'

'It's bribery. I'm hoping you'll come build my deck.' The words are out before I even know where they came from. I think, *What on earth did I just say?*

There is an awkward hesitation. Then, 'Sure.'

Damn! I am a little slow in knowing how to respond. 'I was kidding,' I finally say. I throw up my hands in mild exasperation. 'A joke . . . you know. I wasn't being serious.' My face is burning. I want to disappear down a hole.

'It's OK. I was.' He hangs on to his drink, looking trapped, on the precipice of something.

I hide my face with my hands and say 'Ahhh!' This is a disaster.

If he thinks my behaviour is a little odd, he doesn't show it. 'I'd have to come by and take a look. When's good?'

We meet eyes again. 'This is a little silly. I really wasn't being serious—'

'Tomorrow night?'

We are saved by the arrival of two girls. They form a line immediately behind him and start tinkering on their iPhones. They are in no hurry to be served and he makes no attempt to leave. 'Sure,' I say. I'm about to throw up my hands again, but stop myself, unsure why I'm being so dramatic. I turn and grab the cloth and set about wiping down the steam wand even though it's already clean.

'You forgot something,' he says.

When I glance over my shoulder, his expression is one of slight amusement and intrigue.

'Address?'

TWELVE

We sit on the patio furniture I had to move from the deck to the tiny patch of lawn that's been rendered threadbare in the shade of two dominant cedar trees. He accepted a home-made lavender lemonade, turning down my offer of wine or a beer with 'I'm not much of a drinker'.

'I wouldn't have taken you for a carpenter.' I find myself drawn to look at his hands.

'No.' He smiles, holding the glass mid-chest against his lean upper stomach. Around his left wrist is a curious piece of tough-looking khaki material the thickness of a flexible tape measure with some kind of dull metal running through it. 'When I was at MIT I worked all kinds of jobs. I was a lifeguard, hospital porter, then one summer I picked up litter for the parks department. That was so boring that the next year I was reincarnated as a builder's apprentice where I helped build decks and the odd kitchen.'

'You went to MIT?'

'For aerospace engineering. I wanted to be a SEAL for as long as I can remember but my dad said he'd disown me if I pursued it. But in my second year of college I made it known that when I graduated I was going to apply to Navy Officer Candidate School whether anybody liked it or not.'

'Yikes. How did that go down? Did he disown you?'

'No. He died of pancreatic cancer before I graduated.' He looks off over the fence with an empty stare. 'If I'd never told him, he wouldn't have left the world so disappointed in me.'

'That's sad,' I say, thinking of the concept of last words being bad words. 'But we're not extensions of our parents, are we. We must do what's right for us and stand our ground sometimes.' I can hear Jessica saying, 'Oh my God! Have you heard yourself?' which briefly throws me off course. 'What did your parents want you to do instead of the military?'

He puts his glass down and the tendons in his wrist flex. 'My mom was a nurse. I think she'd have liked me to become a doctor. But I never saw myself as that. Back then I couldn't stand the sight of blood – if you can believe.' He sniggers ironically. 'Besides, I wasn't smart enough for med school. When you're growing up they say you can be anything you want in life, but the reality is you can't. I was never going to be a quantum physicist; no amount of studying was going to change that . . . I do agree that you can be very good at what you do if you have the inclination for it in the first place . . . I just always thought I would be a good soldier, then when I became one I wanted to be the best I could. My father thought the military was for guys who needed straightening out. There were a lot of things in life he completely missed the point of.'

I want to say that if he got into MIT for aerospace engineering he's definitely intelligent enough, but I let his rather charming modesty lie.

'Where did you grow up?' I ask.

'South Florida.' He waggles the foot crossed over his right knee. 'Lived there my whole life.' He looks back at the house, staring at the windows, at the roof, at the trees beside it. 'It's a nice little place, this. Have you always lived in small towns? You're from England, originally, right?'

'Yup. Born and raised in a village in Gloucestershire. But I've been in the US for over twenty years. We lived just outside of Seattle.'

'Your husband is American? I mean, ex, I assume?'

I nod, unsure why I'm letting his assumption I'm divorced go uncorrected.

'And I'm guessing you haven't been a barista your whole life.'

'Ha! No, I worked for many years in sales and marketing for Westin Hotels. I loved it. Hotels are, well, they're a lovely place to work. Something about the fact that they never close . . . It's a long story but I was passed over for a big promotion and then my heart just went out of the job. I quit to start up my own business as a corporate event planner.' I shrug, remembering how Mark and Jess had differing views on it. 'My husband thought I was cutting off my nose to spite my face. My daughter had a totally different view. She said if they didn't appreciate me then I needed to find someone who did!' I smile, a thought breaking in: she'd supported me. Why did I have to leave her with the impression that I didn't do the same for her? 'I was never more proud of my daughter's capacity to go to bat for me. I'd always tried to instil self-worth into her, and there she was playing it back to me, reminding me . . . In hindsight, Mark was probably right, though.'

'So you started event planning?'

I try not to roll my eyes. 'Hated virtually every minute of it. It's very competitive. I was working all hours, not quite making enough money to justify hiring help. Then I went through some personal stuff – something happened – and, well, I just couldn't motivate myself to care after that.' I harrumph, thinking of an email I sent to a Spanish client who had complained the caterer I'd hired had committed the crime of serving Prosecco not cava.

If this is all you've got to stress about, honey, you'll live a long and blessed life!

Not very professional, I know. Burning bridges is a very bad plan in life. How many times have I instilled that into Jessica, too? The endless setting her up to avoid a lifetime of making silly but costly mistakes, because those were my definitions of costly at the time. 'I'm still trying to wind the business down now. Sometimes I think I'll never be free of it.'

'It's funny,' he says. 'When I came here I had no particular destination. I just drove north on the I5 from Seattle, saw the sign for Deception Pass, made the turn. Saw the signs for the ferry. I just thought, *Ferry. Cool.* And next I was in Port Townsend – somewhere I'd never even heard of.' He looks back at me through a void stare. 'Do you ever get the feeling this might be the place you come when you can't face being anywhere else?'

I think about this. 'I'm not sure.' I say. 'I don't think I want to be surrounded by a whole host of people who have checked out of life.'

He doesn't answer, just watches me as though his mind is rapid-firing through a lot of unwanted thoughts.

I must say talking to him makes me feel I have to throw out all my preconceived notions about army guys. He's tough but not in a bullish, hot-headed way. You couldn't label him the strong, silent type either. I can't quite characterise him. With all he has experienced, he seems abnormally together; I'd have expected someone more emotionally torn up. This is what puzzles me most about him. I want to know how he manages it.

'It's not a bad town,' I say, reaching for the positive. 'This isn't a bad house, really. Other than the rotting deck, and the separate taps in the bathroom. It reminds me a bit of England.'

'What do you mean separate taps?'

I do a double-take on his serious face. 'You know . . . no mixer. Just a cold one and a hot one that scalds your face off the second you've turned it on.'

As soon as the words are out, I realise what I've said.

'Isn't cold water supposed to be good for the complexion?' His intense brown eyes steadily hold mine.

I try not to audibly breathe out. 'I guess we'll find out.'

There is a long pause, then he strums his fingers on the side of his empty glass. 'It probably won't take me much more than a week if by some miracle we don't get a lot of rain.'

'Seriously? I still feel bad about this! I hope you're not doing it to be polite.'

'Why would I be polite?'

'I don't know. Because you're a nice guy? Because you felt backed into it?'

'I'm not that much of a nice guy.' He holds my eyes in a way that takes his comment to a slightly more affecting level. Or perhaps I am imagining it.

'If you tell me the cost of everything, I'll let Nanette know.'

He stands now. 'Well, it's only really the cost of the wood. I'm not charging you for my time, obviously.'

'What?' I look up at him in surprise.

'You did a good turn for your landlady, now I'm doing one for you.'

I am momentarily speechless. 'Of course I'm going to pay you! Good heavens! There's no other option.'

His expression lightens as though my mini outrage surprises him. 'I told you I'm not a professional. If I mess up maybe we both have to take responsibility.'

My mouth opens, reaching for objections. I have never been good with accepting kindness or charity.

'Look, you might not realise it but you're doing me a favour. Too much time on my hands is no good for me. Plus, I like outdoor work.' He tilts his head back and looks up at the cedars again, towering way above the house. But I sense he's contemplating more than just the trees. 'I haven't built anything since before . . .' He clenches and unclenches his hands. 'If you don't use it you lose it.'

'Are they painful?' I get up and walk with him to the gate. I half know the answer to this. A couple of nights ago I found myself reading about skin grafts and scar tissue online, then I had to stop because it was more distressing than I'd bargained for.

'No, no, they're fine. I had to have pins put in them to immobilise the damaged joints, or I'd have lost my fingers. After that there was a lot of therapy to stretch the new skin. *That* was painful.'

'Yikes . . .' Goosebumps break out on my arms.

'Hey, you asked,' he says, trying to lighten things. 'Having to fight to get the use of them back was the biggest test of tolerance and perseverance I've ever known. It was the first time in my life that I felt entirely powerless.'

I wonder what his wife must have gone through watching him in excruciating pain. I wonder how that changes a marriage.

'But you did it.' I suddenly feel an emotion I can't name.

'I guess we'll find out.'

THIRTEEN

I haven't gone on to my own Facebook page in a while.

Before 19 May 2016 I would post occasional pictures of our family, holiday shots, beauty shots of the nature around where we live. I dipped in and out perhaps a little too often to call it casual, but not enough to be obsessive, liking people's kids, cats and holidays, inwardly decrying random idiocy, political rants, people who are too self-absorbed, my fingers hovering over the block or unfriend buttons until I reminded myself I was an adult and could easily just walk away.

After 19 May, I started to loathe the window that social media opens on to your life. I'd kept doors locked, blinds closed, switched off my phone, and yet when I clicked on to my page there was a post on my timeline from someone I'd gone to school with twenty-five years ago – Judith Henley – whose only connection to me is that she sometimes runs into my parents at church fetes.

> *Just heard! OMG. What happens now? R police bringing charges???*

Underneath was a string of people's comments – I tried not to read them. But there was one that stood out:

What am I missing?! Liv, RU ok??????

Judith had commented back:

Will PM you. I don't think Liv is active on here at the moment. Understandably.

She was ready to talk about me to a complete stranger! It was beyond invasive and infuriating. There was I, trying my hardest to keep a low profile and this woman I knew a million years ago had suddenly put my horror story out there for the world to see, complete with police and charges.

The last one of the string was from Eloise, my old friend from Westin:

Where are you? Been phoning! Totally understand you don't feel like talking. Going away to Barcelona on Monday. Brad was able to get his shifts covered so trip is on again! Call you when we're back.

I began deleting people at will. With every click of that delete button the sense of my own power returned a tiny bit stronger. Then, soon after that, when the thrill of getting rid of people started to wear old, I shut the account down altogether. Finally I had peace.

But recently I've found myself curious about people again. The little button is there giving me the chance to reactivate my account, which feels symbolic somehow. If I hadn't drunk half a bottle of wine a little too quickly and wasn't feeling adrift on a sea of loneliness, I wouldn't be sitting here contemplating this. As it is, I know I'll probably quickly disable it again once I've dipped a toe in the waters and seen I'm not missing much.

Up comes my cover picture of stunning Mount Baker in the snow. I took it when we went skiing – or, rather, Jessica and Mark skied, and I drank hot chocolate in the lodge and read a novel. My profile is a close-up of my face largely hidden behind Jackie O-type sunglasses. I stare at myself for a while, trying to put myself in the context of when it was taken: our perfect life before. When I look at my Messenger icon I see the same four unread messages, all from Eloise. Not sure I can read them now. Instead, I pull up some friends, to see what they've all been up to.

When we moved to our new neighbourhood, Larry, who lives two doors down, coincidentally happened to be someone Mark had worked with years ago at Microsoft. Through his wife, Deanna, I met a tight circle of women friends – Tanya Waxman, the alpha of the group, is our neighbour whose husband I blasted with the garden hose. If there's a girls' night out or a birthday, Tanya will be the one to propose where to eat, what calibre of wine to order and how much to contribute to a gift. While I like Deanna a lot, there seems to be a certain 'buy one get all of us' mentality among these women. I'm not really into spa days, Botox parties and paint your pet classes, so managed to stay somewhat on the periphery. I tended to dip in and out freely, without becoming too immersed, which worked well. They respected that and still made me feel very much one of them. Until I wasn't.

People behave strangely when they no longer know how to look you in the face and have a normal conversation with you. People just behave very strangely.

I go on to Tanya Waxman's page, and a few others, click through a few recent photographs. Another girls' night on Stephanie's wall. All of them chinking wine goblets. A lot of sleek hair and cleavage. I scroll endlessly through my newsfeed, desensitised to humorous posts, endless pet pictures, political rants. When I tire of this I go back to my own page, to that post from my so-called old friend in England, then to the last comment from Eloise, dated nearly fourteen months ago – where she's blabbing on about going to Barcelona. Now I find myself curious to see what she wrote in the unread messages. So I go back to them and click on them, observing the dates and times.

> *Hey, we're back from Barcelona! Call me. Worried about you!! Your phone is always off. Xx*

08/06/2016 5:22PM

> *Feeling any better?*

28/06/2016 9:06AM

> *Went to Barolo with the girls on Thurs night. Fun! We missed you!*

10/09/2016 11:45PM

> *Merry Christmas, Liv. Hope you're doing well. Hope you get this. I see you came off Facebook months ago . . .*

23/12/2016 11:08PM

It's a strange feeling. I read, then re-read them, aware of a degree of dislocation between then and where things stand now; the insensible Band-Aid of time. Despite myself, I soon fill with profound loneliness and loss. I wonder if she checks to see if I ever read them, or if I no longer feature in her thoughts. I can almost hear her saying, 'Look, I tried.

What more was I supposed to do?' When I think of Eloise, I honestly don't know where I net out. We weathered some of life's storms over the years – most of them her relationship ones. She was from a different part of my life and I quite treasured that. I try to give people the benefit of the doubt. But a real friend knows you need her when you've found a million ways to show her you don't. She doesn't stay away while saying she's there for you, doesn't tell you she's giving you space and manage to make it sound like she's doing you, not herself, a favour. I think of Mark's words when I mentioned another couple of friends I would have thought better of, who pretty much disappeared from my life afterwards: 'You always expect people to do what you would do, Liv, then when they don't you're disappointed. But they're NOT you . . . Maybe they think they're being a good friend by leaving you alone. Maybe they have literally no idea what to say to you . . .'

I listened, and he had a good point, but all I wanted to say was, *Why do you always defend others over me? Why can't you just for once say, 'You're right'?*

What I do know is that seeing Eloise's lame effort at being *there* for me during my living hell stirs up all the old feelings I thought had been muted; they flutter to my surface ready to quash me all over again.

Then I remember I didn't come back online to get upset about this. Instead I click on to Jess's page. Her profile picture has been the same one for a while – a close-up of her hands clasped behind her head, electric blue-painted nails, punkish hair in a messy topknot. This picture always manages to make me smile. There is something so cute, quirky and playful about it. I stare at it for ages until I've a sense of tunnel vision, the world seeming to drop away. *Come home*, I think, urging myself to stop listening to the drone of my own one-dimensional thoughts.

But then I notice something. All those messages from her friends that used to be at the top of her timeline aren't there any longer. Instead, I am staring at all these photographs of Italy! At first I think this must be the proverbial mirage in the desert. How did I not see them when I was scrolling through my news feed? There are so many of them but a few in particular leap out. Jessica at the Trevi Fountain; her hand in the Bocca della Verità. One of her at a patio table laughing, her head flung back, a cigarette in hand. Smoking? Hmm . . . This is new. Though she manages to pull it off like she's a piece of retro art. How strange that not a single friend has liked or commented on any of them. But it's the last one that takes my breath away. This one is a close-up of her face in slight profile. The background is blurred, giving a shallow depth of field. She is gazing at the frescoed ceiling of a church, her long eyelashes curled back by a generous gift of nature, the slightly parted, full lips and dewy cheeks. Her fascination, and the serenity that emanates from her, is palpable. I can practically feel the artistry of the photographer, his keen intent. It suddenly occurs to me: a boy took this. Someone who wanted to capture her when her guard is dropped. I am in no doubt of it; whoever took this photo is in love with my daughter's face. I think back to how many conversations we've had about her crushes, how we'd spend an eternity dissecting all her dates after she'd been on them. It's so strange for me to imagine she must have a boyfriend and I haven't been the first person she's told.

Beautiful, I long to write, to be the first to comment on it, but don't.

FOURTEEN

I am late tonight. Just coming here brings me a certain calm. Just the very act of leaving my house and knowing this is my destination. What is it about a small gathering of virtual strangers joined in a kindred purpose, especially an unsocial and introspective one, that can do this? I've been thinking about it and must admit it's rather mystifying to me.

As before, there is one unoccupied table immediately behind Ned. I try to tiptoe across the wood floor in my espadrilles but the inevitable clop-clop of two-and-a-half inches of esparto rope makes him look up and give me a slow nod. I put my bag down beside the chair, and then go over to the counter to make myself a drink. I am barely reaching for a mug when a hand lands on my forearm.

'What do you do when you send someone a reasonable letter and you wait patiently for a response, and yet still they won't look at you over the garden hedge and their dog keeps barking day and night?'

I stare at the hand. She removes it. 'Tada!' She has pulled something from her purse.

'What is it?' I ask. It looks like a battery block.

'Watch.' She places one side of it to her lips then lets out a low-pitched bark.

Something squirts me in the chest. 'What the . . . ?'

'It's only citronella.' She rubs furiously at the wet spots on my rain-coat. 'It's perfectly humane. No nasty electric shocks.' Then she almost growls, 'Those are for later.'

'Can you stop pawing my breast?' I brush her hand away and take over wiping at the mark. I don't mean to add, 'You're bloody nuts.' It just slips out.

'What was that?' She looks confused for a moment.

'I said you've got some real guts.'

She beams at the compliment. When I catch Ned's eye I'm surprised to see he's quietly laughing, his shoulders sliding up and down.

'Can I try it?' Daniel snatches it off her and tries barking. When nothing happens he throws it on to the table. 'It doesn't do anything!'

'I'm going to send it to him and tell him I don't want payment,' Amy is babbling at me. 'All I want is for him to please give the thing a try. I just can't take it any more! I've contemplated harming myself.'

I give Ned a look that says, *Shame it stayed in the mind . . .*

When Amy finally sits down, I take my chai latte over to my seat. I am wearing a denim pencil skirt that hits just above my knees, showing off about the only part of me I actually like about my otherwise non-eventful figure. Combined with the espadrilles I feel ultra tall and perhaps a little too dolled up: it's a writing circle, not a fashion show. I should have worn flats. As I pass Ned's desk, I note his left hand holding the pen, the clean curve of his thumbnail, the untouched writing paper. I can almost hear words trying to compose themselves in his brain. I pull out the chair, settle myself in. Now what? I don't feel like beginning right away, needing a moment to soak up the spirit of our small gathering and try to get some impetus. We're an odd lot.

Despite Beth's notice remaining on the board, our numbers haven't grown. I am beginning to feel new arrivals would be too much like intruders now.

I stare into the centre of Ned's back without blinking, follow a direct path upwards to his hair, which forms a pristine V at the nape of his neck, where there's a cluster of tiny freckles centred around one larger one, like small planets around Earth. I find myself fixing on those freckles, particularly the big one.

I wonder if he feels my eyes because his head turns a fraction again and he gazes off to the side like someone slyly trying to see what's in his peripheral vision. I look at his unfairly long eyelashes, the cups of his ears, the network of fine scars around the lower part of his face and down his neck. We stay like this for a while – me deconstructing him, and him decoding the fact that I am.

I am the one to break it, rather puzzled by it. I reach down for my bag and pull out my special box of writing paper. When I straighten up, Ned has gone back to whatever he was doing. Just the other day, when Mark and I were talking about Jessica going to Florence, I remembered I had this. I bought it twenty years ago in a pretty little shop immediately across from the Museo Nazionale del Bargello – we had stumbled on it while we were looking for somewhere else, which, in a way, is how many of life's best moments happen to us, I think. It was a gem of a little place that sold quixotically colourful book-marks, blotters, gift wrap, boxes and photo albums and, of course, precious Florentine paper; I had no idea it was anything special at the time. Amazing how travel makes us richer, often in ways that don't feel particularly life-enhancing in the moment. While I had rooted around the shop, Mark stood outside in the sunshine cooing and playing hidey boo with Jessica in her stroller. I was conscious of the companionable white noise of them, of my profound pride in the pair of them, and my love, bigger and more palpable than anything

I had ever known. The paper was buttercream with a border of small cherry-red crests that looked like a cross between a Georgia O'Keeffe flower, a peeled-back banana skin and a cartoon locust. It seemed almost too beautiful to use. Digging it out from my chest of drawers the other day, after it occurred to me that Jessica probably never had any idea she'd ever been to Florence, memories of that holiday sprung at me from all directions. And, oh, the vividness of the detail! I remembered what I was wearing – my short, A-line denim skirt that Mark loved me in. I heard the revolutions of Jessica's buggy as Mark pushed it over the cobblestones, and me singing, 'The wheels on the bus go round and round . . .' I even remembered what we ate that evening – gnocchi with truffles for him, creamy *baccalà* risotto for me. As though my memory had been set the task of drawing a precise map of a city I'd visited only once, I could still find my way to that little restaurant – tucked down a tiny street by a small, dried-up baroque fountain featuring a beautiful sculpture of a young woman standing in meditative serenity with her eyes closed. We were the only two in the place because Italians dine out late, even ones with new babies. I can still see Mark spearing his gnocchi with his free hand, Jessica commandeering his other arm, sound asleep with her cheek pressed into his shoulder.

The box has never even been opened, as though by doing so the sanctity of our bright new days as a family would be marred, the fine points that made up the precious picture of us would be rearranged. Had the paper been used up, that place and everything I'd felt while there would have been just one more thing to have forgotten in time.

I take out a single sheet, appreciating its heft and texture, and pick up my pen. For a while I can't quite find the thread. Then eventually I think, *OK, this is where I'll start . . .*

Just with the very idea of doing this, I am conscious of myself sitting tall, of adopting a certain carriage of my shoulders, of relaxing my hand into a comfortable gait, like a long-lost act of meditation.

Dear Jessica,

I take extra care with my penmanship – I've actually been practicing – wanting my presentation to be as particular as what I have to say.

I know how much you've always been fascinated with Florence. I thought you might be interested in the story behind this writing paper because in a way it's a story about you . . .

FIFTEEN

He throws a rotted plank into the dumpster and the terrier across the street kicks off barking again. I come and stand in the doorway. Someone has lit a barbecue and the smell of steak reminds me of our long summer evenings entertaining in the backyard. How Mark would casually man the grill, spearing and turning steaks one-handed, his other holding his fat crystal Scotch glass. How he'd be holding that same glass, dulled by fingerprints, down by his leg as we saw people off at the door. Then, inevitably, no matter how fun the night had been, we'd collapse on the sofa and swear we were never entertaining again.

'Not bad progress for a day's work,' I say to Ned. He has removed most of the old decking and railing, and is setting about pulling out some nails from the posts with a large crowbar. 'Do you want a bite to eat? I made pasta with some pine nuts and oregano.'

He wipes a speck of dirt from his forehead with the back of his wrist, glances in my general direction. 'Sure. Sounds great.'

He stands while eating. I wait to see if he's going to chat, but it's like I'm not here. The dish is empty in two minutes. I offer him a beer but he brushes it off with, 'Water's good, thanks.'

He hasn't talked at all today. Earlier on I thought perhaps he's just not a morning person. But it's more than that. His silence has a solitary quality to it that's making it bigger than what it is; I'm feeling the need to tiptoe around it, like it's a *thing*.

'Clearing this up then I'll probably head home.' He stands at the back door and passes me his empty water glass with a 'Thanks'.

'OK.' I take it from him. I can't deny I feel a little relieved.

I am sitting on the sofa about an hour later when he taps on the semi-open back door. 'You can come in,' I shout through, wondering why he is being so formal. But he just stands there, waiting.

I move to the door, feeling guilty that he must feel obliged to finish the deck now that he has started. 'Like I said, you really didn't have to take this on. It's way too much work!' I swipe a hand over the entire catastrophe of the backyard.

'No.' He seems slow on the uptake, bewildered almost. 'It's not that. Sorry . . . I just get my quiet days.'

He doesn't meet my eyes – I'm not sure he has even once today. But then it dawns on me and I feel terrible. Here I am making it all about me – my indebtedness about his deck charity, my unease with his silence. I am forgetting he's dealing with his own issues and it's probably true his would give mine a run for their money. 'It's OK,' I say. 'Please don't apologise. I completely understand.' I turn to go back inside, cringing, but he follows me. When I turn around he is standing by the fridge. His presence, permeated with his low spirits, fills up the space, consuming my share of the oxygen. For a moment he just stands there, awkwardly, and looks at me like a person forcing himself to make an effort and finding it nigh on impossible.

'Weather's supposed to be good tomorrow,' he says. There is a desperate plea in his eyes.

I nod overenthusiastically. 'Yes . . . I heard.'

As I clear my throat, his gaze shifts to the silvery pile of garlic skins on the chopping board, the spilt oregano, the shavings of Parmesan. 'I've always enjoyed cooking but I've never been the best at clearing up,' I say.

He looks like he wants to smile but can't manage it. His eyes meet mine again, and there is something in them – a question or comment. I wait for him to verbalise it, but the spell is broken by the ringing of my phone. I'm not sure where it's coming from at first; I'm a little off kilter. We both glance around at the same time. Ah yes. The pocket of my hoodie draped on the back of the chair. 'Tomorrow, then,' he says, before I go to get it, and you can almost read a degree of regret into the whole thing.

'OK.' I nod.

He nods too, then says a clipped, 'You have yourself a good night.'

He doesn't show up for the next three days. Time stretches more so than usual. I try to fill it with naps and long walks and reading but I can't shake off the emptiness. I return to one of my old pastimes from when I'm having one of my insomnia episodes – googling recipes from BBC Good Food. I decide, OK, I'll start making proper meals for myself, ones that require a little prep and a special shopping trip, recipes I can easily quarter so I'm forced to repeat the task the next day. It reminds me of Mark and his bread-making phase. Every morning he'd surface at 5 a.m. to put a loaf in. I remember how beautifully the house smelled on waking. Jessica's and my glee. Then, one day, her saying, 'Mum? Why is Dad's bread machine sitting at the bottom of the drive?' We both went to the window. There it was in a tough plastic bag, sitting on a white plastic stool in the rain with a big FREE sign beside it. 'Ooh, I wonder how long before the vultures take it?' she said, rubbing the palms of her hands together. We had often joked about the ridiculous degree to which one person's trash was another's treasure round here. Jessica saying, 'They've all got enough money to buy their own brand new thirty-dollar wall clock – why do they need somebody's broken one?' She got such a kick out of trotting to the window to see if the bread machine was still there. Turns out it was gone in less than an hour.

On Thursday I venture into a random hair salon and sit on a leather sofa pretending to read a magazine while I wait for the stylist to finish with her current client. Seems luck is on my side and I'm getting a self-absorbed twenty-something who can't stop banging on about the quirks of her boyfriend's Labrador, and the wedding she's doing hair for this upcoming weekend – she won't want to know a thing about my life. When it's my turn in the chair, I watch her sectioning and snipping, sedated by the whimsical dance of her fingers, just like Jessica's used to feel when I'd get her to touch up my roots. Then I close my eyes to the heat of the hairdryer, the companionable tug of her brush being the only thing that stops my chin from dropping to my chest.

I also put in two six-hour shifts at the coffee shop. Although I told Beth I was only staying a week, I've found I quite like the mindless occupation of being behind the counter, the sounds of grinding and churning, air pressure and water flow; the smell of coffee on my hands all day.

I'm at work, taking a ten-minute break, flicking through the Longfellow book, when Beth says, 'You're fascinated by that one, aren't you?'

I run my fingers over its gilt edges. 'Yup. Read it cover to cover. I'm quite besotted with one of his shorter poems, "Loss and Gain".'

'*Defeat may be victory in disguise; The lowest ebb is the turning of the tide,*' she quotes.

'Very good.'

'It was my sister's.' She looks wistful for a second. 'Veronica's.'

'The book?'

'My parents gave it to her when she turned eighteen.' She lowers her gaze, seems reflective, but I'm too busy thinking that I gave Jessica a book of poems on her nineteenth – one my mother had given to me, that I hoped Jess would eventually pass down to her own children.

'I didn't get any such gift myself, even though I was really more into books than she was.' She snaps me back to the moment, pulls a sad smile. 'There was a loose piece of paper in it, with another verse written on it. *The tender word forgotten. The letter you did not write. The flowers you might have sent, dear, are your haunting ghosts tonight . . .* Any idea where it went to?'

Her eyes tunnel into mine, making my cheeks bloom and turn hot. 'Yes. I kept it. Sorry . . . I didn't think it was of any significance to anyone. It was just . . . there.'

She seems to stare me down. All her questions about me now answered because she thinks I nicked a poem about unwritten letters, unsent flowers and haunting ghosts – one I've come to know off by heart.

'I'll bring it back tomorrow.'

'No need. I suspected you might have kept it.'

I'm half tempted to say, *What's that supposed to mean? Was it some sort of trap?* But enough people already think I have a mental disorder. No point in adding one more.

'My sister sent it to me after her husband died. We'd argued about the book years ago – I'd made a point of telling her it should have been mine, not hers . . .' She looks wistful again, and then something else – bitter, if I'm not wrong. 'As for the verse, well, that was no doubt to remind me what an awful person I am, I imagine.' She holds my eyes as though she might say more, but then turns away. I am left holding the book, conscious of latching on to this unexpected little in she's just given me, and juggling a strange mix of thoughts: *Maybe she's not the old harridan I originally thought. Or perhaps she is, if her own sister doesn't like her.*

To ask her more, or not to ask her more? That, there, is the question. But nothing about her says she's inviting my prying. For want of something to do with the book, I place it back on the shelf.

'Keep it,' she says. 'And the poem. What my sister didn't realise is that I never needed reminding. She thought my silence meant I did.'

I wonder if she's being deliberately cryptic. Her words make me think of something Ned said, though. *Is everyone who lives here running away from something?* 'I can't take your book, Beth. Not when it belongs to your family. It wouldn't be right.'

'I have no family.' Her face hardens. But then I see it's not bitterness at all; it's the spectre of chronic sadness. 'Believe me, you'll be doing me a favour. I put it out there hoping someone will steal it but no one ever does.'

I'm still not comfortable taking it but I pluck it off the shelf again to please her. 'I'll hang on to it for now until you want it back,' I tell her. 'So it won't fall into the wrong hands.' In my short time working here I've seen many books that have gone out in good condition, come back like they've done a spell in the gutter in the rain.

She doesn't answer, just goes back to what she was doing as though the conversation never happened. But she is changed. We have walked over a grave. I go back around the counter, bury the book in my bag. Then I set about unpacking boxes of tea. I place the loose leaves into caddies as she showed me, crush packaging and put it in the recycling box, losing myself in the easy sequence of tasks, the silence, and the curious lull of unvoiced secrets, as the earth resettles again.

Just as I'm gathering my things to leave she says, 'Sometimes it's easier to pretend everything's fine than admit differently. But the problem is it becomes habit-forming until it's our new reality. Then we're really just living a lie.'

I'm concluding she's referring to her sister again, but then she meets me fully in the eyes. 'Something you wrote.'

I stare at her, uncomprehending.

'I found it in the trash.'

I have absolutely no idea what she's talking about. I'm about to tell her this. Then my world turns still. The letter to my parents! 'You went through my garbage?'

'Well, it's not exactly *your* garbage if it's on my premises.'

'Hang on . . . You went through the bin and read my letter? You tampered with my mail?' I gawk at her, thinking this must be a joke. 'My God, isn't that even against the law?'

'Not if it rolls out, and someone just happens to pick it up. That's just being tidy.'

SIXTEEN

I am in a most peculiar frame of mind when I get home, after the whole unsettling conversation with Beth. The first thing I do is take the book from my bag and reunite it with the piece of paper that has the verse written on it, which has been sitting on my night stand. But when I go to bed a short time later I can't resist picking it up again. I must lie there staring into space for a while, but instead of it having the effect of making me sleepy, I am suddenly bursting with purpose.

I reach for my laptop, settle it in the right angle of my thighs and tummy. For a second or two I am distracted by the screensaver of my husband and daughter – the panoramic, and slightly other-worldly, photo I took of Mark and Jessica hiking the Haleakala Crater in Maui two springs ago. They're a couple of blunt brush strokes on that vast green landscape – streaks of red shorts and the orange reflector of a backpack. And yet I would know Mark's lanky legs anywhere, and the punkish candyfloss of Jessica's hair. Two days later she went in the ocean on Kaanapali Beach and was thrown by a wave. I don't know what was more distressing to her: the fact that she got her bikini ripped almost entirely off, or that she broke her ankle. I can picture Mark and me helping her hop to our rental car, after I'd covered up her modesty with my kaftan. Mark saying, 'Baby steps up the sand, Jessica Rabbit. Baby steps . . .'

The Facebook app is there. I think, *OK, I'll have one more quick look at her photos from Italy*, but when I go to her page they are gone. Damn technology glitches! Next I go to Sarah's page, hoping it's all still intact.

'You're obsessed with her,' Mark said, the day he caught me poring over her photos. 'Why, Olivia? You need to move on . . . This is not natural.' I will never forget the aversion in his voice, in his eyes. Aversion for her, and for me.

He didn't get it and he was never going to. I accepted that. But I remember the resounding dissonance that was there every time I looked at him. The conviction in me that we had now been blown too far apart by our differences to ever come together again.

I go through her photos again, but out of habit – a little desensitised this time. Once I'm done I stare at the message icon. 7 a.m. in England. How easily I can transport myself to their detached, red-brick home. A mother getting two little kids ready for school. Bread jumping from a toaster while she throws down a second mug of coffee. The radio on as she reaches for apples in the fridge, packs two lunch bags, her iPad open on the kitchen table showing Yahoo news that she scans while scoffing down a cereal bar.

I imagine having some fantastical ability to travel back in time, where I would type: *Don't travel to America. Please, please don't enter our lives.* I might even tell her why.

I imagine the ping of my message cutting through the chaos of her kitchen, causing her to look over at her iPad. That ping changing the trajectory for all of us. But then comes the powerful reminder that no one, and nothing, can.

The message icon almost feels like it's speaking to me.

How do you begin to navigate what is undoubtedly the hardest thing you've ever had to say? Then I think, *What did I once tell Ned? You make a start.* Not just words in your mind, here for a minute, muddled, then gone again, buried once more beneath your fear of saying them.

Perhaps because I have been trying so hard to compose this message at the Correspondents' Club, it's like I've suddenly awakened some sort of muscle memory. Right now it feels quite easy to type *Dear Sarah*.

And this time I don't delete it. Instead I let her name lie there, turning it over along with the image of her that's been emblazoned on my brain. Suddenly it seems fairly obvious what comes next, so I type it before I can forget it or rationalise myself out of it.

> I can't tell you how many times I've come close to writing this – and how often I've told myself that it's pointless. There is so much I would like to say, and the need to say it never seems to diminish. But before I begin I should probably explain who I am . . .

SEVENTEEN

He shows up in the late afternoon. I am on my way back from a brisk walk and as I approach the house I hear hammering coming from the backyard.

'Hi,' he says, looking surprised by my sudden presence, and stopping briefly. 'I thought I would wait until the rain eased off.'

Did it rain earlier? I don't remember. 'Well . . .' I raise upturned palms. 'Thanks . . .' I wait to see if he's going to say anything else but he goes back to his hammering; it's like I'm not there again. Best let him get on with it, then. 'If you need anything just knock on the door,' I say as I pull my key from the pocket of my denim shorts.

There is a short delay before he answers, 'Thanks.' The hammering stops for a beat or two while I walk towards the back door. I feel his eyes on me.

In the kitchen I kick off my sandy pair of Toms, remembering I was supposed to buy some chicken thighs to make a small tagine for tonight but I forgot. Damn! I don't feel like going back out again. I'm not quite sure how you really order in for one; it almost doesn't feel worth any delivery guy's gas. Ignoring the growl of my stomach, I open a bottle of wine, then pour myself a small glass. I stand there for a little while, unable to resist the temptation to watch him through the window while his back is turned. He appears quite content, in a drifter sort of way; a certain methodical quality to how he works seems to put him at peace with the task at hand. Watching him has a meditative effect on me, until I jolt with dread that he's going to look up and see me.

I wander into the living room and fall on to the sofa, feeling restless. Out of habit I reach for my laptop. No new emails. A quick click on to Messenger. No new messages. I stare for a moment at the one I sent to Sarah and am compelled to reread it.

Ned knocks on the partly open back door around seven. 'Bathroom?' he says.

'Sure.' I wave for him to come in, listen to the companionable clonk of his feet.

'You OK?' He sounds a little concerned and hovers there a few steps away from me, looking slightly awkward.

I frown. 'Don't I look it?'

'I guess.' I think more is coming but then he just asks, 'Which door?'

I tell him it's the second on the left. I continue to stand there as he goes in. Then I hear him lift the toilet seat. I reach for the TV remote to turn up the volume to give him some privacy. Given I've never had any guests, it's an unwelcome time to learn that the walls are thin.

There is a small mirror in the front hallway. I walk over to it and peer at myself, trying to see what mysterious thing he's just seen in my face. The dark brown eyes, lashes licked with mascara. The brown, near-shoulder-length, newly layered hair. My minimal pale pink lipstick the only hint of colour against my olive skin. I look the same to me!

When he comes out again, I'm back on the sofa and quickly turn down the news as though I'd been watching it. 'Can I make you a sandwich? Eggs? I haven't had dinner myself—'

'No,' he says quickly. 'I ate a big lunch before I got here.'

I try not to feel snubbed, but then he adds, 'Want to come see my progress?'

I pick up my wine glass and we go outside. With not having eaten since noon I have a little buzz on. 'I'd offer you a glass . . .' I say when I catch him glancing at it, but I remember how quickly he shot down the offer last time.

'To be honest alcohol has caused a lot of problems for me lately. I'm trying to stay away from it.'

'Water then.'

'Much better idea.'

I disappear back inside and get him some Pellegrino with lemon.

He's made good progress. At least a third of the boards are in place. 'This is fab!' I say. 'I can't wait for Nanette to see it.'

'Not too shabby.' He steps down to the grass and plonks himself into a plastic white patio chair. When he looks up at me, his gaze travels rather deliberately along my legs, which, given the lack of forewarning, stuns me a little.

'I'm sorry about the other day. I can't regulate my moods sometimes.'

'It's no crime to be quiet. You don't have to explain.' Now that I am pretty sure he's just frisked me with his eyes, I feel ridiculously self-conscious. I walk over to the chair next to his and pull it out a little way so we're not sitting too close.

He rapid-taps his fingers on the table, then stops. 'I want to, though.'

I wait, aware I'm more curious than perhaps I ought to be. I try not to over-stare at him, to act like this upcoming explanation is almost incidental.

'After I was burned I was pretty messed up. I couldn't cope with my life, my marriage, my son. I couldn't cope with the trivia of our lives, you know; what they did every day, what Lisa talked about, got upset about.' He shakes his head, perhaps at himself. I can't look away. 'For months I couldn't come to terms with myself. I couldn't even stand to look in the mirror. My own son was scared of me. My kid couldn't eat a meal while I was sitting at the table. I grossed him out.'

I think of Daniel's reaction. The honesty of children.

'I had so many surgeries. The doctors kept expecting me to be happier with the progress, but it was almost like they'd oversold me on what the results would be.' He glances at his hands, upturns them as though seeing them for the first time, which I've noticed him do before. 'I got frustrated having gone through all that pain for what was essentially not much difference. I stopped leaving the house. Would disappear into the basement if anyone came over. I only felt normal when I was drinking. It was just in the evenings at first. Then I'd wake up waiting for it to be evening so I could get shit-faced. Then I stopped worrying what time of day it was and just got shit-faced anyway. I recognised I was on a path, but still, somehow, the SEAL in me felt I could control the drinking if I really wanted to. The thing was – I didn't want to.'

He looks at me now but doesn't seem to be seeing me. By the expression of frank disgust on his face, I believe he's too busy seeing himself.

'The army doesn't have a lot of resources to deal with PTSD. You're kind of out there with a self-help sheet . . . I drove my truck into a brick wall in a total alcohol-fuelled fit of despair. I don't know whether I just wanted an adrenaline rush again, or whether I seriously wanted to end it . . . I came out of it so dazed I thought I was back in hospital in Germany, right after the accident. My wife said she couldn't do it any more. She thought I was a danger – to my son, to myself . . . I don't know if I was seriously a threat to anyone's safety, but she was right, there was no point in trying to test it.'

He looks away into the body of the trees. I can't tear my eyes away from the picture of the life he's just painted. Because somewhere in this, I see a reflection of mine. How many days did I stay hidden within my four walls to avoid people's stares? How many times did I visualise ways I could end it if only I was brave enough? Found my only relief when alcohol hit my bloodstream? Mark emptying wine down the sink, saying, 'You have to hold it together. What would Jess think?' Listening to

Ned just makes me want to say, *I know, I can relate.* But the fact that I can makes it all the harder to admit.

He brings his eyes back to mine. 'I moved out for a while. Got some counselling. Went to a couple of AA meetings . . . The thing was, I could stop drinking. It was a choice. Alcoholics don't have a choice. And I'm not just saying this to say I'm better than anyone. I fully recognised it was a slippery slope. But once I'd committed to not touching it, I didn't. And I didn't need any God and his twelve steps to help me do that.'

I glance down at that thing he's got tied round his wrist.

'The problem was what it all stemmed from . . . Deep down I realised I was nothing any more. Before, I was always on a mission with my men. I always had a higher purpose. But now my higher purpose was just to exist purposelessly. In reality I was never going back there again, never going to be part of a team again. So I was nothing now.'

I let out a slow breath through pursed lips, trying to disentangle the threads of his story that merge too tightly with my own, tempting me to look at myself. 'But you're a young guy with your entire life ahead of you. A husband, a father. A hero. How can you say that's nothing?'

'I'm no hero. I'm no better than any guy out there and no braver.' He shrugs.

'Can I ask you what that is?' I reach my hand out and tap an index finger on his wrist, wondering if part of me has somehow just wanted an excuse to touch him.

'Ah,' he says, seeming to lighten. 'We closed in on this village outside of Kabul. My teammates had opened fire on this guy in a house – one of our targets. I was searching the rooms upstairs. There was this kid in the corner . . . huddling.' He frowns as though seeing it. 'He was terrified and I realised it was probably his father we'd shot . . . I tried to tell him I wasn't going to hurt him but he couldn't understand English. Then one of the guys shouted that there was a woman downstairs, hysterical. The kid's mother, I thought. I told them to bring her up.' He pulls a mirthless smile.

'When she lifted him in her arms, the kid was stiff as a board. But he kept on watching me. And I could see this sudden shift in his expression – not fear any more: trust. A minute or two later he pulled this off his wrist and gave it to me.' He touches the torqued material. 'I didn't want to take it but he just kept holding it out, so I did . . . Miraculously it survived the explosion, given it was on the side of me that was the most hit, and I've worn it ever since.'

'Wow.' I don't know what to say. Because it said online that SEALs never talk about what they do, this divulgence completely subdues me. I just can't help but think how humanity is the great leveller. 'Did you ever tell your son about the little boy?' I ask.

He nods. 'I did. Left out the bad parts. Spun it better . . .'

I study him and I can tell something has derailed his mood again with the mention of his son. Then he says, 'I let my family down. Lisa. All my son wanted was a dad and a simple family life. And I'm sure Lisa must have thought I didn't feel they were worth fighting for. Because, believe me, a SEAL's wife lives her own kind of war. She had to grow up way too fast. Afghanistan took something vital from her, as much as it took my face and my career. I am sure she regularly wonders what sort of person she might have been without all that . . .' He reaches into the back pocket of his jeans, pulls a small photograph from his wallet, passes it to me. 'This is Lisa and Jamie.' I can almost hear the quickening of his heart.

I take it from him, our fingers grazing briefly. It's hard to sharpen my focus given all he's just said. My brain is a spinning colour wheel processing all this background information. I stare at the picture of a thin, busty blonde woman, someone who might have won beauty pageants then ended up as a checkout girl in Fred Meyer. The little boy is cute with a buzz cut just like his dad's and metal-rimmed glasses.

'Lisa's a registered massage therapist. They're in quite big demand where we live. She earns decent money and gets to pick and choose her hours around Jamie and his school.' He shows me another one. This time, next to Lisa and Jamie is a man: Ned before the accident.

'I wasn't a bad-looking guy, or so people told me,' he says, semi-seriously.

We meet eyes. 'You're still that guy.'

'You're kind,' he says, after a moment.

I want to protest that I'm not being kind; that talking to him just affirms that our looks don't define us. His scars, once you get used to them, are only a part of what I see, like a pattern on a shirt. What anyone looking at him would see is someone who is principled, interesting, strong. Someone who downplays himself, who is completely without ego. I suddenly find myself filling with questions. Is their marriage truly over? What's he really doing so far away? I want to ask him how he lives, how he pays his bills, where real life begins once military life has ended . . .

I must be transmitting it because he says, 'I needed to be on my own. I just got in my truck, started driving, then I was somewhere else, in another state . . . Somewhere along the road I decided it was a good plan to drive across the country. So here I am.' He shrugs again, looks slightly hopeless. 'Anyway, don't be freaked out if some days I'm a hard guy to have a conversation with.' He stands, stretches his arms way above his head, leans back slightly, which makes me look to the area where his T-shirt rides up from his jeans – the patch of bare, unharmed skin. 'And don't ever worry about saying the wrong thing,' he says through a yawn. 'I've pretty much heard it all. You can't imagine how many people have tried to talk to me. When I was back there, in Florida, that's all everybody was trying to do, to give me their opinions. They meant well, of course. But they never actually let me say anything. It's rare for me to just have someone to listen.'

I am struck by how the air between us is changed. How one small divulgence of confidence – the opening of a window and the invitation to look inside – has drawn us a different topography, brought us to a new understanding of each other. How expansive I now feel. Almost giddy.

He takes his glass into the house. I continue to sit here, recast, listening to him running water in the sink.

When I go inside, he has his back to me. I watch him mopping up the tiny flood that collects around the taps with my hand towel. He looks so out of place, so oddly domesticated in this little house, which makes a battered part of me smile.

He turns and catches me observing him, takes stock of me for a second or two. 'Army training. I've been told I'm the tidiest guy alive.'

I smile. He continues to study me. Whatever more was coming stays unfinished.

'I'll see you soon then?' I say, when he carefully hangs my towel back on its hook and makes towards the door. 'Maybe next week at the Correspondents' Club?' I sometimes wonder if my tendency to give people an easy out is why everyone has taken it.

He stops right in front of me, a mite too close – it's like being back in Beth's doorway all over again. I have that same sense of being galvanised by his nearness and yet bemused by why I should be. 'You'll see me tomorrow, Olivia. I guarantee it.' There is a beat of hesitation where he just stands there, his eyes moving steadily, and with pleasure, around my face. Then he slowly reaches for the door handle.

Reluctant to leave?

Or perhaps I'm just finding myself in a strange frame of mind where I want him to be.

EIGHTEEN

My phone rings from under a pile of cushions.

'Hi,' he says.

I seem to momentarily lose my voice. 'Hi.'

'What are you up to?' he asks when there's a canyon of silence between us. He sounds casual, chilled, much like the old Mark – or he's trying to. I'm guessing the necklace business is clearly forgotten about now. Except, perhaps, by me. I just keep thinking of his parting words as I got into my car. 'Show me. Go on . . . If you found something, then I want to see it!' and me cringing as I shut the door.

I pull my mind back to the present and his innocuous question. *What the hell am I up to?* 'Oh? Right now?' I say. 'Not much. Just watching a spot of TV.' I haven't had the TV on in two nights but don't want to tell him I'm just sitting here in space, in case he reads something negative into that. 'What about you?' I ask. It feels surprisingly nice to have an ordinary conversation. We could be coming together at the end of a normal long day. It makes me miss *us*.

'Oh, not much. I was just out watering the plants. Got talking to our favourite neighbours. Tanya was saying she hasn't seen you in a while.'

With the emergence of his sarcasm, a part of me smiles; he can't stand Tanya Waxman and isn't the biggest fan of Bill. All the more reason I would have expected him to rally to my defence the day I saturated the idiot in his garden, I suppose, but never mind. 'What did you tell her?' I ask.

'Just that you'd gone to England to spend some time with your folks.'

As if. My parents were the last people I could have talked to. How do you inflict something as big as what I've gone through on the elderly? 'Think she believed you?'

'No.' He sounds semi-amused.

I snicker.

'Who gives a shit what she believes though?' he says.

And right there is the old Mark: my number one ally and champion.

I hear him taking a drink of something, picture him sitting on the sofa with his Scotch glass containing one fashionably large and slow-melting ice cube. I am feeling almost drugged by tiredness and the comfy familiarity of us, and find no need to root around in my head to come up with anything deeper than, 'How are you doing?' I realise I haven't asked him this in a very long time. Not properly – where I might be giving him the opportunity to actually tell me.

There's a lengthy silence then he says, 'OK. You know . . . What can I say?'

I wait to see if he will say anything else, but he doesn't. So I ask, 'How's work these days?'

'Working,' he says, sounding a little flat. And then, 'How's your letter-writing club?'

'Ah . . . the Correspondents' Club.' I always love saying its name. 'Good. I like it a lot.' My thoughts slide briefly to last night, to Ned and his hand reluctantly on my door handle. 'I never really expected to, but I hugely look forward to the meetings. There's something very calming about the environment, the company, the busy silence . . . It's cathartic somehow.'

'Good,' he says, after a pause. Mark is never one to really get into conversations about catharsis or anything vaguely resembling it, so it doesn't surprise me this topic is over quickly. 'Oh, by the way, I spoke to Cassie the other day,' he says. 'She was asking how you were doing.'

I feel like saying, *Bit late!* Sadly, I am somewhat inured to his sister's name. I can't really say I've ever been all that close to Mark's family. We're polite and we get along; our relationship has just never gone very deep. Cassie is a successful chef. Her restaurant, in the Bay area of San Francisco, regularly wins national awards. No Michelin stars yet, which, after her comment about how my chicken noodle soup is *the only thing* I can make, ensures I don't lose any sleep over this. Bitchiness aside, my biggest criticism of her is that in all these years she has never made any attempt to be close to Jessica – despite having no kids of her own and Jess being her only niece. Not a single card, gift, text or phone call on birthdays or Christmases. Jess has never once been asked down for a visit. Then when my daughter suffered a Grade II concussion after a skiing fall two winters ago, Cassie spoke to Mark but never thought I might have welcomed a little show of family support. And of course it goes without saying that after everything that's happened lately, she has rung me a grand total of twice.

'What did you say to her?' I ask him.

'The truth. That you've had to go away for a while to be on your own. That you're still not doing too well. She said she'd call you some time.' Mark always has faith in his sister, and I don't want to rob him of that.

'That's nice,' I say. He may be waiting for me to add *I won't hold my breath*, but instead, with being on this topic of people's support or lack thereof, I find myself telling him I finally got around to reading some old messages on Facebook. In particular Eloise's.

He sighs. 'Ah, yes, that was kind of sad, I must admit.'

'Kind of?' I say, with a stab of surprise.

'You were going through a very tough time, I realise. I'm not blaming you.'

I have absolutely no idea what he's talking about. 'Blaming me? For what?'

'For pushing her away.'

'I'm confused,' I say, after trying to think through a few accelerated beats of my heart. 'How do you make out that I pushed her away? She never came near me. Four messages on social media in all that time.'

'I don't know what you mean by that,' he says, after a long pause. 'Eloise came to our door every night for days, weeks, but you refused to see her. She was the one who organised all that food to be delivered from Westin. Remember? There was a full month's supply of meals for the freezer because you were in no state to even get up from the chair.'

I find myself staring into space and blinking. I don't know why he's saying this. Eloise visited? Often? If that were true, I would have remembered.

'Anyway,' he says, changing tack, as though that little blip on our landscape isn't worth pursuing further. 'The reason I was phoning – one of them, I mean . . . I wanted to know if you would send me your address.'

'Why?' I ask suspiciously.

'Because I've got something I want to mail you.'

He sounds like he's enjoying being a little mysterious. 'Like?'

'I don't want to tell you, or . . . It's just something I thought you might like.'

There is a loaded silence while we wait for me to reply. If Mark had been wanting to find out where I lived and somehow come and haul me back to Seattle with him I think he'd have done it by now. Besides, hauling me anywhere isn't really his style. So I don't think this is a ploy. I give him my address.

'OK,' he says, sounding a little flatter than when this conversation started out. 'Gonna pop it in the mail tomorrow, hopefully. Keep an eye out . . .'

It's a guarantee.

NINETEEN

'Wow! This is so cool!' Daniel gawks at Beth's latest find. 'What is it?'

We are gathered around it like it's an artefact from a previous century or possibly from the moon.

'I kinda feel I should ask that myself,' Ned chimes in, sending me a sly smirk.

'It's a typewriter,' Beth says. 'The very one Anne Bancroft used in *84 Charing Cross Road.*' She is giddy like the cat who got the canary.

'How can you possibly know that?' I ask, then when I see her expression, follow it with, 'I'm not being funny with you! I'm genuinely fascinated!'

'It was advertised on Amazon as movie memorabilia. The seller's deceased aunt bought it at an auction years ago. I paid him three hundred dollars for it.'

'It's probably not the typewriter from the movie and you've probably been had, but it is beautiful.' I touch its shiny top. 'I loved that film, by the way. Anne Bancroft was everything I wanted to be.'

'A schoolboy's fantasy?' Ned doesn't miss a beat. There is something quite flagrant about the way his gaze drops over me as he says it. 'I believe you could pull off that role very well.'

The boldness of this hits like a tiny electric shock. My cheeks pulse and burn. It's as though everyone has stopped and is looking at me. I try to pretend to be quite unaware of it.

'She was beautiful.' York saves the day. 'And not far off my age. Which would make her a bigger relic than that machine.'

Beth prods my arm. 'Watch the film again. I can promise you it's the same one. Besides, the guy had no reason to lie.'

Ned's eyes hitch on to mine and we smile.

'How does it work?' Daniel plonks down in front of it.

Beth inserts a piece of paper. 'You strike a key like this.' She punches out today's date. 'The key hits a ribbon made of an inked fabric and this creates a letter on the page.'

Daniel strikes the D key. 'It's so noisy!' he chuckles. I catch myself enjoying the curious whimsy of the conversation; whatever dull sadness I might have come in with melts away a little.

'About eighty years ago they made a quieter version but it didn't sell well,' she is saying. 'Turns out people liked the clickety-clack.'

'What if you make a mistake?' Daniel asks.

'You get rid of it with this stuff.' Ned wags a bottle of liquid paper at him then looks at me. 'I'm barely old enough to know what this is.'

Is this some slightly cheeky reference to our age difference? He is staring at me still, so I look away and try not to smile.

'When you use a typewriter you have to compose your thoughts and your words carefully,' Beth tells us. 'It's a very good exercise. You design your path before you tread it, cutting out the fluff and focusing on what really matters. It's a great metaphor for how we should live our life.'

'Can I have it to write to Irsad?' Daniel asks.

'If no one else wants to use it,' York says, and then, 'Daniel thinks life is all about getting what you ask for.'

I find myself smiling as I go over to the counter to make myself something to drink. 'Maybe Amy will want to use it to write to the poor next-door neighbour,' I tell them playfully.

'I wonder where she is tonight,' Beth says.

'Hopefully not under the neighbour's floorboards,' I hurl over my shoulder, and it gets a laugh.

'What's the movie about?' I hear Ned ask right as I'm cutting off the top of a package to shake out a fresh batch of organic, fair trade cocoa powder. I hadn't realised he'd followed me. When I turn he is leaning on the counter. There's something keen and alive in the way he gazes at me. I feel very zeroed-in on. And now I have to try to scoop out the chocolate powder without spilling any on its way to my cup, which seems like an impossible feat.

'It's about an American writer in Paris who corresponds with an English bookseller in London who sends her hard-to-find used books.' My voice sounds spry. 'Their friendship lasts twenty years. It's platonic but you're left with the sense that it could have become more under the right circumstances.'

'Why didn't it?'

When I glance at him again he appears highly engaged by the topic.

'Because he was married.' I turn and face him properly now. 'In the very best cases of what might have been, somebody is always married.'

After everyone has left, I offer to help Beth clean up. 'Were you close with your sister?' I say to her back, recognising a certain liberated air about myself tonight. 'You mentioned she wasn't into books and you were.'

Her hands briefly stop what they're doing and she becomes very still. 'No.' Just when I think she's going to tell me to mind my business, she adds, 'Unfortunately. Far from it.' She turns and meets my eyes. 'Have you any siblings?'

'Nope.' I prod at the dishwasher settings. 'I always wished I had. It was lonely growing up. We lived on a farm that was quite a way outside of the village. Other kids didn't really want to schlep all that distance to play with me. I spent a lot of time on my own. Books were really the only friends I had – or at least, they definitely felt like more available ones! Then when I moved over here I felt guilty that I was leaving my parents behind with essentially no one there for when they got older.'

'Families can be a curse.' She cocks her head as though she's thinking more on that topic. 'We were a classic example of the terrible destructive nature of jealousy.'

I lean back against the counter and contemplate her. It's a pretty face when you really study it. The clear green eyes, the pert little turned-up nose and neat, bud-like mouth. I wish I knew how old she is. I'd probably say early sixties, but she could be younger. Perhaps we'd all look older if we didn't cut and colour our hair, if we rarely smiled. 'She was jealous of you?'

'No.' She says it without reaction. 'The other way around.'

'Oh.'

I think about this. It's quite a thing to admit about oneself.

She picks up a tea towel and absently twists it between her hands. 'When your parents always praise one at the expense of the other, it becomes a breeding ground for it.' She puts the tea towel down then places a Saran-wrapped dish in the fridge. I watch her back. Though her shapeless clothes do her no favours, she has big boobs and slim hips; she'd be the kind of person Jessica would say needs an extreme make-over. 'If you'd like I can loan you the book,' she says, as though making clear that wander into personal territory is over.

I stare at her thick salt and pepper braids with the uneven milk-white parting. 'Book?'

'*84 Charing Cross Road*. If you haven't read it I think you'll probably find it's one of those rare cases where the film is better than the novel.' She pulls a wistful smile. 'Anthony Hopkins is outstanding in it.'

I am not tired when I get in. I make a cup of tea and check my email and Messenger app. No new messages. In bed, I replay the entire highly charged, somewhat offbeat evening. His homing in on me with his eyes. The schoolboy's fantasy. Did he really say that or did I imagine it? I find myself smiling, a little bemused. For some odd reason I reach for my laptop and click on to Facebook, type *Lisa Parker* into the search box. But there are so many Lisa Parkers and trawling through all of them suddenly seems so absurd that I click off and stare into space. And his face returns to my mind's eye.

It does occur to me that it would be a very odd thing indeed, after all these years, to be intimate with someone who wasn't Mark. A very final thing for my marriage, no doubt. I've had three sexual partners, and, as I once joked to Eloise, Mark has been all three of them, though it's not strictly true: the others were just so short I can barely remember them now, except for Sebastian, my uni love. But even he feels like a blip, something I must have dressed up in my mind to be more signifi-cant than it was. Mark is who I think of when I think of love. I have never desired to be unfaithful, nor do I now even care to fudge where the line might be in order to righteously cross it. I have a feeling that sex with someone else would be less about them, and more about testing the waters of walking away.

I try to cast the entire matter from my mind, willing sleep to come, but my subconscious seems to want to run with the ball. Ned and the schoolboy's fantasy comment again. Ned's eyes. And then . . . Not Ned's eyes. Mark's. A memory, suddenly. Mark's arms around me. My sense of profound release, of dissolving into him. A memory drawn from grey space, a twilight place that is never illuminated enough for me to fully see it. It is just there – that feeling of myself needing him in my worst hour. Of melding into him as though we were one body and my heart was his heart.

Distantly I hear the ping of a text and I think, *He knows!* Somehow we've undergone a form of thought transference and he's had this urgency, suddenly, to call me. I struggle to sit up and reach for my phone.

But it's not Mark at all.

Got your letter. Crazy I never knew you guys honeymooned in Florence! I love this city! Wonder if your little shop is still there?

My little shop?

I try to get my head around this, make sense of what my eyes are seeing. Jessica replied! She's talking about my little shop and she's friendly and perfectly normal – no hint of any wedge between us at all. It's like I imagined it, dreamed there's ever been a reason for it to be otherwise. I sink back into my pillow, practically warbling with gratitude. *Thank you! Thank you!*

I find myself turning over ways to reply. But everything I can think of is overly wordy, or too loaded with intensity, like I'm in some sort of rush to build too many bridges with one brick. *Keep it casual, keep it simple, like she did.* So I settle for:

If you run into it, take a photo for me! xx

TWENTY

'I made a pot of fish stew this morning,' I say to Beth as I wipe up muffin crumbs from inside the display counter. 'Jamie Oliver's cod, shrimp and chickpeas in a wine and tomato broth. It's very good.'

'I don't eat shellfish.' She reaches into the oven. 'Got a nasty poisoning when I was in my early forties. Couldn't eat for three months. Lost thirty pounds. Never felt quite the same after – digestively.'

'Lovely.' I sigh. 'So I suppose picking the shrimp out and just leaving the white fish wouldn't exactly chime with your digestive sensibilities?'

She stops what she's doing and straightens up. 'What?'

'If I invited you to supper. Could I pick out the shrimp and we just pretend they were never in there? I'm guessing I know the answer.'

She studies me for a moment as though unravelling a riddle. 'But you're not inviting me to supper?'

'You're right, I'm not. Not the easy way, in any case.' I try not to let her see me smiling. 'See you at six . . .'

She shows up with flowers. 'Are you a red or white girl?' I ask her, taking the bouquet from her – they are quite gorgeous, though I've no idea where Nanette stashes her vases.

'In the top right cupboard.' She nods to the cabinets above the small pine hatch, like a mind reader.

'You've been here before?'

'For Philippine adobo night.' She smiles. 'But it was some time ago.'

I shake my head. Is not even the inside of one's cupboards private around here? Good grief!

'I'm not much of a wine drinker, to answer your question,' she says, watching me busy myself with the flowers. 'I tend to only drink vodka when I drink at all.'

'Damn. I don't have any . . . Nanette had this place well-stocked when I moved in but there wasn't a drop of booze to be found. Because, believe me, I looked.'

'Red would do just fine, then,' she says, sounding mildly amused. 'Thank you.'

I dig in the drawer for the wine opener and reach for the bottle. She watches me place it between my knees and pull.

'Like an old pro.'

I glance up. 'Less of the old.'

She has made an effort with her appearance – smart black pants and a plain white T-shirt dressed up with a hefty, low-slung silver pendant. I'm surprised by the transformation. The wine glugs into the glass. 'What's this?' She spots the small dish on the counter.

'It's called *pangrattato*. Breadcrumbs, lemon zest and parsley fried in some olive oil. You scatter it on top of the soup.' I pass her a decent-sized pour, then turn my attention to setting the table and slicing a fresh baguette.

'Can I have a little more of this?' she asks after about five minutes, and I see she means the wine.

Not bad for someone who doesn't normally drink it. Maybe this evening won't be a washout after all. I pour her another decent measure, then lay the rounds of baguette on a baking sheet, drizzling them with olive oil and a sprinkling of grated Parmesan. When I look up from popping them under the grill, she has wandered into the living room and is standing by my coffee table holding the Longfellow book.

'I read a bit of it most nights . . .' I say, following her into the room. 'I found a new poem I like. "Autumn Within".'

She glances at me coyly. *'It is autumn; not without, But within me is the cold. Youth and spring are all about; It is that I have grown old.'*

I think of the words. 'Hmm . . . Yes. Well . . .' How different it sounds when I'm not just saying it in my head. 'Bit of a depressing soul, was Longfellow, eh?' I scratch my head and grimace.

There is a beat of suspense while she stares at me as though I've said something utterly outlandish, and then she titters. Then she completely cracks up. The laugh seems to just burst from her, like it's been a long time contained. It's the oddest sound – both guttural and musical. I've never heard anything like it. It must go on for a good thirty seconds. She has to place both hands on her belly, as though she's in pain.

'Shit!' I say.

We must clue-in at the same time. I run to the oven, yank open the door. She runs after me. We stare at the cremated bread. 'Goodbye, cheese toasts,' I say.

'That wasn't the entire dinner though, was it?' She continues to peer over my shoulder.

'Not quite.'

She dabs her sweaty brow with the back of her hand, clearly not fully recovered from her laughing fit. 'Well, then, we're fine.'

Our bowls are empty. She stares at the six shrimp tails in mine – all that's left of my dinner. I made a separate shellfish-free one for her, which impressed her. 'I once went out on a first date many years ago and we ordered shrimp,' she says. 'Like you, I left all my tails. He reached over with his big hand and hoovered them all up.' She wrinkles her nose. 'I thought it was philistine behaviour. Needless to say, there wasn't a second date.'

I smile. I don't feel like saying that's exactly something Mark would have done. 'Have you never been married?' I ask, instead.

'No.'

I wait for more but there's silence. 'Right . . . Shall I open another bottle of wine?' Her glass has been empty for ten minutes and I've noticed she keeps staring at it, as though willing it to kinetically refill.

'It's probably not necessary,' she calls after me. 'Unless you really want to. In which case one last glass might be quite nice.'

I grab some cheeses, crackers and dark chocolate for afters, and a bottle of port, and she follows me into the living room. 'How very British,' she says.

When we are sitting with the fire on low, she tells me, 'My father was from England, you know. He grew up in a village called Haworth, in West Yorkshire. Where the Brontë sisters were from.'

'I've been there!' I say. 'To the parsonage! It's a museum. I was an English Lit major, so one summer I drove all over the country visiting the homes of my favourite writers. Kipling's, Robert Burns' house, Wordsworth's Dove Cottage, the Brontës', and Jane Austen's Chawton Cottage.' I smile. It seems like yesterday.

'We visited the parsonage as kids. My sister and I had the most horrible fight that day. I don't even really remember what it was about, but I was so angry I stormed off and left her. I wandered the village until dark then found my way back to my gran's. I didn't want to worry them. I just wanted to know if they'd actually care that I was gone. Everything was always all about her, you see. She was the only one they had eyes for.'

'Veronica.' I remember her name. It sits there like the elephant in the room.

'Yes. Did you know it's because of Veronica that I set up the Correspondents' Club?' She stares deeply into her wine glass like someone poised to tell a story with a nudge of encouragement. There's a few cracker crumbs on her chest and a whole collection of them on her black pants.

'How come?' I curl my feet underneath my bottom. I love how someone else's tale of woe gives me a break from thinking about my own.

'It's a very hard thing for me to talk about, and because of that I essentially haven't. Not for many years.' She looks off into space. 'Heartbreak never truly goes away, you know. But it does get easier to navigate with time . . .'

I can't help but turn this idea over in my mind. Sometimes someone will say something that reminds me I am not walking my path alone. My instinct is to fight that bare truth, to argue that my journey is the hardest, my path peppered with greater land mines ready to blow me apart – way more so than your land mines. And yet lately I have had to accept that this is something I just don't get to feel so righteous about.

'You said it was about jealousy,' I prompt her when I sense she's reluctant to go on.

She meets my eyes briefly. 'Yes. As I told you, I was jealous of her. Not because she was more beautiful or cleverer or any of that. She was just an ordinary, unremarkable girl like me – that's what makes it so hard to understand why she was favoured, why I could do no right and she could do no wrong. I was four years older. It was really up to me to rise above it but I had a Bette Davis mean streak in me. I think I actually enjoyed having something to hold against her.'

Her eyes wander off across the room again.

'She was eighteen and I was twenty-two. He was right in the middle of both of us . . . Samuel.' She draws out the three syllables of his name. 'When she brought him home I remember he stood in our kitchen like a typically awkward twenty-year-old meeting his girlfriend's family for the first time, and I said something provocative like, "How's it going

Sammy boy?" and she was very annoyed. "No one shortens Samuel's name," she said.' She smiles. 'I didn't like him. I saw the way he was always looking at me. The very way he shouldn't have been looking . . .' Her eyes are tinged with bitterness and pain and I think of what she just said – why is it that physical pain almost always passes, but heartbreak never dies? It seems so unfair.

'There are things we do in life that we know, right as we are doing them, will have consequences. I knew letting him kiss me was wrong. And when he did more than kiss me I felt . . . nothing. The sense of pleasure I'd anticipated from taking one thing away from her, well, it wasn't as great as I imagined. There was hatred – for myself. Disgust. I truly had done my worst deed now . . .' She shakes her head. I'm not sure she's going to go on. 'We were all outside on the day of the barbecue – the 4 July long weekend. I had gone back indoors. It was so hot. There was so much noise outside but inside was just so stifling and silent . . . I was in the living room by the open window. I had taken off my dress because I knew he was going to follow me – it would be our second time. I never wore bras in those days. He was staring at my body in my pale blue panties. I remember I could hear a noise like a knocking sound, and then I realised it was my heart . . . I think what I remember most was the expression on his face when she walked in. But then, it was very odd, he just started screaming at me: "Disgusting slut." He backed away and held up the palm of his hand. Then he said, "I just walked in and she was standing by the window. Before I knew it she started taking her dress off."'

'My God,' I say. 'He completely sold you down the river.'

'Oh, it was very convincing. His acting was superb. I remember how she just stood there looking from me to him. Looking for a reason to doubt him, possibly. I don't know. I remember how he took her in his arms and kissed the top of her head, and how she stared at me hard over his shoulder – the anger and disgust.'

'What did you do?'

She looks down at a lap full of crumbs. 'I could have said no, that's not the way it happened at all, but by the entire convincing act of him – he looked so morally outraged, I've never seen anything like it – I knew he'd do this with my parents and I knew I'd never be believed.' She shrugs. 'So I said nothing.'

I try to process the logic of this, wondering what I would have done. Does illuminating someone else's guilt help mitigate your own? If you stay silent, are you noble or foolish? Either way, I find it very hard to believe I'd have let him get away with his lie.

'She told my parents, naturally. I don't even want to get into the outcome of that. I knew I had to leave. But it was a very strange feeling. The minute I walked out of that door I knew I was on my own now, there would be no going back . . . I wasn't self-pitying. I'd brought this on myself. I'd had sex with him knowing full well she was in love with him, that they were going to be married. Nice people don't do that.'

'So that's why you kept quiet about it? Because letting her believe you were bad and he was innocent was the best way to punish yourself?'

She looks at me as though seeing a new angle she hadn't seen before. 'I'm not sure if it was that . . . I could see what I was up against. He was a better actor than Harrison Ford. How were they ever going to believe me when they were disinclined to give me any credit at the best of times?' She takes a sip of her wine and looks quite resolute again.

'But if you'd said something it just might have cast doubt. Then maybe she'd have been spared marrying a liar and a cheat.'

'The way our relationship was at that time – and believe me it really was not very good – I actually thought they deserved each other. And they were married thirty years.'

'Were?'

'He had a stroke seven years ago. They were living in Austria.' Her eyes go to the Longfellow book. 'When I found out, I suppose I could have got in touch with her to express my condolences but I couldn't bring myself to. We hadn't spoken since that day. But I imagine my silence after his death must have stung . . . A couple of years ago she sent me the book with the handwritten poem in it about letters you didn't write and haunting ghosts.'

I frown, completely baffled. 'Didn't you ever want to set the record straight? Why allow her to think that way about you for all these years?'

She picks up her wine glass but just holds it. 'I had a son. His name was Thomas. I found out I was pregnant almost as soon as I left home and moved to San Francisco. I was young, single, virtually penniless . . . I didn't even have a job and I didn't know how I was going to raise a baby without one, or how we'd cope if I got one – who was going to look after him? I wanted him. I didn't care that Thomas was his child. He was mine too! A part of me! Perhaps the only precious thing I'd ever have who would love me . . .' She breaks off and I sense she's going to cry.

I can't help but think of Jessica. Beth and I would have been pregnant at virtually the same age.

'I thought of every possible way I could make it work. I gave him up through a private adoption – a fluke, really; someone who knew someone who couldn't have a family . . . I paid for that terrible decision my entire life. So that's why I never sent any letter of condolence. I felt I had lost way more than she had.'

I'm surprised to find my eyes flooding with tears. 'That's just awful. Good heavens!' Beth is mourning a child, but one that lives. I want to tell her that all is not lost. I have a sudden urgency to fix this for her. 'Have you ever thought of trying to find him? He's out there somewhere, maybe not all that far away. There are lots of ways these days, with the Internet! Endless resources. New laws.'

She smiles. 'The one condition of the adoption – I signed a legal document – was that I never try to make contact with him. They had insisted on meeting me. I'm sure they saw how ill at ease I was . . . They probably didn't want to be always looking over their shoulder. Or perhaps they sensed I was bad news.'

I frown. 'Why would you say that?'

'I didn't do a very nice thing to my own sister. And then I gave my baby away. Maybe I'm just a bad egg. Maybe people can see it the moment they look at me.' She sounds neither melodramatic nor self-pitying.

'That's ridiculous,' I tell her. 'I am sure if your parents always favoured your sister it must have done a real number on your self-esteem. Kids always know who love them. Genuinely love them . . .'

'Yes,' she says. 'And I am sure my son had adoptive parents who showed him that love. And I'm sure that deep down in his heart he's never quite gotten over the fact that his real mother gave him away. That is, if they ever told him . . . Perhaps they never did.' She turns very pale. Even in this light I can see the colour drain from her face.

I suddenly remember something. 'You said it was because of Veronica that you set up the club?'

'Yes. There are two letters I've been toying with writing for a very long time. One to Veronica, finally saying what I should have said all those years ago. You see, my failure to speak up somehow broke my spirit. It was the rot that just ate away at me. Not a day has gone by when I haven't wished I'd just told the truth. The truth is still the truth even if nobody believes it . . . In some ways I feel she needs to know that his lie and my silence had huge consequences – not just for me but for a child. And then the other letter I'm thinking of writing is to Thomas's adoptive parents asking them if they might let me contact him. I don't have to be in his life if there's no place for me in it, but I just want him to know that there was never a day when I didn't think about him. That I should have done anything – steal, starve, or sell myself – to avoid having to give him away. That my failure to find a way to keep him is a failing I wouldn't wish on anybody.'

'You don't know that there's no place for you in his life!' I sit up, spine straight, suddenly fanatical on her behalf. 'You can't say that. You don't know how he thinks or feels . . . You're his blood! Forget about what you signed and didn't sign; you weren't in your right mind. You have rights.'

'What rights?' She sounds a little exasperated.

'You're his mother! Whatever the circumstances were doesn't change the fact that you gave him life! And you loved him – *love* him. Don't ever imagine that's less than what it is.' From her face I can see she doesn't believe this. She has spent so long thinking badly of her actions that it has formed a shell around her that possibly no reasoning is going to crack. 'Find your son, Beth.' My heart blazes with the need to make her see this. 'Don't overthink it. Just do it. Tell him there was never a day you didn't think of him. Tell him because it's important. Tell him because, believe me, nothing else is.'

After a spell of her being unable to break away from my eyes, she says, 'Did you say you were offering port?'

When she leaves I can't help but go on sitting there in a fug replaying her story. I can't get baby Thomas out of my head, nor a picture of Beth the day she had to give him up – the very thought of this is coating me in the most horrible sadness. I find myself closing my eyes and picturing Beth here in her coffee shop, and Thomas out there somewhere, and trying to join them like they're dots – magnets somehow attracting each other, with a little bit of help from trusty Google and a dose of divine will.

I simply can't imagine the guilt, the loneliness, the sense of loss she would have suffered all these years, and it suddenly occurs to me how very, very lucky I am. I was never in a position to have to give my baby away. Mark stood by me and even if he hadn't I would have still had my parents to fall back on until I got on my feet again. I got to be a mother to my daughter. I got to be close to her. I got to have memories. I've never really viewed any of that as a gift before.

Then I think, *Damn it, it might be a cliché but you must tell your loved ones you love them! Say it. Show it. Do it every day.* I have such a crushing urge to say it now. So I jump up from my seat and rush to the kitchen where I think I left my phone. In the darkness I fumble with passcodes and when I can't immediately find that last text she sent me, I start a new thread.

I love you, I type. Sorry for everything. And then after I let a little heat out of me, I add, No need to reply. Just be well. Be happy. Xx Mom.

TWENTY-ONE

A squirrel is perched on the green mailbox at the bottom of the garden as I come in the gate. I have to get almost right up to him before he gives me a hard blink then flits away. There are two letters for me. Or rather, one of them is a small package and I recognise Mark's writing on it.

I pluck at the padding as I walk back into the house, closing the door with a donkey kick. Then I go to get the scissors and cut the end off. Inside is a sheet of paper folded into four. I open it curiously like a piece of delicate origami.

> Dear Liv,
> I was downtown and happened to see this in one of those gift shops in a hotel. It made me think of you and your Correspondents' Club.

His handwriting is big and sprawling. It is surreal to think of him writing to me, even if it's short.

> I hope you like it. I hope you know how to use it – it'd be more than I do.
> Mark.

Inside is a thin brown box. Once I open it I find myself staring at a fountain pen. It's a thing of beauty – tortoiseshell and shiny. Everything about it speaks of quality and a bygone era. When I pick it up, it's heavier than I was imagining. I love the feel of it between my fingers. Like I could now take on the world. At the very bottom of the envelope is something small and square: a tiny pot of navy blue ink.

The next envelope is a letter. I don't recognise the handwriting on this. I tear into it and read.

> Dear Olivia,
>
> I am sitting here trying to write to Lisa and failing mis-
> erably. Daniel is banging away on that typewriter that's
> straight out of the movies. I've the sudden urge to be
> ten years old again. Then there is you, Mrs. Bancroft.
> You are sitting right behind me, and I suddenly want
> to watch *The Graduate* all over again – maybe for the
> wrong reasons.

Mrs Bancroft! I fumble my way into a chair.

> So now I'm finding myself writing a completely
> different letter. I realise I don't really know you all
> that well, despite the fact that I've told you stuff about
> me that some might say is far too much information.
> What's more, I recognise you for being a private per-
> son, much like myself. But I learnt something in army
> training school that became the truest and most useful
> thing anyone ever taught me and I thought I would

share it with you. You don't have to be a soldier to benefit from it, even though we are all soldiers, fighting our own wars, in our own way, aren't we?

The army has this programme. It's called Master Resilience Trainer. It's designed to train resilience skills in sergeants in order for them to pass this training on to soldiers. Resilience probably means different things to different people, but to the army it means the ability to persist in the face of challenges and to bounce back from adversity.

More than a million soldiers have come home from Iraq or Afghanistan over the last decade. Many of them bring home the grotesque memory of war. I read a good quote from an army general that puts some things into perspective. He said that the average soldier is twenty-four years old. He's been in the army about six years. He's bought a car and wrecked it. He's married and has challenges there. He's been deployed two or three times. He's responsible for a dozen or so other men, overseeing not just their training but pretty much whether they'll live or die. Oh, yeah, and he makes less than 40K a year.

The programme tries to teach soldiers to make sense of their lives, to focus on what they can control, and not to catastrophise everything. There are many components taught over the ten-day period. I won't go into them all or this will become a long letter, but one of them is simply called Hunt the Good Stuff. On one level it's just a way of looking at life. It might sound simplistic, probably because it is. And yet I've actually seen it work, first-hand.

Basically, there's a common simple truth. If you don't realise that there are good things that happen to you every day, and if you happen to be under a lot of stress, you can gravitate to only seeing the negative things in your world and at the extreme end of this you can land yourself in a place that you can't find your way back from.

Most of us are good at this already. We spend so much time focusing on our personal failures that we don't realise there's actually been triumphs. Have you noticed that we're never plagued by the things we did right in life? They are forgotten fast. They're inconsequential almost right at the moment we are doing them. We worry so much about what's gone wrong that we don't actually notice anything's gone right. Hunt the Good Stuff is about recognising these things through a couple of easy tasks.

Task 1. Make a list of the things that make you lucky.

Task 2. Think of three good things that happened to you today. Think about what they meant to you. Think about what you did, or what someone else did, to bring these good things about. Think of what you can do tomorrow to bring about more of this good thing. Then tomorrow, do it.

After I came home from Afghanistan I couldn't believe there was any good stuff and I wallowed in that headspace for a very long time. But then I forced myself to do the exercise, and I did it every day. I did find that one small shift in my attitude helped me make bigger shifts and for me that's the only way I go forward. I am writing this to you as the rain is starting to come down on to the water. I am used to sunshine. I can see how this place could get depressing if you let it. I've given up trying to write the letter I was supposed to be writing. For now, anyway. So I've decided to pen this instead. I hope you read it in the spirit in which it is written. And don't worry, I will finish your deck. It's slow, off and on, but I am getting there. You may doubt me, but I promise.

Ned

TWENTY-TWO

'It's beautiful,' I tell Mark.

'I thought you might think so.'

'I've been practising my penmanship.'

'I figured it would take some getting used to.'

'In a good way.' I smile. 'I've got this poetry book and I copy verse out. It's kind of like homework. It's hard to believe that these days something as simple as a pen could bring me hours of joy!'

'I'm happy,' he says. Then he playfully adds, 'You were always easily pleased.'

Just as I'm grasping for something witty to say, his voice turns more serious. 'Hey. I wanted to mention something the other day when I rang . . .'

'Am I going to want to hear it?' I try to keep the lightness going.

'I don't know,' he says. 'I've been thinking. If you come home – if I can persuade you to, anyway – I'd like us to go get some counselling.' He sounds slightly nervous, if that's the word. 'Plenty of people do it . . . I don't know, I think it might be the only way forward – for our marriage.' After another pause he says, 'We need some guidance.' He is quiet while he waits for me to say something but I am taken aback and can't really speak.

'Anyway,' he says, after a time. 'I just wanted to put it out there. I'm just asking you to think about it. And even if you don't come home – I mean, I want you to, obviously, but I'd come there. Maybe there's someone there we could see. Or even . . .'

I don't know what the *even* is. He dries up, probably catching himself giving up.

I am so blindsided by this. I thought we were talking about pens. I don't want to get into a debate about this issue again so I simply say, 'I don't want to go to counselling.' I'm not the one who went looking for something outside of my marriage. It makes me want to add, *Why don't you go?* but I don't. I thought we were at the point where we could have normal conversations again. *That* would have been my idea of a way forward.

'I have to hang up now,' I say. 'Somebody's at the door.'

TWENTY-THREE

'It's looking amazing.' I tug at the bell sleeve of my blouse. I'm astonished how fast he's finished. 'You've done a fantastic job.' For the last
few days the weather has been great. While he has worked I have made
a point of being out – in spite of him being here, not because of. Or so
I tell myself. I have walked so much that I've had to bend over until the
nerve pain up my leg stops throbbing. I've read at the library until my
eyes burned from dryness and tiredness, the state of my marriage on a
never-ending loop along with this perpetual, tireless confusion. I have
made several trips to the grocery store to buy one-off ingredients for all
these different recipes I keep trying out. I am both enjoying the point-
lessness to my days, and terrified of losing myself to it permanently.

'Just need to get the railings on, but yeah, it's not bad.' He looks
pleased with himself.

'You have some dirt . . .' I indicate my left cheek. He rubs it away,
holds my eyes for a second – or perhaps I am imagining this now.
'Thanks.'

'Well, I kind of feel this calls for a celebration.' I do an about-turn,
hear him set the drill down.

'What did you have in mind?'

I glance over my shoulder. 'I'm thinking let's push the boat out and
have two glasses of lavender lemonade.'

'No way. If you're not having a glass of wine I'm leaving.'

I stop and look back at him properly now. 'Is this your roundabout way of telling me you know I'm always secretly clamouring for a drink?'

'Ha,' he says. 'No. Actually, not at all.' Then, 'Are you?'

I huff a small laugh then trot inside. When I come back out with his lemonade and my vino I say, 'Yes and no . . . To answer your question.' I kick my sandals off and plonk my bare feet up on the opposite chair. 'Not so long ago I was probably consuming a little more than was good for me. I mean, not compared to how much my friends can sink . . . My friends actually send each other birthday cards joking about how they all belong in AA.' I suddenly miss Deanna and the neighbourhood circle on a visceral level. I firmly believe there's a part of a woman's being that can only be fulfilled by friendships with somewhat like-minded people her own age. You don't have to bare your soul and confide your darkest secrets. But knowing they're there, and you can, is everything. Mark's words ring true suddenly. Maybe I could have made slightly more of an effort to be closer to them. In fact, I doubt there are any maybes involved.

'Wine was the only thing that helped me sleep,' I add.

'This was back when your marriage ended?'

After a moment, I nod, sensing he can see right through me but for the first time not minding. It might not be the most natural segue to this, but I find myself saying, 'I liked your letter.'

'There's a but coming.' He pretends to grimace.

I smile. 'No! It's actually interesting because I came along to the Correspondents' Club not really knowing why I was, except that, perhaps a bit like you in Afghanistan, I've always found some harmony with myself when writing things down. I can detach and take all emotion out of what I want to say when there's no actual human being in front of me . . .' I look down at my right hand clutching the fingers of my left. 'Anyway, two meetings ago I wrote a letter to my daughter not really thinking she'd reply. But it just occurred to me that the very night you'd have been sitting there writing to me was the night she sent me a text.' I smile again, feeling my eyes tear up. 'It was one of the good things that happened to me – maybe the only thing. I did your exercise and I realised all I'd done to bring it about was to stop fixating on why she should probably hate me forever more, and just try to be the old me again.'

'Mothers and daughters . . . it can be tricky. I know. I have a sister.'

I suddenly see us sitting at opposite ends of the sofa reading the same thriller on our Kindles the very night before my actions changed everything for all of us, our feet docked into each other's sides. Jessica saying, 'Oh my God! Are you up to that part yet?' I can't pull my eyes away from the image of it.

'It can be a challenge,' I say. 'You can be close but you don't always get on – I'm her mother, not her best friend.' The memory of our quarrel is trying to push to the surface but I stomp it down. 'Sometimes you have to be firm and that doesn't always make you popular. But I always aimed to lift her, not put her down. I hope I made her a confident young woman who has the quiet ability to never devalue herself . . .'

I don't really know why I'm saying all this or even if it's true. Is it wishful thinking, to make myself feel better? I didn't exactly lift her before she ran off to Europe, did I? 'You said in your letter you were sitting there trying to write to Lisa.' I change the subject.

'Yes,' he says. 'We're not good at phone calls. She just gets upset. But try as I did, I didn't even know what I wanted to say.' He stares off into the distance, as though he might be searching for it right now. 'A long time ago I told her I couldn't promise to change. That's just too big and probably unrealistic . . . I've done a lot of thinking since I left. It's so much easier to think without the bias of her presence. And yet I don't know what I've really come up with. Some things just feel too complicated to take apart piece by piece.'

I am happy we're talking about him again. 'My mother used to say the truest test of your feelings is if you can picture life without that person. Can you picture them with someone else and you being fine about it?' Can I picture life without Mark? Is this what I'm secretly trying out?

'Yeah.' He nods. 'I will probably find it very hard to see her with someone else, if the truth be told, but in many ways that would be the best outcome. It might make things a whole lot easier if she phoned and told me she had a boyfriend. There's part of me would be relieved.' He looks momentarily filled with self-loathing. A shade of him I've seen before. 'I mean, heck, she's told me plenty times she'd have been better off with the first guy she ever dated. The thing is, she never really needed to say it because I already knew.'

I hang on to his words, to the sadness in his eyes, taking me away from my own. Our conversation tends to bounce around a lot, dismantling part of me then welding together other elements. I sometimes find myself marvelling at this.

'One thing I do know,' he says, 'the worst thing that can happen to a marriage is not talking. Ours was built on that. I was either coming down from a mission, or gearing up for one. Distancing myself to make the leaving easier. I could never tell her where I was going. When I returned I couldn't talk about anything I'd seen or done . . . She once said she had no sense of "belonging" with me, and I took that as a huge slight on my character. But it was true in a way; I belonged first to the military. I couldn't be her everything. She deserved someone who could.'

Belonging, I think. That comfortable place of connection and acceptance. Yes, I used to know what that feeling was like. Before Mark and I became epic failures in both those regards. I know exactly what he's talking about.

'But she was with you,' I say, not wanting to wander off down paths that lead to self-reflection. 'She obviously loved you. Maybe you're projecting on to her what you think she feels, but maybe that's not how she feels at all.'

He doesn't answer that but says, 'Everybody wants to be somebody's great love, don't they? No one wants to be their biggest mistake. And if you're even thinking along those lines it's probably time to cut out.'

'And that's what you're doing? Cutting out?'

'Well, she's not *my* biggest mistake . . . that's the problem.'

'Ah . . .' I find myself nodding – slowly understanding, and yet not. For a telling second or two I am unable to take my eyes from his. They are separated but he's still in love with her? This smack of reality has caught me by surprise, his honesty almost a little too reverberating. I have to look away because I feel him reading it from me, gleaning what I didn't even realise was there to glean. I stare across the yard with this terrible sense of myself falling between the cracks, a sense of inexplicable despondency.

I had somehow seen him as single, not as a reluctantly divided unit, even though it makes absolutely no sense – why would I have seen him either way at all? Then I remember my own words: things are never as over as we think they are. That's the problem. I see Mark's face. Love has all these roots you just can't kill.

'So you would go back? If she asked you to?' I have the urge to retreat into a corner to pick it all apart and see where the wires got crossed.

'How will it be any different? We'll work for a time until we won't work again. Plus we have a kid; we can't keep false-starting. When he was little you could paint a different sky on his world, but not now. He's a clever little guy . . .'

I love how his face brightens when he mentions his son. But just as swiftly it's gone again. 'It would be impossible for her to forget all the pain that being married to me has caused her. Love isn't enough. Understanding isn't enough. Empathy . . . All that only goes so far. When people hurt you deeply, even when it's because they are hurting, you can't forgive them. Or if you do it's way too conditional – and it's hard to live the rest of your life waiting for the next let-down to happen.'

This makes me think of Mark and me again. Will I ever trust that if anything else comes along to test us, as this has, he won't want to jump ship? Need to be in the company of someone who doesn't constantly remind him of it?

'We have to admit that we lost,' he says. 'And for a guy like me to do that – it's very hard, you know. I can't stand all that waste . . . that waste of her life.'

His words both stun and sadden me. Despite the unthinkable he's been through, he's more sorry for her than he is for himself. Isn't that what it really means to love someone? It suddenly occurs to me: in all of this, who am I most sorry for?

He tilts his head back, stares at the sky. 'It's just all so fucked up. A mess.'

'I told my husband I found another woman's necklace on our bedroom floor when I didn't . . . And I did it because I needed to catch him off guard, see if his face was going to contradict his words.' Ned is watching me with a whole new level of intrigue. 'So that's it on a very basic level. But the crazy thing is there's even more to it than that . . .' I try to shrug it off with a little laugh. I am still rebounding from the realisation that I've been finding myself spinning a bit of a fantasy about this guy, probably to take me away from what really matters. Only he wasn't really taking me anywhere at all. He's in no position to.

'And you have no idea what I'm talking about,' I say. 'And I couldn't even begin to explain it to you even if I tried. So how's that for messed up?'

'What did he say?' he asks, surprising me.

I smile. 'He didn't flinch. He just said, "Come on, you and I both know you didn't find any necklace on our floor! Because she's never been in our bedroom. Because she doesn't really exist." Then he added, "You need to get help."'

'That's pretty messed up,' he says.

Not talking is the worst thing that can happen to a marriage . . . Ned's words won't let me settle or sleep. I suddenly panic at the thought of what we have come to and conduct a ragged search under laundry and a stack of sofa cushions for my phone. When I find it I pull up Mark's cell number. My finger hovers over the call button.

But I have no idea what I want to say when it comes down to it. I don't really know what the particular straw was that broke us, so I wouldn't know how to fix us either. I also can't promise to change – too much has happened to make me anyone other than who I now am. I can't promise anything at all. And deep down, even though Mark wants to believe, I know neither can he.

After a few erratic beats of my heart I click out of there.

I find myself staring at my Messenger app and then for something to do I open it. The last message I sent was to Sarah, her name is still at the top of the list. But – how strange! – beside it there is no longer a little icon that indicates it hasn't been read. Instead there's a small circle that contains her profile picture, indicating it has. I click on the message and scroll to the end.

Seen 19 July

I blink a few times. No, it's still there.

Every hair on my body must be standing up.

TWENTY-FOUR

'I'd like to take you out for dinner tomorrow night,' I tell him as I oil one of Beth's cast iron pans. 'A token of my appreciation for the deck.'

He appears rather taken aback, then vaguely amused. 'You're *taking* me?'

'Yup.' I stop what I'm doing. 'You show. You eat. Me pay.'

'Hmm . . . Never gone on a date where a woman's paid before. Doubt I can do it.'

Beth suddenly comes in, tugging down a sunflower-print umbrella. I'm just about to tell him it's not a date, it's a thank you, when she says, 'You're becoming quite the coffee drinker.'

'It's working . . . Clearly.' He glances me over deliberately. 'Olivia just asked me out for dinner.'

Beth wags a finger at me. 'The hired help are not supposed to fraternise with the customers. But where are you planning on going if I might ask?'

'So you can put word out?' I quip. 'Inform Yurt from the B&B? Maybe he'd like to squat nearby, armed with his telephoto lens?'

'Burt,' she says, smiling. 'And I hear the crab shack is popular.'

'That's where I was thinking of, actually,' I tell her.

Ned winks at me. 'Ah! No one said anything about crab . . .'

'You're sold.' I mop my hands on a paper towel. 'Lovely to know it was a dead bottom feeder from the ocean floor, rather than my scintillating personality, that won you over.'

Beth titters.

'What time were you planning on picking me up?' he asks.

We are shown to a quiet corner – a dark cedar booth warmed by a Tiffany lamp. The booths form a raised dais around another dining space that looks like it doubles as a dance floor. There is a jukebox in the corner. Fats Domino is singing 'Blueberry Hill'.

When I come back from the toilet it's a fairly long walk to our table and for the course of it I can't take my eyes off his back as he sits there. As I get nearer, I realise we're the object of scrutiny – four women closer to Ned's age, seated on the dance-floor level. I shrug off my black blazer, throw it on to the leather seat and try to ignore the heat of their gazes.

'You look great by the way,' he says, having the courtesy to stand up as I approach the table.

The compliment takes me aback and I unnecessarily look down at the fitted little black short-sleeved shirt that I've paired with my jeans – the one Jessica always steals off me. It's plain except for a funky thick cotton hem that's all frayed like the dog might have chewed it, which explains why it cost two months' worth of groceries.

'I like your hair up too,' he adds.

I resist the urge to touch my messy French pleat. 'One more compliment and I'm going to have to leave.' I smirk. Little does he know it was a down-up, down-up, *ah! Just leave it!* sort of decision that I'm feeling self-conscious about now he's drawing attention to it.

'Lisa won't leave the house until her hair is lacquered to perfection and she has a face full of make-up,' he adds, cocking his head as though seeing her right now. 'It makes her look a lot older, I think.'

With the casual way he inserts his wife into the conversation the butterflies in my stomach stop their flitting around. In fact, they might die altogether. A young waitress arrives bearing water and a bread loaf. She looks at Ned and her eyes immediately drop to his burned hands. 'Can I get you guys drinks?' She blushes crimson. We order tomato juice for him and a large white wine for me.

'I'm going to insist you have three of those,' he says to me, just as the girl is leaving and I catch a flicker of a grin from her.

'Then you'd have to carry me home.'

'I would have said it's OK, you're tiny, but that nearly got me into trouble once.'

'You have a memory like an elephant.'

We smile. We reach for our menus at the same time, peruse them in pleasant silence.

'So what's a SEAL like as a child?' I ask when I've made my mind up what I'm ordering. He is wearing a blue and red checked shirt with a button-down collar. In his efforts to smarten up for dinner, he looks even younger and more clean-cut than before, every bit a soldier.

'This is totally first-date conversation, by the way.'

I grin. 'Less of the wishful thinking! And I actually do really want to know – I'm not just being fatuous.'

He closes the menu. 'OK, Barbara Walters. Well, I guess I can only speak for this SEAL. But I think I was pretty normal. Once I got straightened out, that is.'

'Ah-ha!' I find myself de-stressing a little. 'This sounds like a story I must hear.'

'Well,' – he seems to relax a little – 'when I was seven, this kid came at my head with a brick in the schoolyard, so I threw a punch that nearly broke his jaw. The school wanted to expel me. It didn't matter I hadn't started it, all they cared about was it wasn't a fair fight; we were the same age but I was bigger.' He shrugs. 'It took me a while to get it. Just because somebody hurts you, you don't have to hurt them back worse, which you might think is odd coming from a guy in the military . . . I guess I realised I was strong, and I had to be careful how I used my strength. But once I got it, I felt so wholeheartedly responsible for who I was and how I acted. But nobody seemed to believe me. I remember wondering, are you ever truly forgiven? Are we all just the sum of our worst actions? Since then I've had recurring dreams where I'm always trying to convince someone of something but they never believe me.'

'Wow,' I say. A shiver grips my spine at the thought of worst actions. 'I used to always dream I'm about to be shot. I googled it once. It said it means if you continue on this path you'll die.'

'But we're all going to die.'

'Well, I know that . . . Of course, like everything you read on the Internet it can also mean the opposite, can't it? Being shot in my dreams might mean I'll get to live a rich, long life!'

The waitress returns with our drinks and I try to affect some class and not lunge on mine. I am conscious of being like a wire trying to uncoil. We order the crab, a salad and the potatoes baked in Gruyère and cream.

'So you were a reformed human being after your childhood misde-meanour, were you?' I say once she's gone.

'Yup. Never had much of a stupid side. No drugs, drink. Never kissed a girl until I was sixteen, and I was an old man of eighteen before I lost my virginity.'

'To Lisa?' Just a sip of the wine has loosened my nerve. I rest an elbow on the table and place my chin on my upturned hand, aware of feeling flirty.

'Now that would be telling you far more about me than I know about you.' He holds my eyes, steadily, like I am a challenge to him.

'What's to know?' I pick up my wine glass again, hold it in front of my face, stare through it.

'I don't know, Olivia. Tell me something. I'll take whatever you give.' Then he adds, 'Why the US? Why Seattle?'

'Ah . . .' I set the glass down. 'Well, that's easy . . .' I smile. 'I'd finished uni in London. A 2:1 in English Lit. Zero idea what I was going to do with it. I quite liked the idea of a year of travel to, you know, maybe help focus me. Seattle seemed cool. It had a great music scene. I loved *Frasier*! BA had a seat sale. Voila! It was a done deal.'

'And how did you meet your husband?'

A tiny tug of nostalgia and sadness threatens to break my stride. 'Literally the day I landed. I'd just rented a car at the airport. First time driving on the other side . . . He was driving his dad's black pick-up. We'd both come to a four-way stop. He was making a left, to my right . . . I can vividly see his big, shaggy-dog head hanging out of the window as we passed each other on the turn. He said something I didn't quite catch.' I smile. 'I'd always gone for academic, buttoned-up types. And there he was – this big, leering . . . mess, really, for want of a better word.' I let out a little laugh. 'He was so shameless, so male. I just had this overwhelming desire to be pursued by him to the moon and back.' We've told this story so many times – I will start it and Mark will usually finish it – that I forget it's all that special. Right now, though, it besieges me, like a quiet reminder of everything we have been and are. 'I ploughed right into the back of the car ahead. I was probably jet-lagged and tired. Nobody was hurt, of course. Mark pulled over and helped me sort out all the insurance stuff. And that was it, really. It evolved from there.'

'Sounds like he was the one. Love at first sight.' His leg jiggles briefly then stops.

'Hmm . . . My mother once said there's only the one you choose. In her mind, if I'd stayed in England I'd have married an Englishman and been just as happy. And how do I know she's wrong?'

What I do know – that I can't begin to say – is, if I hadn't come here, one thing wouldn't have happened. What would I sacrifice to turn back time?

'Are you OK?' he asks, and at first I'm not sure why he's asking. I am staring off into space. I only realise this when I feel myself coming back from it.

'Yes.' I nod, refocus. 'What was I saying? Ah yes . . . I can't say I went around thinking, *Ooh, I'm in love*! We just blended and we complemented one another. We had deep conversations, we challenged each other, and we laughed. Mark gives you his all, and he's surprisingly more of an introvert than you'd first think. He has this truly amazing gift of being able to be annoyed with you while staying amiable. And you sense that no matter what terrible thing you're about to tell him he's going to find a bright side.' Until the one time he couldn't, of course.

Emotion makes a stab at overcoming me. I don't believe I've ever had cause to sum him up before. Or to properly articulate his good qualities, even to myself. It's as though familiarity has given me licence to forget them.

'It wasn't as passionate as my one-year relationship back in uni but somehow it was more real. With Mark, I wasn't walking around aware of how big it was. I wanted him without desperately needing him. I was still very much my own person. I still knew who I was without him. It felt healthy . . . He always made me feel I had choices and freedom. And then I got pregnant and he didn't encourage me to be anything other than a happy young mother, and he took it on with me and pulled his weight every step of the way.' I briefly think of Beth again and the loneliness of her dilemma.

He says, 'He sounds like a fine guy.'

When I look back at him his eyes are asking, *What causes a good marriage to end after all that time?* I dip back into the wine, after raising the glass and staring through it again, avoiding his eyes.

'Fish swimming around in there?'

'Sorry,' I harrumph, swelling with sadness. 'I'm not good with trips down memory lane.' Now that Mark has invaded this space I can't see past him, I can't peer around him; he's blocking everything, even my air.

'Go on,' he says, 'I love listening to you.'

But I can't go on. Twenty years of marriage are filling in before my eyes. All I can see is the shadow of what love was and how happy I was. I was wrong in my take of it all those years ago: I *don't* know who I am without it.

'What are you thinking about?' he asks. I can tell he is banking every beat of this change in me. I've been rendered mute. I stare hard at the bread, aware of my eyes being ready to spill tears.

When I look up, the waitress is walking towards us. 'I'm thinking here comes dinner.'

TWENTY-FIVE

'The truth is I don't know if my marriage is over,' I tell him, as we share a piece of warm pecan pie.

'The necklace on the floor?'

Hearing that makes me feel ridiculous now. 'It was actually something I did as much as what he did.'

I can tell he's puzzled. He is searching my face as though trying to decipher my code. 'What did he do?' he asks, tactfully picking the better question. 'I'm guessing from the little you've said he had an affair.'

I stare at an oil spot on my napkin. Clarity is pushing in where there has been a void for so long. I just want to go with it, let it direct me to a higher truth because I'm tired of my judgement always being so clouded. 'It wasn't quite that, I don't think. Not in the way you mean – though I thought it was at first . . . And, of course, I was pretty convinced for a time that the minute I moved out and came here I'd paved the way for it to become that.'

'Tell me,' he says.

I don't quite know where to start, so I say, 'Well, I saw them together. I mean – just talking. But I saw enough to make it hard for me to believe his claim that it was just a friendship . . .'

Someone dims the lighting a degree or two – remarkable timing. I can no longer see the intensity of his eyes, which makes it easier somehow.

'I'd boarded a bus that was due to leave in about ten minutes for downtown Seattle. I used to do it once in a while when I didn't feel like the hassle of driving . . . Mark's office is close to the bus terminal. I saw him walk past – it was around 2 p.m. so I just figured he was on his way back to the office from lunch. I went to knock on the window, to surprise him . . . But then there was a woman walking towards him.' I can picture it vividly. Mark spotting her, then his legs just seeming to stop. He swung around and said something to her that made her face suddenly burst into a smile. 'She was a very striking girl. Early thirties. Beautiful figure. She's actually part Fijian.' I tell him how they chatted for what felt like a while – seemed quite engrossed. 'I remember thinking he looked so utterly smitten by her – and the way she was tossing her hair and laughing . . . I don't know, it seemed quite mutual.'

Ned's face is a picture of scepticism and intrigue. I try not to let it put me off my story.

'Mark can be a bit of a ladies' man. Not in any bad way. Women like him. Something about him being bovine and a bit sensitive – it seems to be a winning combination.' I snicker. 'I've never really been threatened by it. It's completely unrealistic to think that just because we're married we go through life immune to the appeal of others . . . He's never cheated, of course, or I'd not have been with him. And nor have I . . .' It strikes me that any rational person would say I can't know this for sure, and it's true. But as far as I'm able to know it, I believe it. 'Anyway . . . this felt different. There just seemed to be this intimacy, like they were a little under the spell of each other . . . I can't really describe it. But it's one of those things you know when you see it.'

'He didn't see you?' Ned is resting his chin on the back of his hand, looking at me intently.

'No. Like I say, his attention was more than occupied.'

'So what did you do? I'm sensing this is leading to something big.'

I'm not sure he's taking me all that seriously. 'Not really.' I shrug. 'It was like a time warp, really. A bit like how he'd looked at me that first time we met. Like I was the sudden centre of everything, the change . . . I felt sad.' My explanation is inadequate. In the interests of not over-dramatising it, I've actually played it down, done myself a disservice. It sounds even more absurd than it probably even was. When he doesn't immediately react, I say, 'I rang his cell.'

'You did?'

I can picture the moment he heard it. The slight disappointment, tinged with annoyance. 'When he saw it was me, there was this studied hesitation. I thought, *Interesting! He's not going to answer!* But then he did. When I asked him where he was, he said he was in a meeting. I said, "You're in a meeting right this second? At work?" And he said, "Yup" . . . I didn't realise he could lie so effortlessly. So then I kind of lied too and I told him I was in Neiman Marcus and I thought we could grab a coffee – we used to do that occasionally during the day once I started working from home; I'd meet him in the little courtyard of The Shops at The Bravern . . .' Summer or winter we would sit in front of that same outdoor fireplace, either in the shaft of a warm sun or by the glow of the fire. It was kind of like stealing together-time when we weren't supposed to be doing it. 'When he's not being truthful he gets a little lisp. It drives him mad but I've always found it endearing. It gave the game away every time. When he said, "Look, I don't have time. Just got way too much going on right now . . ." I could hear that little lisp. But what really struck me was that the entire time he was saying all this, he never once took his gaze off her face.'

As Ned hasn't, from mine.

'Anyway. That was it. They said goodbye. I watched her walk past me sort of looking like she had a little buzz on. He walked a few steps and then he turned and just stood there for a moment watching her from behind.'

166

Ned whistles, then finishes off his drink. 'Did you tell him you'd seen him?'

'Over dinner. He was speechless at first. "You were sitting on the bus? I thought you'd said you were in Neiman's?" As though my white lie was bigger than his. He played it pretty cool, said she was the new head of their legal team – which I doubted at first because she looked way too young, but it turns out he was right – a high-flying brainbox as well as a beauty . . . He said he'd mostly just dealt with her on the phone but just a few days beforehand they'd met for the first time – they'd been seated in a boardroom together for a couple of hours. So he was shocked she'd just walked past him like she'd never seen him before. He said she was embarrassed when he called her on it. She'd had a little laugh.'

'Sounds plausible, I guess.'

'But if she'd been three hundred pounds and his age, I doubt he'd have cared if she didn't remember him.'

'Maybe not. But that doesn't make him a cheater. It just makes him human.'

'Perhaps,' I say. 'He certainly didn't understand why I was making a big deal of it.'

Ned is looking at me as though neither can he. At the time I couldn't bring myself to say, *Well if it was nothing, then why were you turning and gawking at her legs as she walked away?* It felt beneath me. As does putting too much emphasis on it now. 'If it had only been that . . . But I found some texts shortly after. His phone was on the table and one just popped up and I happened to glance at it and then I was, like, hmm . . . They were meeting for lunches. I think he'd also grabbed a drink with her one night after work, because there was one text from her that said, simply, *Six?* And then his reply. *5:30?* And then she sent him a winky face . . .' I remember how hopping mad that emoticon made me! 'Then I found a bill for a restaurant – it had fallen out of his pants pocket and was just lying on the floor. He'd ordered a pretty pricey bottle of wine.' I have never known Mark to drink booze in the afternoon, no matter what the circumstances; he says it makes him feel unwell in his head. 'He got quite defensive about that.'

'Did he admit it was her?'

'Not at first. Then he said they were just friends – that he'd needed someone to talk to because, well, he and I weren't exactly talking . . .'

'Why not?'

I give this question a wide berth. 'Apparently he nipped it in the bud when she told him her husband and kids were out of town one weekend and she wanted to go out for dinner with him on the Friday night.' He didn't exactly volunteer this. I had to pry it out of him. I remember thinking, *If you've nothing to hide then why are you being so cagey about it?* I didn't understand. 'He said at that point he knew they were probably about to cross a line.'

'And you believed him?'

'Like I said earlier, back then I didn't know what to believe. I was very fragile, emotionally. Half the time I didn't know what was real and what was fantasy in my own life, never mind his . . .'

'Well, I guess it sounds reasonable to me. If he'd been going to have an affair, surely he'd have had his opportunity right there. Sounds like she was putting out all the signals.'

'Yes, but to admit he knew they were coming close . . . how do you think that made me feel?' I remember his words, once I'd pushed him on the topic: 'OK, so I liked being in her company! I got to be normal around her, feel normal. I wasn't always reminded . . .'

'Besides,' I continue, 'some people think an emotional affair is way more threatening than a physical one. Once you're looking forward to your cosy long lunches together, and texting each other about it afterwards . . . When you're enjoying being in that person's company and finding you can talk to them more than you can your husband or wife . . . And I honestly do think that even if he was truthful and it wasn't physical at that point, it would only have been a matter of time if I hadn't tumbled to it – he would have weakened eventually.'

'Not fair to hang him for what he *might* have done, though.'

I frown. 'I'm not hanging him.' I actually thought I was being quite objective.

'Sorry,' he says. 'I guess I'm just trying to keep some perspective. He knew when to pull back, and he was honest when you asked him about it.'

'When he knew I knew. I'm not sure that's being honest – more like saving your ass.'

He doesn't seem to have a reply for this.

'It's hard for me to explain and you probably had to be there . . . I was going through a bad time. I was so careful that no one knew how bad, because I'm a very private person, and he was probably blabbing about it to some gorgeous young woman over tuna tartare and a bottle of Sancerre . . . It stung. But what hurt the most was knowing he was relishing being in her company because it was just so hard for him to be in mine.'

'Why?' he asks. 'What bad time? Tell me.' Then he adds, 'I've known for a while that there's something.'

The question takes me completely off guard, despite my having almost led him to ask. Then I think, *This is the problem: you can't tell half the story. This is precisely why I should have stayed quiet.*

'Sorry, that's not something I feel like getting into.' I shake my head, seeing it before my eyes, trying to edge my way around it like it's this thing that's always blocking my path.

'It might help,' he says. 'And I'm sure you know by now you can say anything to me. I'm a pretty unshockable guy.'

A cold sweat has broken out on the back of my neck. I cut him off with a firm shake of my head. 'Thanks. I know I can. But I . . . can't.' Emotion is like hands around my throat and I can't sit here any longer feeling put on the spot. The waitress is passing. I almost leap on her for the bill.

'Hey!' he says. 'Let's not go. Let's just forget I asked. I really didn't mean to back you into a corner.'

I just keep on shaking my head. I can't look at him. Someone has moved a few tables aside and made room for a dance floor. One or two people are shuffling around to a male vocalist singing a touching version of Dolly Parton's 'I Will Always Love You'. 'I just need to get out of here,' I say, searching for the girl, praying for her to come back quickly. 'Sorry,' I add. 'I really don't mean to be melodramatic . . .' Part of me thinks, *Then don't be! Just tell him!*

We sit rigid with anticipation while I try not to have any more of a meltdown than I'm already having. Or perhaps I am the only one who is rigid. He looks more sorry than uncomfortable. The instant she returns, I go to intercept the black bill folder but he beats me to it.

'Please.' I hold out my hand.

'Sorry.'

My arm is trembling. 'You're going to make me feel very bad if you don't let me pay.' I am overwhelmed by my own drama and just wish I could climb into a manhole and pull the lid across.

He lifts up from the seat slightly and reaches into his pocket for his credit card. When the waitress comes back she looks at us as though we're having a bit of a blowup.

I watch him pay, aware of an utterly debilitating helplessness. As we leave, the women at the table for four are paying up too, but they stop to perform a synchronised jaw-drop at us as we pass. I suddenly hate small towns again. But then Ned's hand touches the small of my back and something in me says, *Nothing lasts forever. This too shall pass.* That hand stays there, making me feel a tiny bit less like imploding, until we get outside.

The air feels so good. I don't want the night to end this way – with me having ruined it. Under the unflattering glare of a street lamp, he turns to face me. His bloodshot eye seems sore and tired, and he's pale, probably because I have made him pale with my behaviour. I am sure

I must look like an old harridan to him. Then again, it's not a beauty contest.

I could scream until my vocal cords snap beyond repair.

'Walk you home?' he says, trying to be a good sport about it.

I stare at a point past his arm. 'I'm going to put you out of your misery and walk myself.'

'Why am I in misery?' He sounds genuinely puzzled.

I meet his eyes and become transfixed by his gaze – the questions in it, the concern. It suddenly occurs to me that I came to this place to escape my prison, and yet, at the same time, to remain in one. And yet somewhere I lost my way and joined a writing club. I started granting myself tiny pardons, finding intervals away from my pain, opening myself up to the possibility I could feel human again. Nothing has really changed. And that's because I refuse to let it.

'I think I'd just like to be alone,' I tell him, trying to match his cheeriness and failing abysmally. *Tell him!* a part of me screams. A cord of opportunity stretches between us and holds us fast. I can't seem to break it and neither can he. Then I find myself turning and starting to walk away.

'Don't,' he says. 'Come back to my place. I don't want you to be alone.'

And then, when I don't respond, I hear him say, 'I'm totally not happy with this . . .'

Without turning to look at him again I throw a casual wave over my shoulder, meaning, *I'm fine.* My misery is swallowing me from the inside out. As I start my climb up the hill I'm aware he's still standing there watching me; I can feel how confounded he is. How we both are. Eventually I hear his firm footsteps going off in the opposite direction.

TWENTY-SIX

It's raining heavily by the time I reach the house. I stand in the darkness of the interminably quiet kitchen, unable to take off my jacket, unable to move an inch for thinking how I just did the wrong thing.

The opportunity to tell him was there all night. It nudged me and yet I let it walk on by. Rain lashes the window – even the weather seems to be annoyed with me – and for the first time it hits me so powerfully that I don't want to be here in this place. This is not my home. I can no more go down that hall, lie in that bed . . . I want to be with my family. Mark and Jessica. I need my husband and daughter more than I need air. The yearning makes me stifle a gasp with my hand and bite down hard on my palm.

The pavement is slick and shiny with rain and street lights. I don't know how I got outside, out of the gate. All I do is put my head down and walk, rain thrumming a tattoo on my hood. My legs move quickly to a rhythm of angst in my head. I don't look up until I've located his street. House number 6524 is harder to see in the dark. On the crest of the hill there is little illumination except for the moon.

He told me he rents the main floor and there's an older couple living upstairs so I only look for two-storey houses, ignoring the ranchers. After a hasty extrapolation from the one house number that has a light above it, I land on which one is probably his. There is a glow coming from the front room. Brown horizontal blinds not fully dipped. A number that's visible only when you're up close.

A flurry of nerves turn me nauseous. Anxiety causes me to involuntarily blink. I stop several feet before his door. I cannot reach out a hand to knock. *For God's sake, yes you can,* I think. I take several deep breaths, hang my head, and then just do it. My heart is barrelling. Seconds pass, and then the sound of feet on a creaky floor. I have the urge to run, but it's too late. The door opens.

'Olivia,' he says. And we are face to face again.

I open my mouth to speak, but with the prospect of saying it I am utterly frozen.

Those three little words. I have never uttered them to a living soul. But they inhabit every cell of my being, worse than any terminal diagnosis. I have often thought there's no feeling more sobering than the realisation that, of the many things I could change about myself – my hair, my weight, my marital status, my entire identity if I wanted – I can never change this. These three little words stick with me for the rest of my life. They have become me. I am unable to separate me from what I did. We are one and the same.

He waits. And I think, *Yes, he was right.* What's my story to the heinous things he will have witnessed and done? I doubt it will even give him pause.

My heart ticks wildly. Suddenly my blood rushes with the prospect of saying it. I am a river about to burst its banks.

Tell him, my inner voice says. *Just damned well say it.*

I am on the verge. But before I can get a word out I burst into tears.

TWENTY-SEVEN

19 May, 2016

I am arranging her stargazer lilies on the window table when I see her walking up our drive, her white-blonde and bubblegum-pink hair in a sloppy updo. She's wearing her skinny, ripped blue jeans and schlepping a file folder under her arm. There's a purple bra strap peeking out where her thin, grey sweater has slid off her shoulder. Close behind her is the UPS man and his eyes are glued to her backside.

It's come! Hurrah! Talk about cutting it fine!

She sees me watching and gives me the victory smile. I let out the breath I've been holding for the last few hours. Phew! In a few short weeks she will be off to college, depending on how she performed today. No one else has been holding their breath. No one else was worried about this. My daughter and my husband expect the expected. I am always on the lookout for something to jinx it coming around the corner.

'All good then?' I ask as I open the door to sign for the parcel.

She pulls her earbuds out. 'Totally. I aced it.'

I must be smiling from ear to ear. The delivery guy beams one back, clearly thinking I'm very happy to see him. I sign for the parcel, then close the door with a sharp donkey-kick. In the kitchen, Jessica is tipping juice down her throat straight from the carton, one of her mannish habits that would probably send the legions of her male admirers running for the hills. 'Happy birthday!' I plonk the parcel down on the granite.

There's an instant where she looks genuinely stunned. 'Huh? But I got my present already!'

'That was from your dad.' When in doubt, Mark buys a Tiffany pendant. 'This is from me.'

She rapidly fans her face with a hand and pretends to pant like she's just about to give birth; Jessica has always got ridiculously excited over gifts. Then she runs for the scissors. 'It's something to wear. I just feel it.' I watch as she pierces the thick plastic.

'Wrong!' I try to throw her off the scent. Jessica has an almost supernatural ability to guess gifts.

As I observe her diving into it I am peripherally aware of the ambient scenery – the sun streaming in the tall windows, the potent scent of lilies drifting from the front room. The black-and-green-covered hardback book of poems I gave her this morning, still sitting on the end of the bench, that opens with 'Reynard's Last Run'. I will come back to this moment in my memory many times when life has gone to pieces, less than a couple of hours from now, wishing we could have frozen time right there, like stopping a ball mid-air.

It's wrapped beautifully in silver tissue, tied with a silver satin bow. 'Oh my God!' She looks at me with wide eyes. 'I know what this is!'

I feel silly-overjoyed and can't help but smile.

'This is unreal!' She spies a hint of peacock blue. Her cheeks flush. Jessica has the kind of rare alabaster skin that always has a bloom of pink like a pompadour doll. Something she inherited from my mother, that completely skipped me. 'I can't believe you did this!' She gawks at me in disbelief. We had joked as we'd come out of the shop, 'You could feed a small country with what that thing cost.'

'This is crazy!'

'Don't worry. It got reduced. I was watching it for a while.'

'You devious person!' She squints. '*How* reduced?'

'You don't ask the price of your own present!' I tut. 'But, it was a lot reduced, as it happens. They were practically giving the thing away.'

'You are so lying!' She beams another smile and gives a little squeal of glee.

I watch her unpick it from the wrapping. The fitted silk bustier bodice, with the softly capped sleeves in lace and peacock sequins. The floaty folds of skirt. Jessica was always mad about fashion, even as a kid. There would be drawings all over the house of stick models with boobs and big hair, dressed in all manner of her outlandish designs, some of them quite inspired. She could sketch and colour in for hours. I was convinced she was going to be a fashion designer until she ended up being more left-brained like her father.

'I can't believe I'm actually holding it and it's mine!' She stares at it like it's her newborn baby.

We had seen it in Neiman Marcus. 'Plenty other gorgeous grad dresses besides that one!' my pragmatic daughter said when we saw the price tag.

'Oh my God, I have to try it on!' She scoops it up and bounds off upstairs.

I'm scrunching wrapping paper when my phone rings and I see it's Deanna.

'Hey!' she says. 'I just saw the UPS van. Did the birthday girl like her gift?'

'She loves it! She's trying it on now.'

'I must see her in it. You free to pop over for drinks on Saturday? Just us, and maybe the Waxmans.'

'Damn,' I say. 'We can't. Mark's going away tomorrow to another conference. Maybe next weekend?'

'I'll have to see. I believe we have something on. What about a walk and coffee, Monday?'

Since I started my own event-planning business people often assume that work is one of those things that can get fitted in between muscle pump class and matcha lattes at Starbucks. At first it irritated me; I wanted people to take me as seriously as I was taking myself. But now that I actually hate the damn job, I'd cheerfully have coffee with a lamp post if it means not having to deal with another complaining client. 'Sure!' I say. We agree on 10 a.m.

My phone beeps and I see Mark on the other line. 'Hi!' he says. It's amazing how Mark can make possibly the world's shortest word sound so expansive.

'Hi, you . . . Guess what? It came!'

'Ah. World crisis over then? Are we still on for dinner tonight, babes?'

'Of course! I changed the reso from 6 to 7 p.m., though. Give us a bit more time.'

'Hmm . . . Time for what?'

I grin. 'Not that.' I always appreciate how after all these years Mark still flirts with me and there's nothing contrived about it; it just comes naturally to him. 'Or, then again . . . maybe that . . . If one of us is lucky.'

'Haha. You're so funny. One of us . . .' Mark will always explain the joke. 'I can't leave yet, though. Sadly. Got a meeting at five. Hope to be out of here by six. Long day.'

I look up and see Jessica at the top of the stairs. 'Ooh! Hang on . . .' I fumble for FaceTime. Within a second or two his big blonde head fills my screen and then his patient face transforms into a cheeky grin. 'What do you think of your stunning daughter?' I turn the phone so he can see her walking down the stairs.

'Wow!' She puts on an entrance for him then flourishes a curtsey when she gets to the bottom. Mark looks genuinely stilled by the sight of her, as though he too can't get over the wily passage of time. 'Beautiful. That dress was definitely worth the arm and two legs it cost.'

'You said it was on sale!' Jessica gawks at me again.

'It was. From a fortune to slightly less of a fortune.'

'I feel bad now!'

'Let's take it back then,' I try to deadpan her.

'It's OK. I recover quickly!'

'You girls still need me? Hmm . . . Getting a little busy here . . .'

'Hey, where are you?' Jessica peers into the phone. 'That's not your office!' Behind his head is a velvet sofa and fireplace. She chuckles. 'Busted!'

'OK, OK . . .' He affects his 'caught out' face. 'I'm at the Hyatt. Been here since lunchtime. But I really am having meetings.' He wags his Manhattan glass, his eyes dancing deviously. 'It's a shitty job but somebody's got to do it.'

'Long day indeed!' I say and blow him a kiss. 'See you in a few.'

'Drop me at Cara's?'

I look up from blow-drying my hair. 'What? Right now?'

'Pu-leese? I want to show her my dress!'

A sigh is almost on its way out. I get a bit tired of playing chauffeur, but it is her birthday.

'Can you give me five?' I say. 'You know if I don't dry it properly I'll be wearing a bird's nest by dinner.'

A short time later we are in the car. Then, because we're so immersed in conversation about Jenna Bowles, who walked out of the exam in tears,

I accidentally turn right at the traffic lights. Damn! Now we're destined to pass the high school just as all the kids are piling out and all the super-charged Range Rovers and convertible BMWs line up to collect them.

'Sorry! I wasn't thinking,' I tell her when she groans at my silly error. We are stuck with it now for a mile or two. I stare at the frustrating congestion ahead.

She puts the radio on then starts texting with Cara. I'm peripherally aware of her thumbs flying over keys as she sings along to The O'Jays' 'Use ta Be My Girl'.

'Hey,' she says, when she's finished her chatting, and has thrown her phone back into her bag. 'There's something I want to talk to Dad and you about tonight. I was going to save it but Cara thinks maybe it's better if I break it to you first.'

I glance at her. 'Break what?' It's not like Jess to be mysterious.

'You're not gonna get mad at me?'

I have to stop now because a tribe of teen boys are waiting at the crosswalk.

'Promise?'

'Mad?' I look at her again but she won't meet my eyes. 'Why would I get mad? What have you done?' The boys amble across and I press my foot on the gas again.

'OK,' she says dramatically. 'Here's the thing . . . I'm not going to Europe for six weeks. I'm going for a year!' She squeals with glee.

'What?' I shoot her another quick look.

'I'm sorry! I changed my ticket a few days ago. Cara might be join-ing me. We're going to work our way around all these different coun-tries, and we'll be able to share a room to save some money, although she might only stay six months, by then I'll have met some people . . .'

She rabbits on about her plan excitedly. My brain is slow to process this. I need to pull over but there's no safe place. 'Hang on . . . You changed your ticket? Without telling us? What about school?'

'I deferred my place.'

'You . . . ?' My heart hammers. I must have slowed down because the car behind me gives a toot for me to move on. I return my foot to the gas pedal.

'I'm sorry!' she says. 'I really didn't want to go behind you guys' backs but I knew if I brought it up again there'd be all that drama, just like the first time I mentioned it, so I paid for the ticket change out of my own savings and I'm going to find jobs and fund my own travel. I'm not asking for any money off anyone . . .'

'I can't believe this!' I say. I'm less bothered that she's going for a year than I am about the way she's gone about it!

'It's my life.' The excitement has disappeared quickly, and now she's strident. Jessica can have a short fuse. 'I'm so sick of studying! I'm sick of never having any fun! I want to see the world. *You* did it at my age! Remember? And I'm not actually doing it behind your backs. You guys don't have any right to tell me what to do. I'm nineteen now!'

'Don't we?' I realise she's worked very hard, as good marks don't come naturally to her. But it still doesn't stop me saying, 'Until you're out there earning a full-time living, we are the ones filling your savings account and funding your education – so we actually do have some rights here, you know.'

Damn. I don't mean to make it about the money.

I switch the radio off as the music is getting on my nerves. There are several beats where she refuses to add anything as my disappointment must fill the silence, and I try to just focus on driving. 'And I didn't do it at your age,' I say, after a moment or two, still fuming over what she's just said. 'I'd already done my degree.' Now I sound like Mark. I think, *Calm down and keep it in perspective – it's not worth getting into some blistering fight over, plus it's done now.* I change my mind and put the music back on just to distract myself.

The road bisects the park now for about two miles, a thicket of tall cedars on either side interrupted every couple of hundred kilometres by a break in the footpath from where runners, cyclists and dog walkers will emerge then have to wait until all is clear to cross to the other side. Not far off, a pack of teenage boys dawdle along the road; I watch them clowning around with each other, probably because they're all excited there are three or four girls in ultra-tight jeans up ahead. Normally this would make me smirk.

I'm aware of her staring out of the window, pissed off. *She* is annoyed with *me*? Ha! Then I hear her mutter, 'Fuck.' As though her brain is still rattling all this stuff around, and she can't help but spit a little venom out. 'Happy birthday to me,' she says, more pronounced. I feel her glare at me. 'God, Mom . . . You're such a hypocrite.'

At first I don't think I heard straight. Hypocrite? That's the last thing I am! I'm about to retaliate but . . .

It happens so fast.

I am aware of form. Of something large sailing across my field of vision in a flash of colour. The dull bump. The pitch of myself forwards and the soft leather firmness of the car seat against my shoulders as I'm thrown back. The squeal of something. My brakes.

Oh my God. I have hit a deer.

I am past it, though. Please don't let me have killed it. It occurs to me to just keep driving. But what happens next is surreal. My car has come to a full stop. I am straddling two lanes, turned slightly in the wrong direction. Jessica is babbling but I can't pick out words. Everything is remarkably still and green, like I've driven into a landscape painting. Nothing is moving, not even a tree leaf. Oncoming cars are not honking impatiently. Instead they are slowing down from a distance – a long line of them. My first real indication that something is seriously amiss. Instinctively I switch off the music. Voices filter through the open roof, a flurry of them. A steady tightening of doom in the air, an intense gathering of dread. I turn my head slightly and stare through the back window, but I'm not sure what I'm looking at. There is a cluster of people standing around, forming a loose circle. A fellow in Lycra on a bike, his bottom raised from the seat, frozen, looking down on something like a wind-hovering bird. There is movement now, a slight clearing. I see legs on the ground.

Someone is lying on the ground. A person. As far as I can see, they don't appear to be moving.

TWENTY-EIGHT

Other drivers are getting out of their cars. Anxious faces. There are people on cell phones. I see them through a fog of remove.

Somehow, even though my legs are sponge, I manage to get out of my car too. There is a man hovering by my door. His hand is just above my elbow. The dampened feeling in my head clears. It's as though someone has just switched on sound.

I hear the terrible scream. No, no, no.

Then I realise it's mine.

'It's all right,' a voice says. This man. Fatherly. 'It's all right . . . Calm down.'

But it's not all right. I am walking towards the person on the ground.

I have hit someone.

Hit someone.

The incongruous arrangement of arms and legs. The long blonde hair.

'I thought I hit a deer,' I hear myself saying. Over and over.

This man is trying to stop me but I need to see this for myself. I need to see she is OK. I shake free of his hand.

But as I get closer I can't focus. I am toggling in and out of comprehension. She is face down, prone. The position of the head doesn't look right. I make an inventory of the tight black exercise pants, the black and silver running shoes that are at odd angles; I don't know how her feet can look like that in relation to the legs. I can't take my eyes off them until I work out how.

There is a hand on my back, rubbing in circles. 'It's all right . . .' the same voice is saying.

Her eyes are staring hard, and for a moment I think, *OK, this is good. Her eyes are open so she's OK.* I am trying to will myself to do something productive, but then someone is placing a black thing over her, a jacket. I can't see the eyes any more. They have covered her entirely from the waist up.

But how is she going to breathe?

I place a hand over my mouth, look from her to this man beside me. Vaguely I hear Jessica crying but I am unable to comfort her because I am looking up at everything from a new perspective. I've fallen to my knees. The man on the bike is still hovering high above me, only higher now, frozen in time. Far off, the dim scream of sirens.

I am on eye level with her lower body. The long, slim legs. The under curve of her bottom. Soil on the soles of her runners. Her left hand. The olive skin. An orange reflector-type sleeve that covers her knuckles. I want to touch her curled fingers. Someone needs to comfort her until help gets here! I look up at people, wanting to communicate this but I am cold, so very cold. My teeth are chattering; I don't think I can speak.

I don't know what happens next, if I have fainted. A paramedic called Andy is telling me to drink this. I stare at the paper cup he's holding out. I am clutching a huge sheet of foil draped over me like a blanket. I am half aware of needing to hold my daughter but my head is a fog, my field of vision shallow. The sound of my pulse rushes in my ears. A policeman is asking me if my daughter and I can manage to answer a few questions.

All I can do is shake my head. 'Please call my husband,' I hear myself saying. I am very calm. 'Please call my husband.' Andy tells me to sip my tea.

The tea is warm and sweet. I concentrate on doing what I'm told. One sip. Two. But it makes me want to throw up. I hold it out to him, lower my head. I feel the graze of his warm fingers as he takes it from me. My ears are fading in and out. Periods of sound blocked by periods of silence, where realisation and disbelief want to collide but can't just yet. When I next look up, when the urge to puke has worn off a little, there is a stretcher and a lot of emergency vehicles – I count two fire trucks and two ambulances. The paramedic, Andy – he keeps telling me his name – removes something from my nose. A long tube split into two prongs; I hadn't felt it in there.

'Is she going to be OK?' I say to him. To Andy. I am getting a grip on things now. My voice sounds so very far off, though, like I am out of my body. She is being lifted, raised, like one of those effigies of saints carried through European streets. I can't peel my eyes away. About three inches of blonde ponytail dangles off the end of the stretcher. 'No, ma'am,' Andy says. I can't stop staring at the hair. 'I'm afraid she didn't survive.'

As the words imprint I look up and see Mark and, at the same time, Jessica tumbling into his arms. There is an implosion inside of me while I watch him hugging our distraught daughter and then his arms are around me and my face is buried in his armpit, in the soft merino of his pullover. He is holding both of us. We are both crying. I try to breathe like I'm breathing into a paper bag.

'What happened?' I hear him ask.

My brows are knitted tightly; I can't release them. Jessica just keeps saying, 'It was my fault. It was all my fault.' I just keep shaking my head. I can't unsee the image of her face pressed into that ground. 'I'm not sure.' I look at both him and the policeman. 'I thought I hit a deer.' It sounds absurd.

'No pressure but just tell us everything you can recall, if you can,' the policeman says. 'In your own good time.'

The man who told me it's all right is talking to another policeman, who is making notes. He seems to have a lot to say. I strain to hear but can't. I tell them all I am able. There's not much. Another officer is taking photographs of the road; I watch him, trying to work out why he's doing it. Mark tells me to take a sip of my drink that the paramedic has given him to hold – and I do, obediently, focusing on the sweet taste and the deliberateness of my swallow to get it down, concentrating on not throwing up.

The guy on the bike is talking to the policeman now. The ambulance with the woman in it leaves in a slow roll. I watch it until it's out of range. The policeman asks me a few more questions but I sound vague. Then he starts talking to Jessica. I manage to finish the tea. After a time – I don't know how long – the scene that was before my eyes starts to recede. Gradually, everything reverts to as it was before, a blackboard wiped. The only evidence that anything happened is my car half turned in the middle of the road, and a police car.

Eventually the policeman says, 'You're free to go.' I hear him saying something to Mark about leaving the car behind for now, and how they'll give it back later.

I stare from one to the other, uncomprehending. 'Go where?' Aren't they arresting me?

'Home,' Mark says. He cups my neck and softly rubs my cheek with his thumb.

I look at the policeman for confirmation of this. I want to argue but recognise I don't quite know which position to take.

'It was an accident,' the policeman explains. 'There were witnesses. You were not at fault. It was the pedestrian's mistake, ma'am, she ran out in front of your vehicle. You are not being charged with anything at this time. You and your daughter are free to go home.' His words are precise and formal but he is not hostile.

'At this time?' I hear the worry in Mark's voice. His hand has moved to my back.

'There will be no charges,' the policeman clarifies. He looks at me as though he's very much on my side. 'It was an accident, Mrs Chapman. You've had a tremendous shock. You should let your husband take you and your daughter home now.' He gives a short nod meaning there's nothing more to be said.

I watch him walk off. There is a certain 'business as usual' quality to the moment, to life. Mark and I look at one another, waiting for the caveat that never comes.

TWENTY-NINE

Present

'She was a thirty-six-year-old paediatrician from England.'

I pull up her Facebook page on my phone and find the photo of her at the Christmas party. The one of her in the teal dress, where she's reaching down to her shoe, making a face. 'Her name was Sarah.'

He takes the phone from me and studies her.

At some point he made me a cup of tea but I have let it get cold. He lit a fire because I was freezing. It spits and crackles, filling the depth of the silence that occurs when I just can't go on with the story. On a small table a salt lamp gives off an orange glow, the only light in the room, save for that of my phone.

'She was over here for a conference on meningitis and septicaemia in infants.' My brows knit together. The pain is like a headband, tightening. 'Apparently she's a leader in her field and flies all over the world for speaking engagements . . . She was staying at the Sheraton in Bellevue.' I gaze into the glass top of his coffee table where the salt lamp is reflected. I can see the road that bisects the park, the thicket of tall cedars, the path that exits the trail right on to the road.

'She just ran out. I honestly didn't see her. I don't know how I couldn't have. I've asked myself this so many times. *How could I not have seen her?*

He passes the phone back to me. I am powerfully aware of the shaking of my hands, of an echo of Jessica calling me a hypocrite. 'Sometimes I think maybe I go through life a bit zoned out or something . . . Or maybe I'm just not a very safe driver. I mean, I've had times where I've almost not seen someone . . . Maybe I should never have been given a license in the first place.'

'That's insane,' he says, as though he can hear the peal of my despair. And in a way verbalising these doubts and fears that have until now only played in my head makes them sound more hollow than resonant – almost absurd. 'Every driver has had some kind of near miss.'

'Mine wasn't a near one.'

'No. But you weren't charged with reckless driving. They took statements from witnesses. They found no fault with your conduct. There was nothing you could have done differently.'

'Wasn't there?' My heart beats hard. 'Why did I let anything she said bother me? Why didn't I just tell her, "Look, I can't talk about this while I'm driving"? Instead I sat there fuming and turned the damned music up. And then *I killed someone.*' Those three little words beat hard on my temples.

An unvoiced despair for me registers in his eyes. 'We've all had hot words in a car before. And it wasn't exactly a raging argument . . .'

I can't listen to any well-meaning attempt to tell me I'm not guilty. 'A couple of weeks or so after it happened, the man who had been very kind to me and Jess at the scene – John Hemmings – came to visit me. Mark had taken his phone number. He'd thought I'd want to hear an eyewitness account . . . You see, I wouldn't accept appeasing words from him because he wasn't there and none of it was happening to him – not really, not in the same way. He hadn't been behind the wheel. He didn't have that unspeakable guilt . . . I used that against him for a very long time, which wasn't fair.' I restrain my impulse to digress. 'This John Hemmings said he'd been out for his usual pre-dinner walk. He'd been coming off one of the trails that joined the one she was running on. He said she'd glanced in his direction but kept going . . . "I suppose I'm neither Brad Pitt nor an axe murderer," he joked. Anyway, he said it occurred to him that she should have been slowing down given the road was coming up. He said he thought to say something but it just happened so quickly. He saw her run out and look to the right.' I swallow hard and for a second it seems to paralyse my throat. 'He said, "I just thought, *Oh my god, she's looking the wrong way.*"'

I can tell Ned doesn't get what I mean.

'In England we drive on the opposite side of the road. She was expecting traffic coming from her right. I was coming from her left.'

'Jeez,' he says, and rubs his palm across his mouth.

How many times have I gone back to England and been aware how much more vigilant I need to be when crossing the road, because looking left is now my default? It is particularly treacherous in London, where black cabs hurtle around corners. It is one of the reasons I never drive there any more – it just isn't worth the stress.

'She ran right out in front of me, not expecting me to be there. Other eyewitnesses said the same – that she just bolted out . . .' I shake my head in despair. 'To make matters worse, she was wearing earbuds.'

'So she wouldn't have even heard the traffic to have had any kind of warning.'

'No.' My brows knit, picturing her in the last seconds of her life, as I've done a thousand times before – trying to rewrite fate. In my version she would have realised it was dumb having them in, and would have taken them out at the last minute. In my version that would have spared us.

'This John Hemmings said the whole thing was plaguing his mind and he decided he had to force himself to stop dwelling on it, and I should too. I remember looking at him and thinking, *A woman is dead and you're bothered because you've been thinking about it for two weeks?* I meet Ned's eyes now. 'It was easy for him though, wasn't it? He hadn't killed her, had he?'

He sighs. 'Look, Olivia, I know all about beating yourself up. You've found every possible way to blame yourself but, like I said, the reality – the sad reality – is you were actually as much of a casualty as she was.'

'I wasn't.' I stab a finger into my chest. 'I get to live. No one took that away from me in the blink of an eye.' A fresh surge of sadness and self-reproach ambushes me.

'People are victims of freak accidents all the time. Not everybody gets a long life. You were in the wrong place at the wrong time. And so was she. In her head she was back in England.'

No one has said anything quite as humanising about her before. No one has attempted to imagine what might have been in her head. My eyes tick around his face like the second hand of a clock. There is a suspenseful moment where he returns the same scrutiny, and we are held there in a bubble of anticipation, in an alliance.

'I just can't stop thinking, *What if?* My voice comes out so quietly it's barely there. 'If I'd gone the other route? If I'd let another driver cut in so they would have hit her, not me. Or maybe they'd have reacted faster! If we'd never moved to that damn house I'd not have been driving down that street! If I'd just told Jessica, "I can't take you." If I had just reacted better when she told me about stupid Europe . . .' My heart judders. Sometimes reality hits and I am thrust, slam-bang, into it – a mind-splitting outing from the sanctuary of the half-knowing. It happens now. Tears burn a trail down my cheeks. I taste them pooling around my lips. I am aware of that same quiet panic starting up. At one point the silence is broken by the short keening of my breath.

He slides his left hand along the sofa cushion. I'm not expecting the movement so I find myself staring at it, oddly fascinated. It stops just an inch away from my leg. The long, tapered fingers, artistic for a soldier. The pale pink patches on the knuckles, like bleach spots. Gingerly I reach out my own. The tips of our fingers meet and stay met. There is a moment or two where we both just stare at our hands, like they're their own life form.

'I'm sorry,' I tell him once I've gathered myself a little. 'I didn't know what it would be like to talk about it. I've never done it before . . .' In the back of my mind I am remotely pleased with myself, and then I think I have no right to be pleased about a small nudge in the direction of progress. I have no right to ever feel better. I need to pay for this until the day I die. Through the ceiling I can hear the canned laughter of a comedy show – the older couple who live upstairs, who he thinks might be deaf. I gaze at our hands there, our fingers still touching. The disarming tenderness takes me out of this. I long to preserve it, to just stay like this forever.

When I feel I can, I show him the rest of her pictures. He lets me, which is already more than Mark ever did, and I don't even sense he's humouring me. I explain who I think everybody is, going through them one by one, until we arrive back to Daisy in her water wings in the pool. 'I felt so heartbroken for them! These two lovely little kids lost a mother because of me. Because of my actions, they'll probably only ever have very sketchy memories of her. They'll end up wondering if they're real or if they've invented them, if they've invented *her*.'

I can tell he's thinking hard about what I've just said. 'You've taken a lot on board,' he says eventually. 'You've thought of the impact of this in ways a lot of people wouldn't have. You've made her very real. And that's a hard thing to do with someone you know nothing about.'

So different to Mark saying, 'You're obsessed with her. Don't you think your energies are a little misplaced, Olivia?'

I don't tell him I've watched videos of Sarah giving a speech at a conference. That I've listened to her voice until I've fallen asleep. That I've practically memorised the cadence of her Welsh accent. I don't tell him I've seen a YouTube video of her at a friend's wedding where she's doing a brilliant if slightly comical karaoke performance of ABBA's 'Thank You for the Music', with the camera cutting away to Glen's face and holding there because the person filming it wanted to make sure they caught his expression, the smitten pride. I don't say I've read an academic paper she wrote from start to finish even though there's barely a word in it I understand. That I've scrutinised all thirty-five of her patient reviews on ratemds.com, Google Earthed her house, her office, the hospital where she performed her surgeries, even the church where they got married. That I know the colour of her front door. They've got an abundant tiny blue flower decorating a rockery. I even know what that flower is called. Blue lobelia.

That I've been stalking a dead person. That in many ways I still am.

'Then it was the one-year anniversary and I found this online.' I show him the article in the *Eastbourne Herald*. 'So his wife goes off to a conference and never comes home. But he's a dad and a doctor and he's got to get on with it. But he isn't superhuman – there's a minute or two when his head isn't on the job and he reads a CT scan the wrong way round. He operates on the wrong lung, and the patient could have died because of it, then he would have been sued and probably struck off.' I suddenly find a voice for what I've wished I could have articulated better to Mark. 'You see, it was all this horrible domino effect. I felt so guilty about all of it. If I hadn't hit her, none of this awfulness would have happened for any of us. And I know you and everyone else will tell me I am not responsible for a doctor's ability to do his job, and you might well be right, but at the end of the day, it's how I think and I can't help it.'

'Jeez,' Ned says. I can see him contemplating an effective response and probably realising there isn't one.

I pluck at the frayed hem of my shirt. 'A few weeks later, I just couldn't accept that there were no consequences for what I'd done, that my life was just meant to . . . resume. So I got in my car and I drove to the police station. I asked to speak to the officer who'd taken my statement at the scene. I told him, "You see, there was already a lot going on in my head that day. My daughter was about to embark on a new phase of her life and I was sad that I felt like I was losing her."' I'd always said it's our children's job to grow up and leave, and our job to let them go. It had felt, in a way, like a team effort. Her part. My part. But all I could think was, where would my team be when she walked out that door and began her adult life? Who was I without her? 'I told him I was already a little fragile and then she dropped this bombshell about how she was actually going away for a year!' I can't swallow the lump in my throat. 'I told the officer that we had words and my attention clearly must have not been on my driving. I told him that was why I'd come to the station – to tell him that it absolutely was my fault and it was completely unacceptable that I got to walk away scot-free.'

His wipes a hand across his mouth again. 'Man . . . What did they do with that?'

'Well, they listened. They were kind. They gave me a cup of tea. They rang Mark. Mark came and took me home.' He couldn't open his mouth in the car. How do you remember silence more than words? 'We went back to doing what we'd been doing all along – I slunk back to my corner of the sofa and he padded around the house in a bewildered netherworld then shut himself in his office for hours on end.' And that's what I remember most about that time – the silence, that sense of being stonewalled, punished – or so it felt at the time.

'I read about survivor's guilt, blameless guilt,' I say. 'I suppose I went searching these online forums and chat rooms to see if there was anyone out there who felt like me or if I was entirely alone . . . It was fascinating to discover there were so many other people who had caused accidents, taken lives. I felt I had a strange kinship with all this some-what anonymous confessing and baring of souls on the Internet . . . And yet I could never have joined in, put myself out there into the ether of similarly circumstanced strangers. They were different. They walked in similar shoes but not *my* shoes. It really just confirmed to me that I was entirely alone. And some people had done some pretty terrible things and had bounced back fairly easily. That just made me feel even more hopeless.'

The tears have dried now. I am surprised how good it is to talk, how I have a new ability to breathe, as though there is now a soft clearing in the forest of my head.

'No one knows why two people can experience the same thing and react so differently,' he says. 'The military have done a lot of looking into this. Some of it's to do with your life experiences, previous trauma, how many stressors there are after the event, and how you've been taught to cope – are you someone who shares and seeks help, or do you isolate and avoid? But some of it even lies beyond rationalisation. Generally, though, for soldiers, they've said that the person who is able to verbalise his experience is the one who is most likely to manage his moods and eventually make positive steps forward . . .' He gazes at my upturned hand on my lap and in that instant I feel his heart go out to me. 'Didn't they refer you to anyone? You were suffering from post-traumatic stress disorder. You should have had help.'

'My doctor said that. And Mark. I didn't understand it. I thought, *No, that's for people who've fought wars or plucked dismembered bodies from car wrecks. Not for careless drivers who somehow didn't manage to see someone crossing a road right in front of them.*' I see objection in his face but don't give him a chance to speak. 'The truth is I didn't think I deserved these resources that would help me feel better. I'm sure, looking back, this is why I pushed friends away too. I didn't think I deserved anyone's pity, kindness, anyone's attempt to make me feel that I wasn't one hundred per cent responsible.'

'And now?'

It takes me a moment to work out what he's asking. I force myself to really think before answering. 'And now . . . I have to admit I'm tired of all the guilt and pain. It's just so very relentless and oppressive. There is part of me that would like a tiny little reprieve from it.'

'I'm proud of you,' he says, which is the very last thing I'm expecting. 'You've said this, and it was hard for you. This is progress even if you might not recognise it.'

My face must show my scepticism. I can't remember the last time anyone said they were proud of me. The garden hose episode blazes in my mind – Mark's shame. The first time I've ever felt how very unproud someone was of me. Until then I would have thought that if there were to be any show of etiquette around grief, it certainly wouldn't be on the part of the one in mourning. It was a wake-up call.

'You have got to move on, and I think you might be realising this now. You've allowed all this to alter how you see yourself, and you've got to force the shift back.'

'I thought I was moving on. A little. Since I came here.' Sarah had stopped being the first thing I thought of in the morning and the last thing before I went to bed. She had ceased to occupy the entire space in between.

'I think you need to start by reframing the way you think about it. For example, instead of saying, "I killed somebody," you need to start saying, "A woman ran out in front of my car and she died." You've got to do it every time you get a thought about it, until it's second nature.'

I ponder this for a moment, trying to exercise an open mind, but my brain is both wired and tired, and refusing.

'Take me, for instance. I ticked every symptoms box for PTSD and yet I constantly asked myself why am I *not* more messed up from the shit I've seen? But I think it's because I've done a good job of compartmentalising it. There's my civilian life and then there's my job. I've blocked all my emotional responses by blocking my triggers. It doesn't work for everyone but it's worked for me . . . Whatever works for you, whether it's blocking it or talking about it, you've got to force quit. You've got to forgive yourself because you finally accept there is nothing *to* forgive. And you've got to believe it not because I'm telling you. You've got to believe it because you know it's true.'

I mull this over. Yes, that last part is the hard part, I must admit.

He tucks a strand of hair behind my ear that must have fallen out of my pin. 'Healing is an act of persuasion, Olivia, believe me. There comes a point where you have to decide it's what you're going to do because you fully recognise what the alternative is. Do you want the alternative?'

It's a rhetorical question. He doesn't need an answer because he knows that in some place far inside of me I don't want the alternative. My instinct was to die but I didn't die, and I realise now that all that's left is to live, for the living.

'You don't have to go,' he tells me, after he has made me another hot drink, after we have sat here for a while, all out of tea and conversation. I had just been thinking that I do. 'What I mean is, if you want you're more than welcome to stay here tonight. You can take the bedroom. I'm happy on here.'

I look at his long legs, the foot he's thrown over his right knee, the patch of fair skin where the top of his slipper ends, imagining myself sleeping in his bed. 'I'm sorry, this isn't at all how I expected our evening would go.' I angle myself to better face him and our knees are almost touching. Did I even pay the bill? I'm not entirely sure. My head is fog again.

'The evening's gone just fine, Olivia.' His eyes circle my face slowly. I feel more is coming but he breaks the suspense by looking away.

After some time where we both must conclude I actually am going to stay the night, he switches on the TV. I sit there with a degree of relief and peace as he surfs through a few channels, his sleeved arm grazing my bare one; I can feel the smallest of muscle movements fired by each press of his thumb and am hyper-attuned to them. At a channel that has no picture, only sound – the gentle, bluesy riff of Ray LaMontagne's 'All the Wild Horses' – he stops. We stare at a blank screen and listen through a full first verse, Ray's weathered, captivating voice fading into the background before disappearing altogether. This is replaced by the distant din of street noise wafting in through an open window, soft footfalls across a bare floor.

And then a woman's gently coaxing voice asks, 'Who was she?'

Someone gives the smallest sigh. A male. 'She's the ex-girlfriend of a friend.'

'Is she a model?' this woman softly teases. They sound like they might be in bed.

'No.' Another tired sigh. 'She's a fashion designer.'

'Does she have a name?'

It seems like he might not answer, then, 'Harriet.'

There's a weighted pause. 'You weren't expecting to see her there, huh?'

Muffled sound of him getting up and moving around. 'Yeah. Want some coffee?' The clap down of cups on a counter top.

'Seems I don't get this channel,' Ned says, unnecessarily, while we continue to stare at a black screen and wait to hear what happens next. He glances at me sideways. It's odd to be so intrigued by words without a picture. Then the woman asks, 'Did you sleep with her?'

'Leave it. It's good,' I tell him, placing my hand on his forearm. I want to hear what the guy's answer is.

I am aware of Ned's gaze lingering on my side profile and then of him looking down at my hand there and seeming to study it curiously. It makes me look at it too.

And I never actually hear whether the guy slept with his friend's ex-girlfriend who looks like a model. Because Ned leans in and he kisses me.

THIRTY

When I wake up it doesn't immediately dawn on me where I am. Then it does, and I lie there blinking at the ceiling, last night rolling over me like a slow tidal wave. The touch of his hand at the back of my neck, my head tilting into it, letting myself fall. My eyes close involuntarily to recreate it, and then reopen and tick around his room. To press the memory of him closer I inhale in the gentle secret scent of his sheets, finding myself caught in a spell of deliverance. It's as though time and everything elemental has shifted, moved on slightly. I am bathed, for the now, in promise and peace.

After a while I think I should probably snap out of this and get up. The house is silent. Perhaps he is still sleeping. I have no idea of the time, except that daylight has broken. When I sit up I see my jeans and T-shirt are in a heap on the carpet and there's a shoe peeking out from underneath. I perch on the end of the bed in my bra and pants, orientating myself. Last night, as I was sitting here just like this with my heart raging to a beautiful burst, he knocked on the door. 'Need a nightshirt?' I heard him say, after a suspenseful pause. When I said I was fine, he continued to stand there for a beat or two – or perhaps the beating was my anticipation.

Come in, I was silently chanting.

My God, don't come in.

Then I heard him walking slowly back down the hall.

Right now I could use the toilet. I pull on my top but don't bother struggling into the jeans. If he's still sleeping on the sofa I'll just come back to bed. Before venturing out I take a quick gander in the cracked mirror of an old-fashioned walnut dresser. My eyelids are fat from tears. There is a band of red across my nose, making my under-eyes appear starkly white, like I've tanned with sunglasses on. I do a quick finger-comb of my hair. Not great, but I'll have to do. I creep out of the room trying to minimise the squeak of the door and listen for breathing sounds coming from the living room, but there is nothing. Going into the bathroom, I quietly slide the stiff lock shut. After I use the toilet, I turn the cold tap on and let the water run until it's properly cold, then splash my face twenty times, paying particular attention to my eye area. An old trick, but the older I get, the less it works. His toothpaste is lying on the side of the sink – squeezed from the bottom, as all toothpaste tubes should be and Mark's never are. I squeeze a bit on to my finger and dash it around my teeth, finishing off with a gargle.

As I'm coming out of the bathroom, he's coming in the front door. There is an instant where we seem to startle one another. 'Oh,' I say. '. . . I thought you were sleeping.' He is a glowing picture of health, and so very young. Memories of our kiss wreak havoc with my stomach.

'Sleeping?' He gives me a playful *as if* look. 'Just been for my run.'

He is wearing navy track pants and a burgundy T-shirt.

'I didn't hear a thing.'

He smiles. 'That was intentional.'

'What time is it?' I rake fingers through my hair again, think of him pulling away from me, looking into my eyes with such lively keenness in his, and saying, *hmm* . . .

'6 a.m.' His eyes go to my stomach, where my top has risen up with the movement of my arms.

'That's super early to be out running.' I tuck my left foot behind my right ankle like a bird.

'Force of habit. Mornings are great.' He seems spellbound as he looks at me. 'No people.' Then in one swift, unselfconscious move he reaches a hand round to the back of his neck and tugs off his damp T-shirt. In that second when his face is covered I can't help but glance at his lean torso. There is a web of scar tissue down his left side, but the rest is healthy skin on a beautiful, fit body. I have a sudden yearning to touch the damaged area, to touch all of him, like I almost did last night but stopped myself. To slip seamlessly into some sort of other deliciously distracting dilemma that we came so close to. 'Need to get in your room for a change of shirt?' I ask. I feel like I've just emerged from a two-hour massage; my body and mind are loose and free-flowing.

'Nope,' he says. 'Got one here.' He reaches into an airing cupboard. 'I'm gonna put some coffee on then take a quick shower. Want some?'

'But it's still the middle of the night.' I sound flirty.

'6 a.m. Half the day's over.' He smiles then slides past me into the kitchen.

I follow him and stand in the doorway, doing that the bird thing with my legs again. 'I should probably go. I'm sure you must be getting sick of me by now.'

He turns, holds my eyes quite deliberately. 'Never.' He glances at my legs a second time, and I feel the charge of it right through my lower belly. And then, 'Eggs will be ten minutes.'

Back in his bedroom I sit on the side of the bed once more, feeling rather restless and redundant. After a few minutes I hear the shower being turned on, the gush of water on the other side of the wall, its interrupted flow a few seconds later as it hits his body. Rather than just carry on sitting here, I go to the mirror again and try to put my hair into some sort of order, combing it briefly then raking it back into a stumpy ponytail. I've some nude lipstick with me so I dab a bit on both cheeks, rub it in until it almost disappears, then put a little on my lips. As I do so I'm aware of the pushing and muting of the water pressure next door, of something being unfinished and something not quite begun. The thought of him on the other side of the wall right there. I just want to stop and place my palm to it.

When I sit on the end of the bed again, my heart is jumping out of me.

Nothing happened because something was stopping us.

We were stopping us.

I hear the water being switched off. To distract myself, I pull out my phone and power it up. One new message.

Unbelievably – Mark.

Where R U?

I don't quite know what to make of the question or its timing, or what to really say. It doesn't sound like there's any great emergency, so with only the smallest twinge of guilt I shut my phone down and slip it back into my purse.

By the time I go back through to the kitchen I am slightly nauseous, perhaps because I ate so little last night. He is standing at the stove with his back to me. A tea towel hangs over his shoulder. There is a weak early sun, and he's opened the back door a few inches. I don't know whether it's him or the fresh air I can smell, but it's good.

At the sound of my feet, he glances over his shoulder, smiles. I pull out a chunky chair and sit in the single stream of light. 'A chef as well as a carpenter. I'm impressed.'

'Chef would be stretching it, but I suppose I'll never starve.' He has changed into a white T-shirt. He mustn't have towelled off thoroughly because where there are transparent patches I can see the musculature of his back through the fine material. 'Everybody should know how to cook at least basically, is my theory. Or you just end up eating shit your whole life.'

'Some of us feel we've had to eat shit our whole lives even though we're great cooks,' I say, trying to be amusing. He looks over his shoulder again, snickers.

'Here.' He puts a plate down in front of me and pours a mug of coffee.

'Very creative.' I stare at two slices of thick brown toast piled high with scrambled egg and bits of green onion and feta. 'I've never had anyone feed me before.'

'Why not?' he says rhetorically.

It makes me think of Mark and his short-lived bread-making craze, his boasts to the neighbours about how he couldn't think of a better way to start his day – until he could. Ordinarily this might make me smile. But right now I'd be happy enough to open a mental hatchway and let stray thoughts of Mark go sailing right out of it.

He brings a plate for himself and sits down opposite me. Our knees graze under the small table and I notice neither of us moves our legs. I wonder if he's as in tune with this small but loaded detail as I.

'How are you feeling?' he asks.

I suspect he is referring to our conversation, not our kiss. 'Better,' I tell him. It's the truth. This morning I didn't wake up with that same sense of oppression, that feeling of being in a vessel without air. 'Not sure what it means in the long run but I can't deny I feel some benefit from having got so much out into the open finally.'

'Did you manage any sleep?'

I nod. 'Slept like a log. You?'

He looks at me with a steady gaze. 'Not really.'

I scoop eggs on to an upturned fork. We sit without saying anything now, around us an aura of habitude and peace. I absorb the ambient chink-chink of his knife and fork, its own kind of companionable music. Even during our silence there is something so very reassuring about his presence. I've never really known a person be able to restore my equanimity by not even saying a word.

'I ran into a man again who owns the boat yard at the far end of town,' he says after a while. 'You know it?' He's still wearing the towel over his shoulder, making him look so appealingly housebroken. I am alive with the ordinariness of all this, the unlikely, yet easy, domesticity of us.

'Yeah, I think so,' I say. 'I've walked past it a few times. Older fellow. Red hair? Always smoking? He's actually about the only person in this town who's never bothered to give me their best interrogatory stare.'

'Ah yes. No, he's not that type of guy . . . He's an ex-marine. Keeps himself to himself. I've chatted to him a few times. We got talking this morning and he said he's taken on some new projects. I told him I might be able to help him out. Now that we know I'm OK with my hands.'

At the mention of his hands I think of them on the back of my neck, his thumb sliding along my jawline and down the centre of my throat, all the way to the tip of the V of my T-shirt. While my mind goes there he's watching me with a certain mellowed-out fascination.

'So you've landed yourself a job then?'

'Don't know if it's that. I'm just going to help out and he's going to pay me. So I suppose it probably is a job, yes. For now, anyway.'

'The waitress and the carpenter. Sounds like light opera.'

He cocks me a borderline flirty look. 'Ah, but you're not a waitress, remember? You're a barista. The barista and the carpenter doesn't have quite the same ring.'

'No.' For some reason I think of an article I read a couple of weeks ago. 'What sort of jobs do ex-SEALS usually do anyway?' I ask, aware of needing to make the conversation benign. Then again, perhaps this is not the most appropriate topic, either.

'Lots of things.' He seems unfazed. 'Private security, Homeland Security, military contracting, high-level business . . . The list is long.'

'Any of those ever sounded appealing?' I could absolutely see him as a bodyguard. Though, admittedly, my knowledge of this is limited to Kevin Costner and Denzel Washington movies.

'Maybe at some point down the line,' he says noncommittally. 'One thing's for sure, disability isn't going to be enough forever, and I don't want my son held back because his dad couldn't get his shit together.'

With this sudden reminder of the existence of his family we meet eyes. 'Hey,' he says, after what feels like a long time. 'If you're worried about me then don't be. It'll come out OK in the end. I'll be OK.' Then he adds, 'And I know you will too.'

It sounds so final. Is this his way of saying we are two roads that have come together but now must diverge? I look down at the stray morsel of egg on my placemat, stare at it until it starts to blur into a sunshine spot of colour. I am caught between wanting to be glad, and to panic. It's on the tip of my tongue to say I'm not convinced it's going to be OK for either of us. And yet the urge to say this swells up and dies. Instead I settle for just going with his words and being wrapped in his positivity.

Then I'm aware of the movement of his hand across the table. Gingerly I reach out my own until our fingers meet again. I am conscious of us both absorbing the significance of the fact that we are both still drawn to touch one another. But then I look up into his face. There is so much confusion in those eyes. So much confusion.

THIRTY-ONE

'You got mail!' As I walk in my garden gate, Nanette springs from her car. I had completely forgotten I'd invited her over to check out the new deck this morning.

'Human mail,' she says when I must look very puzzled.

'Well then you'd better come on in,' I tell her. I root around in my purse for my keys.

'Ah, not today come in. Today Olibia busy!' She cackles.

'Huh?' I feel like saying, *Are you on drugs*?

She takes backwards steps down the path. 'Tomorrow! Tomorrow I get full status report . . . OK? On *deck*!' She cackles again like we have a dirty secret.

Mystified, I watch her clamber back into her battered car. As she pulls away she waves frantically out of the window then lays on her horn, and it's like I'm watching outtakes from *Chitty Chitty Bang Bang*.

I shake my head, unlock the door and go in.

Mark is sitting on the sofa.

'What on earth—?' Suddenly Nanette's silly business makes sense.

'Hi,' he says, and then, 'Sorry.'

I shake my head in disbelief. 'She just let you in? Because you asked?'

Carol Mason

'If it's any consolation, I had to really persuade her,' he says and then he beams a smile that's trying really hard to be a typical Mark smile but not quite making it.

'God.' I throw my bag down on the chair. 'I bet I could go and live on the moon—'

'And I'd still find you,' he finishes. 'But you did give me your address. So admittedly it wasn't that much of a challenge.'

The pen. I just find myself standing here and shaking my head.

'Hey,' he says, brighter. 'I thought I'd stop by the local café for a latte. You know – Books and Beans. Heard of it?' His expression changes to mild annoyance. 'Got talking to your old pal Beth. You said you had a job, Olivia. You didn't say you worked in a coffee house.'

'I'm a barista,' I say, a little defensive at the insult. It suddenly occurs to me that it's just as well I'm not in hiding, running from an abusive relationship – with all these women freely giving out access to my life and my living room because he smiles nicely at them!

He studies me closely, letting my fit of pique come down a peg or two. 'Where have you been anyway?' he asks. 'Your bed hasn't been slept in. You look like the morning after the night before.'

'You've been in my bedroom?'

'Nanette and I were worried. We thought you might have had a coronary in your sleep.'

I am momentarily speechless. 'If I must explain myself I went for a very early morning walk.'

He glances at my pointed-toe ballet flats. 'Because we know you do that on a regular basis. Because we know you're such a morning person.'

I take off my jacket and throw it on to a cushion next to him, feeling a little hot from the third degree. 'Not sure you've really any right to question what I'm up to.'

'Why?' He narrows his eyes. 'What *are* you up to?' We stare at one another. 'Oh, and by the way . . . your landlady happened to mention

208

you're paying her month to month. You didn't sign any one-year lease. Lies are dangerous things, Olivia.'

'You should know,' I find myself saying flatly. 'You've told a few.'

His face changes. 'That's a low blow.'

'Why did you come here?' I ask, suppressing emotions that are threatening to flood me. 'Really, Mark? Isn't life easier without me in the picture? I thought you'd be relieved . . .'

'I don't know why I'm here,' he says after a moment or two, looking rather helpless again. 'I figured if you won't come home of your own accord I have to come and get you. Because this can't go on. It can't and it won't. I won't let it. Whatever fight is left in me, I'm going to fight for us. Whatever happens, I need to believe I tried.'

I sit down on the arm of the sofa, his indignation suddenly exhausting. 'How do you plan on pulling that off?'

'I don't know,' he says. He looks at me as though he's struggling to find a way to lighten the mood but has forgotten how. The old Mark would have had a witty rejoinder. It's this loss that says more about him than anything else. 'I just . . . I'm worried that the longer this goes, if I do nothing, you might think it's because I feel nothing.'

The old me of not so long ago would have said, *No need to worry there. You've already proven you feel nothing.* But I no longer make myself feel better, brighter, braver by lashing out at Mark.

'I thought you might make it easy for me,' he says, defeated. 'I thought after all this time there might have been some sort of small change.'

I stare at him sitting there, thinking, *Change? But I have changed in some ways! Haven't I?* Though I don't know how I would ever prove it to him, or if I even want to. It's surreal to me that a mere couple of hours ago I was sitting across from Ned in his kitchen, in the path of sunlight, imagining it blossoming into some sort of new life, one that I like. All that is stripped away again and Mark is forcing reality back in my face when I was doing fine with the fantasy.

'To be honest, I wasn't expecting to be having this conversation right now,' I say. 'I am better, I think. Well, not *better*. But . . . better than I was. And that's because I came here. I got away from the daily reminders. And . . .'

I got away from you? But I can't really say that because it isn't exactly true.

I feel my brows knit with a surge of emotion. 'And that's why I'm not really ready to come back. Not yet . . .' I look at him. 'It doesn't mean I won't. But I won't right now.' Then I add, 'I know I sound like a stuck record and I'm sorry.' I have no idea why this man has any patience left with me, why I warrant it.

'No,' he says. 'You don't. You don't sound like a stuck record. And you have no need to be sorry.'

We look at one another and once again I'm assailed by all these confused emotions. I wish, if we were going to try again, that we could be on the other side of the bridge without needing to walk it. I wish I could wave a wand right now. I wish I could know.

'Look, I've been thinking,' he says, a tad brighter again. 'Why don't you keep this place on? I'm sure the rent's cheap enough. Come home with me now. We'll go to counselling as a couple. And if you need to come here for a little break for a day or two I've no problem with you doing that. In fact, maybe we can even come together some time . . . on a weekend – maybe it'll be good for us . . . But I want you living back at home with me, under the same roof; I want our life to go on together in whatever shape and form it has to be for now, until it can be better again. I want you to at least try. I need you to do that for yourself, for me . . . and . . .' He draws a breath. 'I need you to do that for Jessica.'

At the mention of Jessica I stare with a hard vacancy across the room. I think of Ned telling me I was suffering from PTSD, and how valiantly I fought any idea that I might be deserving of help when I was the one still alive. Forces are pushing me towards helping myself right now. All I have to do is to allow the gentle nudge. And yet I hear myself saying, 'I'm not ready for it.' I frown, hating the echo of my own ineptitude.

'I'm not asking you to be ready for it, Liv.' He is firm with me. 'The truth is you're never going to feel you're ready, and after all these many months I think even you know that. I'm asking you to stop indulging this, whatever it is, and to just make a decision. Come home and face up to things, up to life again. Face it with me . . .'

The word *indulging* rings in my brain. I hadn't seen myself as doing that, but maybe he's right. I have never asked myself what it really means to love or to feel loved. But if I did, somewhere in the answer would be this: it's that fine line we all walk between honesty and hurtfulness, guiding and controlling, supporting while being fair. It's seeing past imperfections without pretending they're invisible, seeing the good in someone's heart and remembering that even our most bungled deeds often spring gracelessly from there. Mark loves me. Every cell of my being is saying, *Don't squander this.*

Mark has been my locus, my hearth. Without him the very concept of where I stand in relation to all that is around me is challenged. And yet now he's here right in front of me, the balance is upset again. It would be so easy to say, *OK, I will come home and I will let you help me. Help us.* But a quiet voice is reminding me of the fragile inroads I have made here – they seem so much more pursuable than the giant challenge that awaits back there. So I say, 'No. I'm sorry, I just can't.'

I find him some time later down at the beach.

I join him in standing with our arms touching, a union of two people staring out to sea. It's almost as if he fails to hear me or realise I'm here. He stands like a mast in light air, straight-backed and unmoving.

'Why did it have to destroy us?' he asks. He moves his head a quarter turn in my direction. 'That's what I don't understand. It should have done the opposite, shouldn't it? It should have made us even closer.'

I gaze at the sea trickling in and retreating from the waterline. 'I don't think it destroyed us. I think we just coped differently with it.'

I can almost feel him thinking this through, as though I've said something highly insightful. 'We can try again. To do better,' he says. 'Can't we?' Then as though anticipating my answer, '*Why* can't we?'

I look at his sad, tired face. 'Too much water under the bridge?'

His eyes fix on mine, blonde brows knitting. 'No. I don't agree. What water?'

It's like we've just opened a floodgate and I am hit with the most incredible compulsion to just say what I need to say without always stopping myself, without always holding back. 'I wanted more from you, Mark. I know it's wrong, you had your own stress and sadness, but frankly it just wasn't the same as what I was dealing with . . . I don't feel I had a partner who was truly there. I needed you to listen when I said I needed to talk. To understand that if I was asking for it, when I so rarely have, then you had to try. But you had no patience for it.'

'That's not true. I just wanted you to stop going on about *Sarah. Sarah . . .*'

'Because that was *my* way of dealing with everything! Don't you see? I don't know why you can't see that . . .'

I am feeling a little out of breath but I'm determined to get out what I want to say without letting emotion override it.

'The whole for better, for worse thing . . . I can't help but think you love me, yes, but you love me when I'm fine. You have a limited reserve of sympathy when I'm not. Emotionally you jumped ship when I needed you there as my anchor. You turned to somebody else. And I know you don't see it that way. Perhaps you never will. But it feels like you let another woman into that very private place that should have been just for us, and that makes what we have not so special any more. And I am worried what this says for us going forward.'

'It's incomprehensible to me how you can keep harping on about Meleni.'

I am almost immune to his intransigence on this now. 'It's not really about her or anyone else.' I try to say it calmly. 'It's about you and it's about me. And it's about how we are different now. How we *view* each other differently.'

'I don't view you any differently. Why would I?'

The answer beats there. I can't say, *Because I changed your life. All our lives . . .*

After a time he says, 'I needed someone to talk to as well. You'd forbidden me from speaking of it to anyone who we knew because of this insistence it got kept within our four walls. I was terrified of even running into neighbours, always dodging everybody, heading off their questions . . . careful how I trod. It was a living nightmare. And you know what, *I* was living a nightmare that never got acknowledged because yours got to be bigger . . .'

His face is flushed from the sun. It hurts my ears to hear his side. Yet I can't contradict him. He's absolutely right.

'It's hard living with somebody day in and day out who you can't reach, who is mad at you because you can't feel the sum of their pain the way they feel it themselves. Who you can't even ask, *Can we figure what's going on with us?* Because they've retreated so far into themselves that there isn't an *us . . .* Meleni listened. She had perspective I didn't have myself. She didn't know anyone we know. She wasn't going to run her mouth off to anybody. She had no agenda. I promise you.'

No agenda? 'She knew you were attracted to her from day one. You *knew* she knew and you sort of led her on.' He can't be so dumb as to not see this.

'How do you make that out?' His bemusement says perhaps he is.

'You're older, attractive, high up in your job . . . When you were sitting there in that courtyard outside of Neiman's in front of the fire pit having a nice cosy drink with her, confiding in her about your pain and the state of your marriage, you were basically telling her, *I'm vulnerable. I may be available.* How can you not see it?'

'How do you know about us sitting outside of Neiman's?' He is genuinely astonished. Then he adds, 'Been sitting on a bus spying on me again?'

'I didn't know that, actually,' I say, surprising myself and giving myself a second's pause. I honestly didn't. 'But it's what you would do, isn't it?' I feel like saying, *Because it's what you would do with me.*

'Jesus.' He wipes a hand over his mouth. 'You leave me lost for words, you know that?'

'Well, sadly not lost enough . . .' I say it without even a hint of bitterness.

We stand here, so many paces apart, like we'd be about to duel if either of us had strength for it.

My eyes fill with tears. I want to hit him, flail at him. I want to make him hurt in this one inadequate way for all the unremitting ways I am hurting. 'I am trying not to make it bigger than it is, but I can't lie. Knowing that at the lowest point of my life my husband was wending his way into a relationship with another woman is a hard thing to get past. I'm trying to see why it happened, but part of me feels it just makes a bit of a mockery of us.'

'Wending my way? God, you're such an exaggerator!'

'You oaf!' I don't know where this comes from but I pick up a stone and pelt it at him. It's actually bigger than a stone. More like a mini rock. It bounces off his shoulder and he says, 'Ow! Shit! That hurts!' So I pelt three more at him, bending fast and grabbing anything I can, holding nothing back in my aim.

'Jesus!' he squeals.

My heart thrashes. It's that hot rush of indomitable anger that I've only ever experienced since I drove a car on my daughter's birthday and I killed somebody with it, and lost everything in the process – more than I will ever be able to deal with, more than I can ever say. But I discover something too in my stone-pelting fit. Suddenly it's her I'm angry at. Not Mark, or some other woman. Sarah. Mark was right. Why *did* she have to be so bloody irresponsible? How could a mother – a doctor of all people – be so careless about her own damned safety? Why did she have to be there at the precise moment *I* was passing? Why not the car behind? Why me? Why us? Why didn't she live to be answerable for her utterly reckless behaviour? Mark thought of all this long before I have. Mark wasn't cold toward Sarah. He was angry.

Two teenage girls are passing and they slow down to gawk at us. When they see me noticing them they splutter laughter, folding in on themselves and locking heads.

I try to calm down and stare after them while they walk off. My heart is a fiery ball of fury. It takes some doing. The only thing that balances me is the realisation that this is how Mark has felt all along. Finally, I understand him.

'I'm sorry,' I say, my head reeling. I don't even know what I'm apologising for. Except that somewhere in me I know he deserves it – more than I will ever be able to show him.

After a while he says, 'It's me who's sorry. Everything you said you needed from me – I thought I was being all that. I honestly did. I realise your guilt was something you alone were carrying, not me. I was trying to understand that. But I have to admit it was very hard for me . . .'

For a moment he looks like he's going to break down.

'I just wished you had someone else you could talk to because I was being so very bad at it. A friend . . . anyone. I just wasn't equipped for it, on top of everything else. I just didn't know how to deal with it. It was too much.'

You were the friend I wanted to talk to, I think. *You were the one person to whom I thought I could.* But in a way this feels like bygones now.

He tilts his head back a little, lets his mouth fall open and closes his eyes. We are too old to persecute one another. There is enough wretchedness eating at us from things we can't control, without inflicting that which we can.

I want to tell him that I know and that I understand. Because perhaps for the first time I really do. I want him to hold me and whisper assurances to me I know would be impossible to give, about how we will forget all this in time. But I know that won't happen. If there's one thing all this has done for me, it's made me a realist. All I can do is draw upon Beth's words. *Heartbreak never truly goes away, you know. But it does get easier to navigate with time.*

He looks at me now. 'I am genuinely sorry I let you down . . .' There is a crack in his voice that's so pitiful it makes my ears hurt. 'You and Jessica . . . you have both been my whole life. My world. I would have died for you both. I hope you know that. And if you don't know that then I have let you down in ways that make my failure something I don't want to live with.'

I stare at my feet in the sand, stare until my eyes sting with tears and their suppression makes me choke.

I married a good man, but I didn't get to design a human being or I might have changed a few things. Expecting him to fight the exact battle I was fighting is the first time I've required him to do the impossible. He had his own.

I look up to find him steadily watching me. 'Sorry I threw rocks at you,' I say.

THIRTY-TWO

'Have you seen Ned?'

The boatyard guy is staining the hull of a canoe and gives me the most cursory of glances. 'No.' His paintbrush resumes after a brief pause.

'I understood he was going to be doing some work for you.'

'He was supposed to stop by this morning but he didn't show.' He squints at me from a web of smoker's wrinkles. 'Want me to tell him you're looking for him, if he does?'

'No.' The wind has left my sails. 'That's OK. Thanks.'

I walk by his house for the second time, staring in but being sure to keep moving. Then I think, *You've kissed him, slept in his bed, you've told him things you've never told a living soul, surely you can knock on his door?* So I venture up the path. There isn't a doorbell, so after much ado, I give three hard raps. Nothing. I sneak over to the window and attempt to see in through the half-closed blinds but that's not very fruitful. I have the oddest sense that he's in there. Not that I have any real reason to think he would avoid me. Just as I'm about to head back down the steps I notice there's a footpath that leads to a door around the side – presumably the upstairs tenants' entrance. I follow it and knock. I wait a moment or two but there is neither sight nor sound of life. I'm just turning to walk away when I hear the door open. When I look over my shoulder there is a woman, probably my mother's age. She seems groggy, like she might have been napping. I ask her if she's seen Ned in the last few days. I explain that I'm a friend and he hasn't shown up to a couple of appointments.

'Can't say I have,' she says, after a wary hesitation. She glances me over, seeming fascinated by my hot pink ballet flats. 'He's a quiet type, though. We don't always hear him anyway.' She talks to my shoes. 'We're both deaf in one ear.'

I'm just about to say, *Sorry to have bothered you*, when she says, 'We sometimes hear his nightmares though. We're both very light sleepers.' She glances me over one more time, then shuts her door.

My spine tingles with an unpleasant sense of foreboding. I try to imagine him just having disappeared. Though why would he? A few days ago he was telling me he'd just accepted some work. But now that the thought has lift-off, I can't seem to shake it. And it hits me how much I couldn't bear it if I never saw him again. I've some scrap paper in my bag so I sit on one of the steps and scribble a short note.

Ned. Been looking for you for a day or two. Hope all is OK. Please give me a call. Hope you are coming to the CC tomorrow night. Olivia.

I write my phone number just in case he's lost it. Then I pop it in his mailbox, taking pains to stand it up so it won't get swallowed by all the marketing flyers.

When I get back to the house I am ill at ease and can't sit down. One more try of his number.

Phone switched off.

I sit at the kitchen table but spring back up again. I pace the floor, pour a lemonade, stand and drink it while watching a hummingbird arrive at my feeder. To try to conquer the restlessness I go into the living room, get my laptop and plug his name into Google – not that Google is going to tell me his present whereabouts.

There are lots of Ned Parkers. Then I realise it's mainly the same guy – a journalist. His picture pops up alongside his byline. The Ned I know seems to have no visible online profile. Nonetheless, for want of something better to do I keep scrolling. But then around page eleven the words *Navy Cross* still my hand. The article is from *Military Times*. Aware of the quickening of my heart I open it, read. The story details several SEALs who were awarded the military's second highest decoration for valour in combat in a secret ceremony – Ned being one of them. I can't pull my eyes away from his name. The recognition he received was for saving the lives of eighteen US embassy personnel in Kabul. There's a small picture of him sitting against what looks like a padded wall – maybe the inside of an aircraft or bunker – wearing dark glasses, a beard and a hat with large ear muffs attached. He is dressed in army fatigues. I wouldn't have known him. In fact, I can't get over how different he looks and it makes me think of how he said there was his civilian life and then his job – the two Neds. The article quotes him as saying, 'I accept this award not for myself but for my two teammates who made the ultimate sacrifice that day.'

What did he say to me? *I'm no hero. I'm no better than any guy and no braver.*

It then goes on to say how, less than a couple of hours after the rescue op, he was blown up in a Humvee and two of his teammates died in the explosion. As for how this has left him: 'I struggle with a lot of what I saw in war, more than with what I now see in the mirror. It exists along with me. I don't think it will ever cease to be there in my head. I've accepted it's just a part of who I am and how I'll be. I ask myself endlessly if I could have done things differently. And there are days when that is alarmingly hard to live with.'

This last part chimes in me. I hadn't known it at the time, but in listening to my story he was hearing echoes of his own.

Alarmingly hard to live with.
I bolt up from the table again and grab my phone.

The main drag is busy this afternoon. I pull over and pop into the grocery store just for long enough to know he's not in it. I poke my head into Books and Beans. 'You haven't seen Ned, have you?' I say to Beth, who is scrubbing the counter.

She looks puzzled for a moment. 'No.'

I tell her that if she does she must call me, then I hurry out of there. I doubt he'll be in the bar but suddenly I get a vision of him drinking himself to oblivion, so I duck in there too. Lastly, the crab shack where we ate dinner. I stare at the booth where we sat.

Now what?

I can't go home. I don't feel there's any point in going back to his place. So I find myself driving along the route he told me he sometimes runs though I know this is not his running time of day. With each passing mile it gets more and more fruitless but somehow my mind comes down from its state of panic.

When I get back to the house I sit in the chair by the window, feeling a little worn out. If someone doesn't want to be found you have to respect that. I, of all people, should know this. And yet I just can't shake this feeling that something bad might have happened.

THIRTY-THREE

Dear Amy,

Amy stands before us, breathless, and she has barely started reading it yet. I didn't feel like coming here tonight. I came for one reason only: to see if Ned would be here.

> I would very much like to applaud you for the three letters you've written to me and Bernie. Forgive me for not getting back to you sooner – your letters all said the same thing, so I was waiting to see if the next one might add anything different before I composed a reply. The other unfortunate thing is that I don't write all that well. Even when I have to sign my name at the bank I prefer to mark the space with an X. And Bernie's talents in this department are also virtually non-existent. So rather than waste any more postage stamps, I have a better idea. Why don't we meet for a drink like two civilised adults and get to know one

another a little? Once you realise Bernie and I are both in fact decent human beings, it might aid in us finding an effective resolution to this ongoing matter of Bernie's bark. Sound like a plan? If you re-post this letter through my mailbox then I'll know we have a date.

Sincerely,

Lucas and Bernie, your friendly neighbours

'What are you going to do?' Beth asks her.

I only half hear her giddy reply. All I can do is stare at a single empty chair. The more I gaze at the vacant space where Ned usually sits, the less I am able to connect with being here. And yet something tells me to believe what he said that morning. *If you're worried about me then don't be. It'll come out OK in the end.*

I pull out a sheet of my Florentine paper and my beautiful fountain pen. *Dear Eloise.* Since Mark told me what he told me, I have felt horribly guilty that all this time has passed and I have never delivered any sort of explanation or apology. But my brain can't seem to shape thoughts into the words I want to say. That's the thing with writing the old-fashioned way: it's a cue to mine the recesses of your heart, to set down that which has true worth with a certain grace and decorum. It feels big. But then I realise I don't have to overblow it. Anything I might say is better than silence. And, when in doubt, best to be simple. So I begin.

I am sorry it has taken me this long to thank you for all that you tried to do for me. I am sure in time you and I can sit down over a cup of tea, and it will all feel so much easier to talk about. But for now, please know I am thinking about you and sending you my thanks and my love.

From Liv

When everyone has left, Beth asks if I would like another cup of tea. I am in no immediate rush to get home, so I curl into the comfy chair by the window that looks out on to a black sea while she brews one for us. Once we're halfway through the pot she shows me the letter she wrote tonight. The one to Veronica telling her that her husband fathered a son.

'Do you think I should send it?' she asks, after a steady pause.

I stare at the tiny, tight handwriting, navy on cream, words crowding the page. 'Good heavens, I mean, it's not my place to say . . . In fact, I'd hate to influence you either way.'

'But if I'm asking you . . . What's your feeling? Be honest.'

There is an intensity and desperation in the way she is looking at me, and I know what that degree of helplessness feels like. So I think about it, seriously, before I reply. 'Well, my mother always used to say let sleeping dogs lie, and in many ways I believe that. Little good comes from raking up the past . . . But I think you have to ask yourself, what do you hope to achieve? Is it some kind of atonement? Is it to hurt back? Do you want a reconnection? Because if you do, the letter might not accomplish that. She might well think, *Why is she telling me this now?* and believe you're just trying to sully her dead husband's name.'

'I've thought of all that. I certainly have no wish to hurt her again. And it's not really for a reconnection. I feel that would open up more wounds than it might close. I've often contemplated how I would feel if I were to die knowing the last time I saw her was under those circumstances in that living room . . . It's a horrible question. She's my sister, after all, despite the fact that we never got along.' She stares off to the side of my head, melancholy. 'I suppose I don't really know what I want to achieve.'

'What about the letter you were going to write to Thomas?' I ask. I can't help but feel this one would be the more productive.

I'm waiting to hear her say, *I'm not sending any letter to Thomas,* but she gets up and goes into the back room. When she emerges she is holding out a piece of folded paper. She hands it to me and I read.

Dear Thomas,
I often try to think of all the things I'd want to tell you if we could talk face to face. The reality is, I am not your mother. You have a mother. Nor do I really expect you to understand how I could give birth to you and give you away. No one has told you my reasons, and this is why more than anything I'd like to tell you now because I think you are owed that. So, for what it's worth to you, and I hope it will be worth something, here is my story . . .

There are eight pages. I read to the end. Much of it I know and yet I'm as moved as though for the first time. When I look up she is watching me with anticipation.

'After you and I talked that night I went home buoyed up on wine, port and courage, and I wrote to his parents.' She tries a small laugh. 'I received a reply by email. His mother said that Thomas had been curious about me when he became an older teenager. She said she didn't know how he felt about things now that he was married and had two children of his own. The email ended rather abruptly there . . . But then, curiously, a day later I received a second one from her. All she wrote in this one was his address.'

This lights me up. 'She'd thought about what it must be like to be in your shoes.'

'I suppose. Or perhaps what it must be like in his.'

I feel myself becoming emotional. 'So you're going to send it to him?' I am so excited for her.

'I don't know.'

'You wrote it, so you must want to.' But as I say this I know it's not strictly true. One thing I have learned is letters are cathartic. We write to get beyond what we think we can't get over. There doesn't have to be a destination; it's the journey writing takes us on that is often enough.

'It could upend his world,' she says. 'And if he doesn't reply . . .'

'It'll upend yours.'

She stares into the near distance, sits very still, then nods.

'You have a child, Beth. You have a son. Nothing can take that away from you. Don't you think you owe it to both of you to at least let him see how much his life means to you? Surely whatever chance you might have of being in his life, in whatever shape or form, you need to take it?'

She meets my eyes and smiles.

THIRTY-FOUR

The letter is in my mailbox next morning.

> Dear Olivia,
> Three days ago my son had a fall that put him in hospital with a bad concussion. He's fine, but for this reason I have decided to head back to Florida. They probably don't need me there, but neither do they need me here, at the other end of the country. It was a wake-up call, I suppose.
>
> Olivia, I am trying to think what I would have said to you if there had been another chance. Maybe it'd be something I've said before. I think it comes down to this issue of walking forward. Life doesn't stop and neither must we. No matter what burden we carry, we owe it to this life we've been given, and the family who love us, to just keep walking forward. If we do, eventually we will be in a better place than we are today. Please think carefully about your marriage. Don't expect him to understand what he can't. Even if he could, it would change very little for you. There are just some things we're in alone.

And I wanted to say thanks for listening to me. Thanks for the friendship. I didn't expect it. I didn't think I'd be leaving so quickly but then again it's probably a good time as my staying might have complicated things further for both of us . . . I think you know what I mean.

Travel safe,

Ned

I stare at the address scribbled at the bottom. A PO box in Tampa.

THIRTY-FIVE

The butterflies are back the instant I turn on to Abigail Avenue. Yet I am not as bothered as I was before about kids who might be meandering home from school, mums returning from dog walks. This is my home, and there is something liberating about wanting to come back to it. The nerves in my stomach feel like positive ones for a change.

I am often struck by how with absence we can find much is changed, yet in other ways time stands still. The three blue hydrangeas at the front of the house have sprung up grandly since last summer and now have the bearing of belonging. I planted them the first spring we moved in, digging out some of the existing shrubs with their strong architectural lines to insert a peal of colour. Alfie from two doors down is riding his bike in the cul-de-sac and he waves at me as though he might have just seen me two hours ago, or yesterday. Everyone is getting on with their lives. No one is thinking about me. No one is monitoring what I do.

Going inside is still a little unsettling. Without me and Jessica filling it and giving it life, with Mark at work, it's just like it was that last time – a cavern, unlived-in, oddly silent. I set down my suitcase and travel bag by the front door, lay my purse gently on the small table.

There is a pile of mail – some of it for Jessica. I see an envelope with the University of Washington State logo on it, but I don't touch it. There are a couple of pieces for me. I walk into the kitchen that still smells faintly of the eggs and jalapeños Mark would have scrambled for breakfast. Through the half-open window I can hear Wren barking next door. For a while I stare out into the Waxmans' backyard, waiting to see if the events of the Fourth of July barbecue are going to rush at me again, like before. Nothing happens.

I take my suitcase upstairs to our bedroom. It smells like it hasn't been aired out in a while, so I push the window wide open and take a moment or two to reattach myself to the space. Mark's jim-jams, as he calls them, are splayed on the bed. When I notice them I find myself smiling a little. I realise that bizarrely I've missed seeing his stuff almost as much as I've missed him. I pick up the top and briefly press its fuzziness to my cheek. I wander into the bathroom and unpack my toiletries first, sliding some of his things along the shelf, staking my claim to the space that used to be mine. Unzipping my suitcase, I set out the neatly folded clothing in piles on the floor, then try to work out a more efficient way of arranging them in my drawers and closet than I had before. New beginnings.

When I left Port Townsend I dropped an envelope off at the library for Nanette, containing the next month's rent to give her a little financial leeway, and some instructions Ned gave me on how to best maintain the new deck. For Beth I left an apologetic note along with my phone number. *Please let me know when you hear from Thomas.*

As I sit here on the floor – taking a breather from my inspired decision to layer black T-shirts along with white – it occurs to me that life and love are simply the endless process of letting things pass. Whether Ned had stayed or left, I don't want to wake up every morning beside a hot young damaged guy who is trying out the process of taking steps with someone else, when his heart still belongs to his wife – though I treasure everything that happened that could well have made me arrive at a different conclusion. I want my husband, and the unremarkable every-dayness of life with him again. I do. Since I came to this realisation – to something I've probably always known – it has made me want to push up and reach beyond my capability for it. To do the things I know are going to be difficult to do.

I am lying on Jessica's bed when he comes home. I don't remember coming in here. I certainly don't remember falling asleep. At first I'm disorientated and shrink from having to wake up. I just want to keep lying here, my face pressed into her pillow, into the smell of my daugh-ter's hair. But when I hear him pottering downstairs I force myself to get up and make my presence known.

I open the bedroom door carefully so as not to shock him but it squeals anyway. Suddenly there is an audible silence from the kitchen.

'Jesus,' he says when he sees me appear at the top of the stairs. For a moment all he can do is stare at me as though I'm an apparition. 'I thought . . .'

He has turned white.

'What?'

His face loses its shocked apprehension. 'There was an intruder or something.'

'No.' I emerge from a small emotional pause. 'Only me.'

He continues to stare at me, as though reading meaning into me. I feel we have been here before, only the layers of pain have fallen away a little and I am able to look at him and offer up a smile. 'Sorry . . .' I shrug. 'I wasn't intending some huge surprise. I don't know what hap-pened. I fell asleep.' I am still groggy in my head and let out a long yawn. 'Oh my gosh, what time is it?'

'Eight,' he says quietly. 'I worked late.' There is a question in his eyes that I know he's building up to asking. And an answer I am work-ing my way around to giving.

We stand here, unable to do much but navigate the unspoken. He has a frying pan in his hand. A box of eggs sits on the counter. 'Didn't you have eggs for breakfast?'

He looks at the box as though bewildered by it. 'There's not much else in the fridge. I didn't feel like takeout again.'

'I'm sorry,' I say.

He shakes his head, frowns. 'For what?'

I open my mouth to reach for words and something happens. Before I can answer, Mark puts the pan down and places the heels of his hands in his eye sockets. I watch him stand there like that for a moment, before he inches to a stool by the island. He lowers himself on to it, rests his elbows on the granite, and then he sighs a long breath through his mouth, like a person trying to get a hold of himself.

And then I see Mark do the one thing I realise I've probably been subconsciously waiting for him to do. He cries. I have seen him cry before, when his tears were trying to be private tears. But not like this. This outpouring, this spontaneous dismantling that begins without provocation or forewarning. It goes on and on. I cannot pull my eyes away from him.

'I'll go to counselling,' I say, as I attempt a shaky walk down the stairs. At this point I realise I would say anything to make this better, but surprisingly I actually mean it. 'I'll do whatever it takes. Like you said before – with you, or on my own. I promise. I'll talk to whoever you want me to talk to. We both will. I'll do what it takes.' I am remarkably stoic, but in a good way. I look at the three or four flyaway strands of hair standing up on the crown of his head and my heart aches for him. 'I'll do this for us. I'll do it for Jessica.' I suddenly think of Ned's words. 'I'll do it because I don't want the alternative.'

Still he doesn't look up. I don't know if he's heard me. His head bobs gently between his hands with the force of his emotion. I lay my head between his shoulders. His quiet sobbing has no beginning and no end. I try to absorb its shuddering vibrations, as though by doing so I might have the power to take his pain away from him. I can feel his heart beating through his back. His broken heart, keeping step with mine. Together we can try to mend each other's.

It was all I ever wanted.

THIRTY-SIX

Because I didn't tell Ned the entire story.

So I ended up saying it in a letter.

Dear Ned,

My daughter isn't in Italy. Jessica is dead.

Her head hit the window when I hit Sarah. Not hard. Not even enough for her to remark about it when the paramedics assessed us at the scene. It was much later when we got home – about three hours later – when she complained of a blazing headache. We thought it was tension, shock, but Jessica died later that evening in hospital of an epidural haematoma.

The doctor called it a rare catastrophic occurrence. People Jessica's age don't normally die from a low-impact bump to the temple. But several months before, Jessica had been left with a significant concussion after a fall while skiing. The doctors thought it might have caused a small clot that wasn't present when they performed an MRI at the time. I couldn't make sense of it at first. But Mark explained it to me.

Jessica hadn't died because she'd hit her head when I hit Sarah – not directly. She died because there was already an abnormality in her brain.

I have found this very hard to process. The doctors call what I have complicated grief. It is explained in a certain way that doesn't offer me any explanations at all. Grief, apparently, can manifest itself in a form that's so severe and debilitating that to some doctors it meets the definition of a mental illness.

I have been dealing with shock and a rigid belief that my actions caused two deaths, and somewhere in my head the wiring gets mixed up, my circuit overloads and the breaker trips. Even though I am fully aware that Jessica is dead, sometimes I can trick myself into thinking she isn't. The nice thing about being around strangers is there's no need to enlighten them – like that day you and I first talked at the beach. It was so easy to speak of Jessica in the present tense. And for a moment when I'm doing it, it feels so very real. Other times I will have a sense of her presence that is not related to the five senses. It will be real to me, like a shadow through a glass door. But then I can have beliefs that are a little more troubling. I will think that Jessica lives and is travelling. That she is in Europe – staying away, to get a little freedom from me. That she knew I hit someone with my car, that I shrank so very far into myself afterwards, leaving no room for her or her father . . . And that's the scenario I like to think of best. Jessica living her life, happy in the moment, a bit at odds with me, a little wary, but alive, living, free. I've even gone so far as to imagine she has sent me photos and emails. They call these benign hallucinations. They are extraordinarily real. Though I have a sense, afterwards, that they might not quite have been . . .

Mark suffers no illusions or delusions. Mark's grief is quite straightforward, though not less. Mark didn't kill anyone, you see. It wasn't Mark's hands on the wheel that resulted in a stranger, and our daughter, dying. He doesn't live with guilt and all that self-hatred. We are at opposite ends of the spectrum in what we think and how we feel, and I think those opposites became too extreme for us. Mark couldn't understand why all my energy was spent on grieving for Sarah when we had lost a daughter – or why I became so fixated on her husband and two kids. I can't even really explain it myself. Fixating on Sarah helped me not deal with Jessica. Perhaps my brain would not have stood me dealing with both at the same time. Perhaps it was a coping mechanism. As for Sarah's family, they lost so much because of me. I felt – and still feel – so profoundly guilty about that. I have found myself drawn to them, to know about them . . . Sometimes I convince myself I have the power to change things: if only I stare hard enough at their faces I can turn back time.

I came to that first meeting of the Correspondents' Club with a sense that I needed to write to Sarah. To apologise. To make my peace. And then writing became a sort of medicine to me. No one was making me do it or pressurising me. I was perhaps searching for a way of untangling everything and writing helped me find that thread.

I wish I had been able to tell you all this that night. There was part of me that still couldn't go there – saying it would make it too real. And in a way I have wanted to hang on to my grief and not try to talk my way past it. But it is real, and it is out there now. And I am ready to take positive steps to rebuild whatever part of my life isn't irrevocably shattered. You helped me in that, and I thank you more than I can say.

I will never forget our friendship, nor how you listened to me, and how I was drawn to listen to you. Your story took me out of my own, and I probably needed that. I understand your decision to return home – on all fronts – and I hope your son makes a quick recovery. Whatever life has in store for you, I hope it will only be the good you absolutely deserve.

Olivia

THIRTY-SEVEN

We are lying in bed, facing one another. The sun is streaming in the window, warming my bare back. We have made love for the first time in more than a year. I have allowed him to touch me without feeling like his attention is something I ought to deny myself, without feeling I didn't deserve the comfort it gave.

I imagined, coming home, that we would need to bare our souls to each other. That there were so many things that would have to be said, clarified, forgiven. That being back together was going to have to be this tentative thing we must shape, massage, mould. That each day was probably going to demand effort and lots of energy. But none of this has been true. We have got on with things against all odds, perhaps in the relief of knowing that all that has happened has not destroyed us, which might well mean that nothing ever will.

It took me a very long time to realise that my strength comes from being with Mark, not without him. But I'd allowed myself to imagine the opposite of him. I tell him this now, as best as I can get it out without becoming overly emotional. 'I actually thought that if I left and you felt free to pursue an affair with Meleni, then maybe that would be for the best – then I'd have a concrete reason for us to split up. It's what I thought I deserved.'

'I don't know how you can think that,' he says. 'But I accept that you can. I accept that you did.' He squeezes me and drops a kiss on the side of my head. 'Whatever happened, my future is with you, as it always has been. Of everything that's changed, that hasn't.'

I place my hand on his chest and feel his heart beating steadily. 'I lost everything. I thought I deserved to lose you too. I deliberately pushed you away. I thought you blamed me for Jessica's death, and that you always would.'

'I know you did,' he says. 'Time to myself has made me realise that's exactly how you saw it. But that's behind us now . . .' I can tell he's on a mission to avoid too much reflection, to keep alive our fledgling positive thread. Then he says, 'I have been thinking. I think we should consider taking a vacation.'

I contemplate this strange concept. 'Like where?'

'Everywhere,' he says brightly. 'Maybe Europe at first.'

I wait for a certain mindfulness of Jessica and Florence to alight like a butterfly, pictures to fill in before my eyes, but nothing happens.

'I'm thinking of taking a one-year sabbatical . . .'

'What?' I sit up a little.

'It would give us a chance to go off, have an adventure, see the world . . . We could still keep this place as our base, but who knows – maybe we'd fall in love with somewhere else and decide never to come back here.'

I ponder this fantasy for a little while. 'How would you ever give up your job? How could we even afford to run off and live in another country?'

'Well, the one benefit of owning property in such an expensive part of the world is you can easily afford to move somewhere cheaper . . . I bet we could find a little place in Tuscany or on a Greek island where we could live quite happily and our money could go a long way.'

I am not sure if he's right or wrong about this, but I smile anyway. 'Good heavens, sounds like you've thought this all through.'

'I have in a way. Despite what you think, I'm no longer as wedded to my job as I once was, and to the idea of working like a dog until I'm sixty. I have a whole new set of values and priorities now . . . Plus there would be other jobs in other places. The nice thing is it would give us time to decide what we want from the rest of our lives and we'd get away from here.'

We gaze at one another, and at the possibilities he has put there, that glimmer ahead, enjoying each other's faces, and the spell of calm that has fallen on the house now that we're able to look at one another and see – if only for a few minutes – what we have gained rather than what we have lost.

'It's not a bad idea,' I say. 'I mean . . . I've never really imagined it was something we'd ever do, but it does sound a little exciting in a way.' I picture us plotting places and itineraries, and following seasons. Buenos Aires when it's winter here, where we might learn the tango; the South of France in spring. Perhaps a side-stay in Lyon, where I would take cooking classes . . .

'There's something else I was thinking,' he says. 'About a change that might be good for us . . .' He struggles to sit up, reaches across to the night table for his phone. I gaze fondly at the pallor of his inner arm that's escaped the sun's range, the slightly slack skin under his armpit, the tuft of blonde hairs. I watch with a degree of curiosity as he seems to be searching for something, then turns the phone to face me.

It's an email. At first I don't recognise the address.

And then I do.

Dear Mr. & Mrs. Boyciak, Mark has written.

You may well remember me as the person from whom you bought your current home a little over four years ago. I am writing to you with an unusual proposition. My wife and I realise that selling our house is, for several reasons, something we regret. I know this is out of the blue, but should you be looking to sell, now or in the near future, we might be interested to buy it back at a profit that would be worth your while. Please take your time to think it over; we are not in an immediate hurry. If you are interested, we would be happy to talk. And of course we would be prepared to accommodate whatever time you needed to relocate elsewhere. I hope to hear from you.

Sincerely,
Mark Chapman

'What?' I sit up properly now, tugging the white summer quilt around me.

'You hated this place from day one. I think I knew that but I conveniently thought you'd change your mind, and that was wrong and selfish of me. I'm sorry for that. I should have listened to you. The more I've thought about it you were right in what you said – if we'd never moved here none of this would have happened.'

I try to process this, in my state of surprise. My brows pull together like a reflex that occurs every time I think of Jessica. 'Moving back to our old house won't bring her back.'

He hesitates for a second before replying. 'I know that.' He stares distantly across the room with a certain dismay alighting on his back. Perhaps illusions can happen to the least susceptible; for a moment he's fancied that it might.

There is a silence that becomes so filled with her absence – negating that small spell of promise and peace that came before – but I push it away. I think of Ned's mantra: *Choose to walk forward.* I *want* to walk forwards. 'You love it here,' I tell him. 'You adored this house the minute you set eyes on it.'

'But you mean more to me than a house.'

'I know. But we don't have to sell it to prove that.' I reach a hand to his sad face, drawing it so his eyes meet mine.

For the first time, I am the one who sees things quite clearly. Mark wants to move back because our old house is so full of memories of Jessica everywhere we look. Mark, in his kindly deluded way, thinks that this would be what I need. I think it would be terrible for us. How would we ever see anything else?

'But if they respond and say they're interested maybe we should at least give it some serious consideration,' he says, scooching around so he can better see me. 'More than this, anyway.'

'I've already given it serious consideration,' I say, and hand him back his phone. 'Besides, they've probably done so much to the place we'd barely recognise it now. It was crying out for a good reno.'

'They haven't.'

I frown. 'How do you know?'

'I drove over there and peeped in all the windows when nobody was home.' He throws himself back against the headboard.

'You didn't?' I don't know why but this makes me smile.

'No one saw. And even if they did, who gives a shit?'

I shake my head, turning over the picture of Mark pressed up against walls and poking his head around window frames. 'Good God,'

I say. I take the idea on board again, to make sure I'm convinced of my opinion. 'Well, my guess is, if they haven't responded in three days, they're thinking about it or they'd have said no immediately. I have a feeling they're going to write and say they want to talk . . .' I sit up taller now, to make my point. 'But if they do, I definitely want you to tell them your wife has changed her mind.'

He appears helpless for a moment – like he can't do right for doing wrong. I reach up and kiss him on his cheek, hoping to purge that thought. 'I'm saying we should stay here, for now. Then let's think this travel plan through a bit more, see if it has legs. If we did go off for a year, and then we ended up feeling like we did want to come back to Seattle, then maybe that would be the time to think about selling this place. Maybe it would be good to downsize and buy a gorgeous water-view condo right in the heart of downtown . . .' Then I will never have to drive down that road again. I will no longer see Jess in every room that I look in. It will be as fresh a start as could ever be possible for us.

'I never thought of that, but it's actually not a bad idea . . . A nice condo near everything, so we can go out for an evening, get drunk and just walk home . . .' We have often said that living in the burbs has made us less spontaneous, imposed practical limits on what we do, quelling some of our spirit. He looks at me with a sudden earnest, imperative energy about him. 'I just wanted to give you something you really want. To make you happy. Just one thing that'll be good for you, that's all . . . You're not upset I went behind your back with the email, are you?'

'No.' I shrug. 'Not at all. It was very initiative-taking . . . But the thing is, you're wrong about something.' His hand is resting on his ribcage. I gaze at it, at the wedding band that I'm sure he never once thought to take off. I reach out my own, slide my fingers so they lock with his.

My husband's hand.

'You don't have to give me anything. I have what's good for me already. And I've always had it.' I look up and meet his eyes, hoping I can transmit, through mine, how much I dearly mean this.

'I have you,' I say.

EPILOGUE

I haven't been on Facebook in a while but when I do log on, the night before we leave for our month-long trip to Australia, I see I have two new messages.

The first is from Beth.

> Dear Olivia,
>
> It might surprise you that an old fossil like me is now on Facebook. (I am just getting the hang of this but please see you have a friend request from me which I am hoping you will accept.) The reason I am on here is that Thomas suggested it would be a good idea.
>
> Thanks to you I did send that letter, though not the one to my sister. A week later, he replied.
>
> Thomas lives in Scottsdale. He is a firefighter and has two sons – Donald, who is seven, and Christopher, eleven. His wife, Patti, is originally

from Santa Barbara and they regularly go there to visit her family. Thomas said that when they are next there, likely over Thanksgiving, he would like it very much if they could make a side trip up to PT so that we could meet. He said my letter had given him a lot to think about and that he had wondered about me for years. So I have agreed. And because he encouraged me to get on to social media I have seen all kinds of photos of my son and his family in their day-to-day lives, and the faces of my grand-children. It's quite an amazing thing . . . I attach a small picture of him here – his profile picture – for you to see. While I never would have especially wanted another person to look anything like me, I am quite pleased to see that he doesn't resemble what little memory I have of his father.

I hope you are settled back in your home with your husband. I am most grateful for the letter you sent me a couple of weeks ago, explaining everything. I realised that day you reamed me out (deservedly so) that something awful had happened to you. Being so mindful of my own privacy, I thought it best to respect yours and not ask until you gave me an 'in', which you never really did. I was so thrilled to hear how the Correspondents' Club helped you! And of course it now makes a degree of sense to me why you were so keen that I find my child – because you had lost yours. There is so much I would like to say to you on this subject, but I feel it would be more appropriate face to face, perhaps *over one of our wine nights, if that can stand being repeated. I hope it won't be too long before you will pay PT a visit. My spare room is always there for you. At the very least I would like to pour you a coffee and offer you one of my muffins. I am determined that one day you will eventually eat one.*

Beth

Attached is a small headshot of Thomas in his fireman's uniform. She's right. The same small features and kind green eyes.

The second message catches me completely off guard.

Sarah.

I find myself staring at the tiny little profile picture of her: the close-up of her playfully pulling a face. I am deaf to everything except the whoosh of blood in my ears, the sudden slamming of my heart.

Dear Olivia, it begins.

Thank you for your very kind message. This is Sarah's husband, Glen. Sorry it has taken me such a long time to reply. Your words truly moved me. I had been meaning to deactivate Sarah's page and didn't really understand why I wasn't getting around to it – this turned out to be a positive thing.

I have actually given a lot of thought to what it must have been like to be the driver, to be you. You must try and let go of the tremendous guilt you speak of. It was a cruel accident that probably could have been avoided, as so many of them can – but not by you. Sarah would have hated you to believe it was your fault, and to let it ruin your life. Live your life, Olivia. My advice is live it proudly and profoundly – for yourself and for my wife.

Cheers,
Glen

THE END

ACKNOWLEDGMENTS

Once in a while, when I have been trying to come up with story ideas, I have asked myself, *If I only had one book in me, what would it be?* Every time I've done this, I've come up with the same thing – writing about one of my biggest fears or dreads coming true. I have felt the theme and the mood of the novel, imagined its various dimensions. Then, for some reason, I've convinced myself that the topic is too tragic, too big for me, too different from the other books I've written, and I've run, scared, on to a new idea, with this other lingering like a pilot light in my mind.

Then, several years ago, I wrote twenty thousand words of a book about a letter-writing circle; in the group was an ex-Navy SEAL and a woman whose teenage daughter had caused a terrible accident and was having a hard time getting over it. I couldn't make all the storylines come together, so I set it aside. Last year, when I asked myself the question about what would be that one book I would write, it dawned on me that I had already begun it. The idea was there, only it was buried – I had made it the daughter's story so I could write about it with a degree of remove. What I had to do suddenly became so very clear. I would tell one woman's story – a mother's. I would dig deep into my own fears on the subject, and give it my all.

Once I decided this, the story I'd wanted to write for eons finally had lift-off and it almost wrote itself. Along the way, a very different ending from the one I'd anticipated suddenly came to me. Pulling that off required a significant rewrite. I owe huge thanks – as always – to my tremendous editor and champion, Victoria Pepe, and to the patient and invaluable Arzu Tahsin, for how they guided me so deftly through that process. A novel before it's edited, and after, are two very different beasts. I am eternally grateful for all the creative thinking, and the constant pushing, that helped this book be the best it could be. Indeed, I owe sincere thanks to Sammia Hamer and to everyone at Lake Union who is involved in bringing my books to you, my wonderful readers. It truly is a team effort and a strong team means the world. Thank you.

Huge thanks are also due to my terrific, tenacious literary agent, Lorella Belli, to my mother, Mary, who gets as excited about my books as I do, and who actually came up with my title this time, and to my husband, Tony, for always giving me the space and encouragement to pursue my dreams. If you have read my novels, reviewed them, recommended then – thank you! I am eternally grateful to my readers. I love hearing from you so do please be in touch either through my website, www.carolmasonbooks.com, where you can give me your email so that I can let you know when I have a new book out, or be my friend on Facebook: https://www.facebook.com/carol.mason.1297.

ABOUT THE AUTHOR

Photo © 2018, Tony Capuccinello

Carol Mason was born and grew up in the north-east of England. As a teenager she was crowned Britain's National Smile Princess and subsequently became a model, diplomat-in-training, hotel receptionist and advertising copywriter. She currently lives in British Columbia, Canada, with her Canadian husband. To learn more about Carol and her novels, visit https://www.carolmasonbooks.com.